THINGS I SHOULD HAVE SAID

KELSEY HUMPHREYS

© 2022 Kelsey Humphreys
Things I Should Have Said
First edition, November 2022

Magnamour Press
magnamour.com
kelseyhumphreys.com

Editing: Shayla Raquel, shaylaraquel.com
formatting: Aeyshaa
Illustration: Shana Yasmin

ISBN: 978-1-959428-00-8

*For RomCom lovers who haven't quite seen themselves
in all those sunshiny pages*

*and for Stephanie L. Jones, my real-life Janie.
I love introverting with you!*

AUTHOR'S NOTE

Introvert: one whose internal battery is recharged by being alone

Extrovert: one whose internal battery is recharged by being around others

These two groups are not monoliths, and most people fall somewhere on a sliding scale between the two extremes. I have been told I'm way too outgoing to be an introvert, yet parts of this book were painfully autobiographical. There are quiet extroverts who just like being around people. There are introverts with no social anxiety whatsoever, and so on. Still, tragedy and comedy are found in the extremes.

Enjoy!

PROLOGUE

I had all my necessary defenses in place.

Hoodie? Pulled up.

Noise-canceling headphones? On.

Sleep mask? Check.

Turned toward the window? Obviously.

I even caved and took Dad up on his offer for the first-class upgrade because I knew I'd need the time to recuperate after peopling for a long weekend. Which meant there were extra inches of buffer between myself and whomever sat next to me. If they were like me—*Please, Lord*—they'd take one look at me and read my message loud and clear: don't even think about it, fellow passenger. They'd sigh with relief, smile to themselves to find another introvert out in the wild, and never look in my direction again. If they were someone like Sam—*again, God in heaven, please, no*—and wanted to chat, they wouldn't be able to. Because I couldn't see or hear them. This was not my first high-altitude rodeo.

But then the turbulence started.

I'm not totally afraid of hurtling through the air in a skinny metal death tube. Unless the tube starts jumping and gyrating and threatening to pull apart at those visible bolts everywhere. I can't be the only one who notices all the bolts. Because everything in there has to be bolted down. In case we start to plummet nose-first to our fiery end.

Even a little bump I can deal with.

These were not little bumps.

The clouds between Dallas and New York were clearly pissed. Maybe they also wanted to nap for three hours, and here we were piercing through them. Why were we? Shouldn't we have diverted around whatever fresh hell is happening outside? Is the pilot a rookie? He is. Actually, more and more women are becoming pilots—I bet it's a woman. *I'm proud of you, Jennifer, but give the stick to ole Dan next to you, or you're going to kill us all!*

My mental state deteriorated along with my hold on feminism.

I started to sweat. I had to take the sleep mask off. Then I had to turn from the window to open the little knob of freezing-cold jet stream. I sat facing ahead in my seat with my eyes closed, and it was good. It helped. But then Jennifer did something else to piss off the clouds, and we jerked so hard a woman behind me yelled out "Oh, God!"

I'm praying too, lady.

After that, the tiny beam of arctic breeze wasn't enough. The headphones were making my ears sweat. They had to go. The hood had to come down, and I had to push my sleeves up. I kept my eyes squeezed shut, breathing, wondering if I'd somehow forgotten to put on deodorant.

"Look at the flight attendants," a voice said beside me.

Crap. Crapcrapcrap!

I was bare, exposed in the soft blue florescent wilderness. Which opened me up to be shot with small talk. Is there anything worse than limping through conversation with a stranger when you're already trying not to vomit and/or cry? I sighed. I opened my eyes and looked to my right.

Yes.

There was something worse.

Small talk with a *hot* stranger.

His big brown eyes held mine as he broke up his strong, scruffy jaw with a grin. He had dark brown slightly styled hair and tanned skin that popped against the light blue T-shirt under his gray zip hoodie. He looked about my age, but that could have been due to the relaxed vibe.

"W-What?" I managed to get out.

"Look at the flight attendants. They're totally calm."

"Okay?"

"If it were really serious, they would know, and we'd see it on their faces. And they look downright bored to me."

He had a point. Hot and helpful. Great. How many minutes before I said something awkward?

"I . . . I guess you're right. Thanks."

I continued to focus on calming myself before I sweat through my hoodie. Pit stains on a shirt? Acceptable, even for a woman, if small, delicate, almost unnoticeable. That says, "Oh, cute, she's nervous." Sweating through a shirt *and* a sweatshirt? That, however, says, "Oh, wow, that woman has a Niagara Falls–size medical problem. She should seek pharmaceuticals. Look away!"

"Uh-oh," hot guy in 3A said, still smirking.

"What?" I said a little too loud. Did he know something about our impending death that I didn't? Was he a pilot? *Go help Jennifer, Hot Pilot, I'm too young to die!*

"I shouldn't be helping out a Sooners fan." He glanced down at my boobs. No, at my hoodie.

"Oh." I gave him a smile. It was a gray hoodie with my alma mater's logo printed on it. Subtle. But not subtle enough. The hoodie was huge and super soft, a favorite for traveling. Except it could prompt conversation! Ugh, what was this, traveling amateur hour? The sweatshirt was not going to see the outside of my apartment ever again.

I also realized, in that moment, that my old sweatshirt was not exactly cute or flattering. My plain black leggings were fine, I guess. But they weren't even my *good* plain black leggings. And I'd been so deeply tired from the weekend I hadn't even put on a full face of makeup. I'd put my thick, wavy light brown hair in a top knot and didn't even put on earrings or eyeliner. Am. At. Eur. Hour.

"Hook 'em." His grin grew to more of a smile, which was— wow—hard to look away from. It was warm and confident. But I groaned a bit, despite it. Sports small talk was arguably the worst of all the small talk. It's a ball, they throw it around, catch it, run with it, we get it, very impressive. We're all very impressed. He gave me a quizzical look in response to my odd groan.

That was when the plane lost a wing.

At least, that's what it felt like. Some sort of shudder and dip on the left side that made the praying lady behind me cry out to God again. I gasped and gripped the armrests and squeezed my eyes shut. *Jennifer, girlfriend, get it together!*

And that's when Smokin' McSmokeshow gently touched my right wrist. And I forgot about Jenn and the prayers and my sweating and my own name. His warm, calloused hand dwarfed my wrist, and it . . . did things. It did things to my insides that felt a lot like what the angry clouds were currently doing to my ride home.

"Would a drink help?" he asked, as he held my wrist. I looked at my wrist, and he pulled his hand away slowly, as if willing to keep it there a lot longer. I nodded, unable to speak. Which was good. Not speaking meant not blurting something embarrassing. My wrist continued to buzz as he pushed the button for the flight attendant.

The well-endowed attendant, who I named Betty Boop in my head because I am mature, came over to him and flashed him a brilliant smile. Like, a "she clearly whitened her teeth weekly" kind of smile. I vowed not to show my teeth the rest of the flight. I hadn't whitened in months, and coffee was my main nutrition source. Why, why didn't I whiten my teeth before this flight?

Wait, what?

Was I having a seizure? Who cares about teeth? Up front, Jenn was trying to end my life. Why was I thinking about whitening strips?

"What can I get you?" the attendant asked from her much-too-pretty face, in a much-too-friendly way. It made me a bit irritated, which made me confused. *She's pretty and good at her job, unlike Jennifer. Let her live her best life, you wacko.*

"Heineken for me and a . . . ?" He looked at me.

"White wine." Her face fell when she looked from him to me, and that made me a bit glad. Because I was losing my mind, obviously. He gave her his card, and I tried to protest, "Oh, no, I can—"

"It's all right, easier on her to have one bill," he said, but he winked. I didn't know until that moment that a wink could be so sexy, that when it greets you, you have to cough a bit. You have no choice in the matter.

"I'm Matt." He reached out his hand to me.

"Skye." I coughed back to him, with another small smile. What was with his wizard hands? Why did I feel his hand shake down in my nether regions? *Why did I call them nether regions when I am under the age of eighty-five?*

"First time visiting New York?" he asked, as he angled his body toward me. I braced myself. Okay. Small talk was happening. I told myself to remain calm, say as little as possible, but also maybe smile a bit to combat the resting bitch face Sam said I had.

"Nope, live there," I said with an easy grin as our drinks arrived. I loved that I actually lived in New York City. It was still a dream come true, even after almost five years. "Thank you," I said to her, and then I looked back into those big brown danger saucers. "And thank you."

"Sure." He shrugged it off. "So, do you live in the city?"

"Williamsburg." No, I didn't live in Manhattan, but I had a view of Manhattan, and I loved that about my little place. The plane shuddered again, and I chugged a couple gulps of wine. Which was a very bad idea, some voice told me from the back of my mind. If there was one thing I did not want to be with a hot small talker, it was loose. Next I'd be telling him I had Niagara pits and he had Harry Potter hands and whatever other mortifying thoughts popped into my head.

"Sorry, would you rather not talk?" he said after I had to close my eyes again. Bingo! Dreamy Drink Buyer was catching on. Except . . . he was so captivating, I actually was forgetting about my impending demise when he was looking in my direction.

"No, um, it's helping. What about you, do you live in the city?"

"Chelsea." He nodded and took a sip of his beer. Weirdly, I watched his mouth as he did so. He had full lips and just enough five-o'clock shadow to look intriguing but not sloppy. I felt purple splotches escaping from under the neckline of my hoodie as I looked away. He didn't seem to notice. Instead, he said, "What took you to Dallas?"

"Tulsa, actually. Family." I took a couple more big sips of wine, but this time it was more about the chatting and less about the death trap. Why did simple questions make me so nervous?

"Oh, Oklahoma, right. Did you go to OU?"

"Yep. Did you go to Texas?"

"Yep. You gonna hold that against me?"

"Of course." I said it with a smile. I was flirting. It was flirting, right? Because I honestly could not have cared less about football. As a student, I didn't go to many games because I preferred the extra time in the studio on Saturdays. Still, any living, breathing Oklahoma grad, or even fan, had to hate a Longhorn fan. It was Middle America law.

The last bit of wine jumped around in the glass as the plane reminded me my life was about to be over. I took a deep breath in.

"So why the Big Apple?" he asked, but I was still focused on breathing. "Skye." He said my name softly, like a caress. It was like he'd touched my wrist again. It was such a strong reaction to such a normal thing, as if I hadn't been called by my name my whole life. Like he'd given me a new name and just said it for the first time. "Skye. Why the Big Apple?"

I gave him a slight nod of gratitude. "I'm an artist." I finished off my wine. I was venturing into terrifying territory. I didn't need to talk about real things with a man who had just given me a new name.

"An artist? So my opposite then."

I just raised my eyebrows at him.

"Numbers guy. Specifically ones and zeros." He motioned to my glass. "Want another?"

"No! No." Whoops. I almost yelled it, causing him to look at me with alarm. "One glass is my limit before—" I cut myself off, but it was too late.

"Before?" He was grinning again.

"Before I snap and start oversharing and word vomiting and saying awkward things you shouldn't say . . . even more awkward than 'word vomiting.'" I sighed. Why did I say *vomiting* twice? *Jennifer, fly this thing faster, angry clouds be damned!*

But he let out a little laugh and said, in a voice that was definitely too low and too buttery, "What shouldn't you say?"

See, this was the problem.

People think awkward like cute, funny Zooey Deschanel awkward. Movies and sitcom awkward. So I just cut right to it.

"You know, *not* small talk. Big talk. Religion, politics, conspiracy theories, greatest hopes, greatest fears, realizations from therapy, how I'm dripping wet under my clothes."

Aaaaand there it was.

His eyes flashed wide when I realized what I'd just said.

"Like flop-sweating! Crazy insta-sweat under my hoodie."

Flop-sweating.

Fantastic.

Couldn't have just said "It's hot in here" like a normal person. Zooey Deschanel wouldn't say flop-sweating to a hot stranger. And therapy? Really? I knew I shouldn't be ashamed to be in therapy. But I still was. I actually had to talk to my therapist about it. Ugh. Cringe Level: 1,000.

But thankfully he laughed, a big hearty laugh, too much for the airplane. It filled all the space, and he didn't care. Surprisingly, I liked it, even though it was loud. "Well, now I obviously have to know about the conspiracy theories."

I shook my head and pressed my lips together. I was never speaking again.

He smiled. "C'mon, do you have a tin hat? Are we flying over a flat earth right now?"

I laughed at that. He nudged me with his elbow. Who knew pointy-elbow nudges could be so sexy? "Um, all right, how about the Denver airport?"

"What about it?" He said it low, in a way that I'm sure he didn't mean to be sensual. But he leaned in toward me just a bit as he said it, so my stomach lurched up into my throat.

I coughed out, "Something shady going on in tunnels underneath. Creepy murals. The devil horse. Google it."

He pulled out his phone, already connected to the fancy first-class Wi-Fi. "Wow, that *is* creepy."

"Right!" As I said it, I moved my arms in exclamation, realizing he'd left his arm over on my side of the partition. He was still touching my elbow, and if I put my arm down, we'd be touching from elbow to fingertip. I coughed yet again, feeling my elbow on fire. He had to be seconds away from asking me if I had tuberculosis. *We're done with the wine. No more!*

A man had gotten up to go to the restroom—to Betty Boop's horror—and when he passed us, he tripped a bit from how badly the plane was shuddering. My grip went back to my seat's arms, which Matt noticed. Now my entire forearm was against his. He'd pushed up his sleeves, and a hidden wire of energy now ran down the length where our skin touched. Which sealed the sweaty deal: I could not, under any circumstances, remove my hoodie. I needed the hoodie to remain intact around my blotchy, stenchy, not-cute-pit-stain situation like a Dutch oven shield.

"So. Artist. Like a musician?"

"Like a painter." I winced a bit. Musician is a much cooler answer than painter. I was well aware.

"Wow, a painter. Where can I see some of your work?" He held out his phone and looked into my eyes as he said it.

But I saw it then.

He was smooth. He was handsome and charming, and now he wanted to see my work. No stupid-hot thirtyish guy actually wanted to see paintings by some random chick next to them on the plane. But a man would fake interest to be—*ding ding ding*—smooth. I didn't answer at first, because of the realization. But when I didn't say anything, his face fell in a way that made me feel like a jerk.

"Uh, I guess my Instagram. Skye Morgan. It's at PaintedSkye, with an e." He picked up his phone again, and a rush filled me. I wanted him to look, but at the same time, I wanted to jump out of the plane rather than sit there and look at him looking. I was twisted up with both hope and dread at the same time. And I was sure both would show through my hoodie if I lifted my arms.

"Wow, Skye. You're like a celebrity."

I snorted. I had about one hundred thousand followers. Okay, exactly 104,300 followers. And I hated that I knew that number by heart. And I hated Instagram, but didn't, and hated myself for not hating it. And I hated that I had worked so unbelievably hard for those followers when that number was almost nothing in the realm of social media stats.

"Did you just snort?" He looked away from his phone to me. I just put my head in my hand.

Jennifer, just take 'er down! I've lived a good life!

But then he grabbed my hand and pulled it down from my face and looked straight into my eyes. And while the simple motion prompted me to stop breathing and involuntarily squeeze my thighs together, it also made me remember. Smooth. Too smooth.

"These are incredible." He held my gaze and my hand until he looked back to his phone. "I mean, really . . . wait, what does 'The Titles Girl' mean in your bio?"

Rather than use words, I directed him to an article linked in my profile. I create realist mixed media paintings, mostly thick layers of acrylic, but I always add something extra. My work is hyper-realistic, with neon or glitter or metallic finishes mixed in that take the realism over the line if you look closely.

My most recent series, mentioned in the article, was twenty floral works. I went semi-viral for the titles of my pieces. I did a close-up of a pink orchid with a title "I'm Not O'Keeffe, You Perv." A gorgeous field of wildflowers was named "Gesundheit!" The one that caused a stir on ArtTok—the art community within the app TikTok—had a bright drugstore bouquet of hyper-saturated carnations and roses, still in the plastic wrap, with the rubber band and the flower food pouch. The title of the piece was "He's Just Not That into You."

Some people actually hated me for that one piece, that I was "too good" for drugstore flowers. They passionately disagreed about my premise. And that was fine with me. I became a known artist that day. Their hatred had actually allowed me to rent a private studio space in my favorite part of the city. Also, they were just flat-out wrong. I had been on the receiving end of those CVS flowers.

I turned purply again as Matt read the article next to me. What did it mean, to be incredibly proud of something and also simultaneously want no one to ever see it? Why did we humans long to share our whole souls with someone while also hiding huge pieces of ourselves at the same time? *Ooo . . . series idea if Jenn doesn't crash this sucker: Questions for My Therapist.*

"These are all so funny. And smart. And man . . . I promise not to buy you drugstore flowers." He looked at me when he said it. He didn't blink or back down from the idea. His eyes said "I want to take you on a date and get you better flowers." And he held steady, looking for my reaction. Which I'm sure was a wince or a grimace.

I hadn't realized with all the elbow-touching and soul-baring (also known as showing someone my work) that we'd already started our descent. Thankfully, after he made his suggestion, my phone lit up with a call from Sam, which I promptly rejected. I should have put my phone on airplane mode. My sister *knows*

I'm not going to answer, but she calls anyway. So I sent a text, which caused what I like to call a SamStorm.

Me: About to land

Sam: YASSSSSS Omg!!!

You were gone too long!

I've been so bored!

Let's go out for dinner! Woooooot!!!!!

Matt cleared his throat and spoke into the last sip of his beer bottle. "Lucky guy."

"What?"

He gave me a tight smile and gestured toward my phone. "I saw the call pop up. Sam. He's a lucky guy."

I could've told him Sam was my sister, Samantha. But in that moment, I actually did have a lucky guy, Paul. A guy I hadn't thought of even one time during my death-defying journey with the Brown-Eyed Wonder. So, feeling guilty, I just gave a small, closed smile and looked away. To his credit, Hot Matt changed his demeanor after that. He leaned a little farther away and quit chatting.

I tensed up again as we were about to land. Takeoffs didn't bother me as much as landings did. Takeoffs were gradual. Landings were jarring and always felt like maybe something was going wrong, and you could be about to die, but no one would really know for sure until all our limbs were on fire. Matt noticed my vice grip on the seat.

"Well, I followed you. On Instagram."

"Oh, thanks." I smiled and forced myself not to pull out my phone and look him up right then and there.

"Sure. Can't wait to tell all my friends that I sat by the next Denis Peterson on the plane." He smiled wide again. And my breath caught, because his smile was unfairly gorgeous, yes, but also because he quoted the article back to me. He'd actually read it, not just browsed the images.

Was he being thoughtful or slick? I wasn't sure. The landing of the plane broke my stare because yep, I'd been staring at him. With my mouth hanging open like the village idiot. And he was just staring back, grinning. I smiled and looked down as the plane slowed. *Thanks for the save, Jennifer! Sorry for all the crap I gave you. Girl power!*

We didn't say anything else as I put my sleep mask and headphones into my backpack. He pulled his backpack out from the seat in front of him. Then he stretched, revealing a firm, wide chest and built arms I hadn't been able to fully appreciate. He twisted in his seat, and I sneaked a glance at the spot where his neatly trimmed hair met his tanned neck. I had the impulse to smooth my hand down his head and massage his flight-induced tension.

Which helped me to realize the plane had been piping crack through the air system.

Had to have been. What else could explain my sudden insanity? I was bothered all over, from looking at a plane stranger's neck?

We stood eventually, and he went out into the aisle. I went out behind him, and he turned back to me. Our chests were almost touching, and he didn't back up. He was right on top of me, and not by accident. He didn't back up or apologize—just looked down and asked if he could get my bag for me.

Smooth was an understatement. This man was liquid. His face was so close to mine I couldn't think. He was almost smirking, but he was also smoldering. He knew he was affecting me. He put his hand on my shoulder, clearly grinning now, and repeated himself.

"Can I get your bag?"

I managed to nod as he pointed to my hard black suitcase with purple zippers. He moved farther down the aisle to put my bag between us, and I immediately felt the absence of his body's almost-touch down my entire front. I watched him walk out of the plane ahead of me, taking him in.

His gray backpack covered my view of what I'm sure was a glorious backside, if his chest and arms were any indication. Stylish gray-and-white Adidas popped out from under just-tight-enough jeans. I kept my arms down, realizing I was dripping wet, in all the ways, from just . . . what? An hour of conversation with him? A wrist graze?

It struck me, as two men in suits broke off from our disembarking herd, that I had no idea what Matt did. Ones and zeros, like computers? Surely not. He was too sporty hot to be a nerd and too empathetic to be a programmer. But he did have on a hoodie a la Zuck. Gross. Tech guys and their soul-sucking apps and gadgets. But Matt didn't seem gadgety either. So what did he do in Chelsea? Why had he been in Dallas? What was his last name? Did he have a girlfriend? He probably did.

After we got through the gate, he turned to me and said, "It was nice to meet you, Skye."

As I said, "You too, Matt," he was already turning to walk away. I hadn't even thanked him for talking me through my near-death experience. As always, LaGuardia was a packed, hot dilapidated mess, and he was lost in the crowd quickly, because I was standing still.

"Dammit, move, lady! You're blocking the way!" someone barked at me. *Welcome to New York,* I thought as I smiled and got back to walking, back to normal. I didn't let myself look for Matt as I made my way down to the subway. I had had hot liquid like him before. Like whiskey. It had burned going down and coming back up. Never again.

CHAPTER 1

Three Months Later

"Less than an hour. You already sold three pieces. You got this," I tell myself in the mirror of the tiny, dark single-use bathroom. I pull my gloss out of my dress pocket and reapply. *Thank you, twenty-first-century fashion designers!* With a deep breath, I exit back into the gallery.

I love openings, I do. It's easy to talk about my work and say thank you to supporters. They ask the same few questions, and I have funny answers ready to go. Sometimes buyers ask for a selfie or an autograph, which is a thrill, obviously. I'm living the dream. But also, the nightmare. I simultaneously hate openings and wish I was invisible while they're occurring. I count down the minutes until they're over. All the while I'm also hoping time will stretch so that more people will see my work, and so that more canvases will get little red PURCHASED stickers placed next to them on the wall.

It's such a blast being me.

I walk over to Janie in the corner, my best friend and faithful buffer. She always comes to my events, happy to stand silently with me by a wall. She also covers for me with Maud if I need to go outside and catch my breath. Maud is my manager, who I notice sealing the deal with a young couple eyeing one of my smaller pieces. She is a total New Yorker: sharp, stylish, genius, ruthless. She pushes me, usually in a good way, but sometimes in a way that requires Janie to step in as a human shield between the two of us. Sam also comes to these, of course, but she's too busy flitting around making new lifelong besties to help me if I need it.

"Less than an hour," Janie says with a smile.

"Yep, I'm good."

"Want another water?" she asks, but my voice leaves me when I look at the door.

It's him.

He came.

Not that I was planning he would or hoping he would . . . okay, I was kind of hoping he would. I knew he'd been watching my stories on Instagram from time to time. He didn't post often, but when he did, they were always group photos. He seemed to have a lot of friends, coworkers, double dates, or business meetings— it was hard to tell. I'd refrained from following him or leaving comments. But dadgum those wizard hands and his gorgeous grin. I couldn't forget them. So, I'd noticed whenever his profile photo showed up in my notifications if he'd watched my stories or reacted with an emoji. When I'd posted about the reception tonight, I'd wondered if he'd notice, if he'd come.

And now he had, and thank God I'd gone with my signature high-necked dress because I could feel the splotches breaking out across my collarbones.

"Skye? Hello? Do. You. Want. A. Water?" Janie says, as if I am going deaf, which in this moment, I am.

"Where's Sam?" I whisper to her.

"I don't know, talking somewhere, why?"

"Wave her over here!"

"Why are you being weirder than usual?"

"I'll explain. Get her to come here!"

I pretend that I'm not focusing all my sensory power on Matt and his two friends. Suddenly I'm fine with how small this gallery is. If I'd landed a spot at Culture, I could not have eavesdropped onto their conversation.

A guy with Matt says, "That's hilarious, my parents have those too."

"What?" Matt asks as his friend points to the title card posted next to the canvas. It reads:

My Parents' House Is Covered in Nipples #traumatized

Matt laughs too. It's a painting of a hallway with those light fixtures—the round kind that hang flush on the ceiling and have a bowl shape with a little metal point on them. They totally look like nipples. No one can unsee that. I smile watching them while not watching them. Matt eagerly moves to the next large canvas. It's a dentist's chair. I'm particularly proud of how touchable the worn blue pleather looks, and how the sliver of the metal bars look so real you'd think the paint there would be cold to the touch.

"She's not lying," the other one says with a smile as he reads the title card for the dentist chair:

Preferable to a Seat at the Singles Table

The guys are laughing at the next canvas, but Matt starts to turn his head in my direction. The hairs on my arm stand up as I am suddenly hyper-focused on Janie in front of me. Sam bounds up to us with a wide smile and an anticipatory sparkle in her eyes. "What, what is it?"

Once Sam has joined our huddle, I whisper, "Janie, *he* came."

"Who came?" Sam asks.

Janie gasps. "Hot Plane Guy?"

"Hot Who?" Sam is incapable of whispering.

"Shhh . . . yes!"

"What! Excuse me, who is Hot Plane Guy?" Sam is beside herself. This is why I didn't tell her.

"Listen, coming back from Dallas, I sat next to a hot guy on the plane and we talked and—"

Sam's eyes threaten to bulge out of her gorgeous face. "You *talked* to someone on a flight?"

"Samantha, so help me God, shut up!" My clinched smile hurts my cheeks. "Yes, the plane was going down, so he talked me through the turbulence and—"

"Holy crap! It's a meet-cute! Did you tell Sadie?" She is practically salivating, so I give my younger sister a glare that causes her to visibly wither.

"This was not a meet-cute, Samantha! He talked me through my impending death, and I mentioned flop-sweating and the Denver airport conspiracy." Janie laughs at me, Sam groans. "Then he followed me on Instagram. He must've seen me post about tonight."

"Which one?" Janie asks.

"Seriously? Quit looking! Try to be subtle, you guys." I was grateful for my dress choice again because black didn't show the faucets awakening under my arms. "White shirt, jeans, blue suit jacket."

"Well, hellllooooooo!" I love Sam, but she is just so, so much. Although in this instance, she is spot-on. He looks delicious. In fact, Hoodie Matt was hot. But Jeans and Jacket Matt? A tailored jacket—expensive, made to fit his body—and jeans and . . . well, he is venturing into gorgeous Greek god territory.

"I agree with your sister on this one," Janie says.

"Yes, I know I said he was hot! Now please talk to me like I'm super interesting."

"Skye, you *are* super interesting. You're like one of the most interesting people on the planet." Sam places a sincere hand on my shoulder. I smile broadly. This is why everyone loves her.

"Ha! On the planet? Sorry, Skye, but I can guess to the minute what you're doing on any given day. And what you're eating. And wearing. And watching. False." Janie is not like Sam, she's like me. It's why we're best friends.

I can feel Matt's magnetic presence coming my way, but of course I do not look at him. I fake laugh at Janie, and she laughs too, even though her eyes are telling me that I've officially lost it. *Oh, yes, I'm aware!*

"Here he comes, be cool, oh sh—" I mutter, feeling my stomach squeeze shut like a fist.

"Hey, Skye," he says with some kind of porn-star voice. Seriously, who talks like that?

"Matt! Uh, hi!" I am smiling too wide.

"You remembered," he says with a grin and a small tilt of his head. That grin. I freeze. I am dumb, deaf, and mute now, so Sam takes over, naturally.

"Hi, Matt." Matt looks to her and shakes her hand. "I'm Sam." His head jerks back to me so fast he must've strained something.

He squints a bit and maintains his dreamy grin. "Sam, the boyfriend?" Then he catches himself, "Oh, girlfriend?"

"Ha, the boyfriend! No, that's Paul. I'm Samantha, the sister. This is Janie, the best friend." Sam is so good at this, just chatting away. Janie shakes Matt's hand. Do they feel his wizard powers too, I wonder?

Matt is back to gazing into my eyes with no qualms. Who maintains eye contact this long? Is this some boardroom tactic? "Paul, huh?" He looks around the room.

"Oh, he's not here. He never comes to these things. Never leaves his apartment. He's even more introverted than Skye is, if you can believe that!" I look at Sam with wide eyes. Seriously? What next, is she going to give him my Social Security number? Tell him what brand of tampons I buy?

"What do you think of Inside, isn't it amazing?" Sam is beaming with pride. *Aw! Overshare forgiven.*

"Inside?" Matt asks her.

"That's the name of this exhibit—everything is indoors. Isn't she such a genius?" *Okay, beyond forgiven, must buy Sam a present!*

Matt's back to staring at me. "She is. Congratulations, Skye, this is awesome."

I look down and bite my lip. "Thanks."

"I need a champagne. Can I get one for you?" I shake my head, so he says, "Already had one, huh?" His eyes sparkle in the gallery lights.

He's pleased with himself. And for good reason. He listened and remembered. While he is oozing charm and making the back of my knees sweat, Samantha is just watching us back and forth with a smile like she's at a tennis match.

"You know what, we'll get your drinks." Janie pulls Sam away. *Must buy Janie a present too.* Matt thanks them and steps closer to me. He looks me up and down, and my cheeks burn. At least I look pretty good tonight.

My short, tight black dress covers my chest, which is definitely sporting actual hives at this point, and the long, sheer thin sleeves cover my stupid scars. My wavy hair is piled to one side, and I have on big sparkly earrings. But he stares at my shoes, black and white Nike Jordans. Not sure if it's a good stare or a bad stare, but I don't really care. Killer sneakers are a fashion hill I will die on. I am not about to wear heels to stand on for four hours, and they aren't me anyway.

His eyes take their time coming back up to mine, and I think there might literally be flames in his irises. I look away as fast as possible.

"Thanks for coming out." *Thanks for coming out? That's the best you can do?*

"Of course, I can't believe *Paul* would miss it." Whoa. He just went there. The cojones on this guy. My eyes grow wide while his squint around the edges. I try to find words to defend Paul, but Matt moves on. "Do you have a favorite?" He looks around the space.

"The succulent." I gesture toward a smaller canvas on the right wall, just past where his two friends are meandering. They're trying their best not to look bored, and failing. I smile as I notice them.

"What's the title of that one?" Matt asks. The piece is a small succulent in a teal pot illuminated by a ray of light from a metal heat lamp on a desk. The contrast of the rest of the room and the light just made the piece sing, and I'll be a bit sad to sell it. Janie shoves a water in my hand and gives Matt a flute of champagne and practically runs away. "Thanks," he says to Janie and then looks back to me for my answer.

"It's called 'Better Than Flowers.'"

His smile breaks out. "And what do the TikTokers think of that?"

"I'll find out tomorrow," I say, smiling wide myself. Liquid. Hot liquid. How else do you explain that he actually remembered stuff from the article he read on the plane three months ago? Sexy smooth ridiculous hot liquid. *Danger! Back away!*

Luckily, Maud starts to make her way toward me with the hip couple. Matt sees them approaching.

"Congrats again," he says, then moves toward me for a tentative hug. I open my arms a fraction, an automatic polite instinct, and he hugs me. Except *hug* is not an accurate word for what's happening. We each have a drink in our right hand, so it should be awkward. And we are not even remotely friends, so the hug should be surprising. But it's neither. His left hand wraps around me with zero effort, pulling me in, my cheek to his chest, which is hard and smells incredible. Then that same hand has the audacity to splay across my back as if it's made to be there. The fabric across the back of my dress is sheer, like the sleeves, meaning I can feel every cell of his warm hand against me as if I'm naked.

Then he's gone.

He turns and joins his friends as if fireworks didn't just erupt across the whole front side of my body. *What the . . . ? What just happened?*

Luckily, Maud immediately distracts me. She launches her go-to questions with the potential buyers, and I respond with my clever answers. While I take a few more selfies, sign some collection cards, and answer the usual follow-up questions, I sense Matt and his friends as they walk around and, pretty quickly, they leave. And I'm relieved. *Wait, am I relieved?* Yes.

"Nine out of ten sold tonight! You're such a rock star!" Sam says, which leads to squealing from her and Janie and myself.

"Well done, darling!" Maud says, and we toast the last bit of champagne together.

"Thank you, Maud, seriously. I mean, I can't believe it."

"Believe it, love. You're on your way now. New York better damn well prepare itself!"

In two hours, I'd made eighteen thousand dollars. After taxes and Maud's cut, that number would shrink in half, but still. One step closer to quitting the family business and finally shutting up my father and Susan and everyone else. Maud had pushed me to release sooner and promote harder, and she'd been right.

I squeal again. *Nine paintings sold tonight! Like, what!*

And it's totally about the opening and the money.

Not at all about Liquid Matt who remembered so much about me three months later.

"Let's go out to celebrate, pleeeeease?" Sam gives me her best puppy dog eyes.

I sigh. "I *am* starving . . ."

"Yasssss! What do you feel like? Pizza? Tacos?"

"A big fat burger." I pile my hair up into a topknot, letting my neck breathe.

"You got it." Sam starts looking up nearby options on her phone.

"Let me text Paul. Maud, you coming?" I pull out my phone.

"I need to finish up here, but I'll text you later," Maud says as she gathers leftover printed reception cards from the cocktail tables around us.

"Babe, you up for burgers?" Janie asks Theo, who'd arrived for the tail end of the show. Theo was how Janie and I met years ago. He's a very talented sculptor. At a tiny, shared exhibition, Janie and I hid next to each other in the corner. Theo could keep up with Sam when it came to making friends and conversation. Opposites in so many ways but equally gorgeous. Sam called them Taydaya because he looked like Taye Diggs and she looked like Zendaya. Janie and I had commiserated at that show, started swapping introvert memes, and the rest was best friend history.

"As long as there's a veggie burger on the menu, that's fine." Theo is a vegan, but in New York, that didn't really matter. If the first burger place didn't have vegan options, the next one a block over would.

9:40 P.M.

Me: I sold NINE pieces! We're going out for burgers to celebrate. Want to meet us?

Paul: Wow! Congrats! Why don't you come here after the party and afterparty with me ;)

C'mon, it's just me, Sam, Theo, and Janie and maybe Maud.

I already ate. Come here after?

OK

12:01 A.M.

I'm exhausted, and Sam is a little drunk. See you tomorrow?

12:35 A.M.

Goodnight xoxo

12:36 A.M.

Sam: We need a sister call STAT!

Sam: To talk about Skye and Matt.

Sadie: Matt who? What happened to Paul?

Sally: Who is Matt?!

Sam: Paul is fine. Paul is tall.

Sam: Hey, that rhymes. Paul is tall. Paul is tall.

Sam: lololololololol

Sally: Take her phone away asap.

Sadie: Sally, shouldn't you be asleep?

Sally: [Eye roll emoji]

"Paul is tall. Poor tall Paul hahaha," I hear her cackling on the other side of my bedroom wall.

"Sam, go to sleep!" I hiss.

Me: Surely she is going to pass out any minute now

Sadie: Who is Matt???

Sam: Hot guy she met on the plane! Total meet-cute!

Sam: And he came to her reception!

Sam: Tall Paul didn't come tonight.

Sam: [I'm Just Saying GIF]

Sally: [Animated GIF Anxiously Eating Popcorn]

Sadie: Sorry he didn't come, Skye. Why didn't you say that earlier? That sucks.

No, it doesn't. I didn't ask him to come. Night night now [Waving emoji]

I sit up to head to Sam's room to confiscate her phone, but I can tell from her heavy breathing that, thankfully, she's passed out. The SamStorm is over. But not for long.

CHAPTER 2

I'm already at our little kitchen table with Gus and my coffee when Sam shuffles out of her room. We share an old two-bedroom apartment that could practically fit into one of Dad's closets back home. But the building had been refurbished with giant windows, from which Gus and I could see the full view of the Manhattan skyline across the river. The view never gets old.

"Why did you let me have a third margarita? What kind of big sister are you?" She's grouchy. It took a while for the sun that was my little sister to rise up and start shining.

"The kind that already made coffee and pancakes."

"Mmmm, so the best kind then." She pours coffee into her mug and turns to me. She flashes me an annoying, knowing smile. "So. Didn't go to Paul's last night, after all."

"I had to get you home, you lush."

"Lies. I could've taken an Uber just fine." She stares at me with the same stupid look. I just roll my eyes and focus back on my phone. I mark a couple more images from last night as favorites to post to Instagram before switching gears from my work to *work* work.

"Did you see the latest clapback?" I hope she'll agree to the subject change.

Thankfully, Sam perks up. "Yesssss. Savage. You should just take over the Twitter account."

"Definitely not. I wanted the tweet to say, 'Get back to us when you sprout your first pube.'"

"Ew, Skye, too early for that word."

I raise my mug to salute her. "You see my point."

Canton Cards, the family empire, is a worldwide player in cards and stationery. We have haters. Especially with our "family values" and "Bible Belt roots." Dad and Grandpa expect squeaky-clean perfection in every area, which is why I can't run the corporate Twitter account. One F-bomb, and I'd be not only fired but probably excommunicated as well. *Would that be so bad?*

Normally, I don't care about haters or bad press. But as the world has moved faster and faster toward paperlessness, our family legacy has struggled. We started as an old-fashioned greeting card company, after all. We've adapted pretty well, if a bit slowly. We have a great direct-to-customer, mobile-first website that offers cards, books, gifts, and even digital products. We've partnered with artisans to bring color and texture to all our products that can't be captured in pixels on-screen. I initiated and spearheaded the artist collaborations, which landed us the partnership with Target.

Which must explain why I get so irked that this baby stationery brand keeps trolling us on Twitter. The latest was a reply to a tweet featuring a hilarious birthday card that had an old man on it, and the idiots had replied.

Reply @NewCardsOnTheBlock: Look, it's a pic of Old Man Canton—probably stopping by the mailbox on his way to 5pm dinner.

Like, what the hell? Where does this media intern get off? We are one of the most loved and respected brands in the industry! So, I suggested my somewhat vulgar response, which marketing turned into:

Reply @CantonCards: We'll be sure to congratulate you when you post a proud pic of your first chest hair.

Which honestly was a good compromise. My responses—with their censoring—have brought us some great press. And by us, I mean Dad. Of course.

"Hello? Skye? Can we please talk about Paul?" Sam starts tentatively, pulling me from Twitter.

"What about Paul?" I'm already defensive.

"I love Paul!" She shoves a chunk of plain pancake in her mouth and keeps on talking. "Paul's the best! Great guy, super cute, very tall. Like six-three or something? Love that for you, for sure, for sure . . . *buuuut . . .*" I sigh. "Just hear me out, Skye. Hear me out."

"But what? But he's not one of Sadie's secretly romantic brooding billionaires ready to whisk me off to Tuscany? Give me a break, Sam. None of that crap is real. Meet-cutes aren't real! Paul is real!" My gray, speckled, four-legged soulmate feels the mood shift, hops down from the windowsill, and makes his exit. *Take me with you, Gus!*

Now it's her turn to sigh. "Um, you literally had a meet-cute on the plane. In real life! But even if you forget about that, it's just . . .

last night, the way you lit up with Matt . . ." I start rolling my eyes. "C'mon, admit it! You couldn't stop smiling. And he looked at you like he wanted to lay you down and make you scream right there in the middle of the gallery."

I can't shake my head hard enough. "You're insane."

"I'm not! He was all like, 'Hey, Skye.'" She mimics him in a low, manly voice with lidded eyes. "Congratulations, I stalk your Instagram, and I want to take you home and hump your pretty little brains out." She raises her normal voice. "I think I had an orgasm just watching you two talk."

"One, gross. Two, hump my brains out? Really? And three, no, he didn't—doesn't. He's just another classic player. He knows what to say and how to say it, probably to the entire city. I'm surprised he didn't ask you for your number once he found out I had a boyfriend."

She raises a brow. "He came to your opening."

"Yeah, because he's smooth, Samantha. Too freaking smooth."

"Ohhh, okay, so any guy who's hot and thoughtful and outgoing is automatically an asshole?"

I laugh, but it sounds more bitter than I mean for it to. "Finally, you're learning."

"That's really sad, Skye. Ryan was a douchebag, but that doesn't make all hot guys douchebags."

"I know. Paul is hot, and he's not a douchebag," I say calmly, happy to have won. She stares at me, her mouth in a flat line, baiting me. "What, you don't think Paul is hot?"

"Paul is cute. Maybe even hot sometimes, but last night, you were, like, glowing. Like the clouds parted and angels were like,

'Ahhhhh!'" She sings it out like an opera singer. "And in two whole years, you've never looked like that around Paul."

"That's because Paul doesn't make me feel uncomfortable!"

She slams down her coffee cup so her hands can fly up with abandon. "Paul doesn't make you feel *anything*! You two have about as much heat as Susan's deep freezer."

"We have heat, we just have it in private." She cocks her head in disbelief, and I'm getting pissed. "And you know what? Remind me to pick apart the next guy you date, see how you like it. It's been, what, thirty seconds since Josh? It's early, I'm sure you'll be madly in love again by the end of the day."

She doesn't show how hurt she is, because I've hurt her with mean comments so many times it's second nature now. I feel bad after the words are out, as always. I sigh, about to apologize.

"You're right," she says softly, grabbing another plain pancake. "Paul is great, and I don't know what your relationship is really like. Forget I said anything." She walks back to her room and shuts the door.

I focus back on work. I crop and edit a photo of myself, Maud, Sam, and Janie from last night and post it to Instagram, along with a few cool shots from the reception. For the caption, I just put the gallery information and show dates, hoping more people will go by and see it before it comes down in a month. I respond to a few messages and comments and hop up to change. I will apologize to Sam later.

Right now, I need to run.

I can feel anxiety building in my chest. Adrenaline from last night, pressure with my dad, guilt for hurting Sam, and the questions that always pop up after I finish a project. *What next? Was that the best I can do? Do I have more ideas in me? Do I have what it takes to do that all over again in three months? What if I don't? Does Paul make me feel anything?*

———————————

I still feel a rush of excitement running around Brooklyn. There's no better place to be invisible than the crowded streets of New York. Turns out one of the loudest, busiest, densest cities in the world is an introvert's paradise. And while I'm not in the city itself, I can see Manhattan across the East River to my right. My feet hit the pavement, which pulls my anxiety down into the concrete and away from my brain. I can think again.

There are always more ideas. I'll be fine. I've never run out of ideas. And Maud and Janie will keep me accountable to actually create, not just dream. *Must text Maud another thank-you when I get home.*

Dad is staying out of my way. He's not supportive, but he's not holding me back. And I'm making real progress now. I'm following my plan. Closer every day. Left, right, left, right, keep moving.

Paul. He never texted me back last night, now that I think of it. He fell asleep, I guess. But he didn't text me back this morning, either. Although, if he got into an early flow, it's not unusual for him to zone out for hours. Like I do when I'm painting. He edits novels, mostly fantasy and science fiction, and he can get lost in words like I get lost in paint. It's what makes us work. We can go for days without talking. We can go for weeks without a date. Wait, when was the last time we went on a date? When was the last time we . . . ?

Holy crap. It's been over two weeks since I've seen him. My boyfriend of two years. And he hadn't even asked for a booty call in all that time. *Remember to google symptoms of low testosterone.*

But what if it wasn't him? What if it was me? I'm cute, I have good days, even great days, but I'm no Barbie. Not a sultry sexpot either, that's for sure. I'm not a prude, but I wouldn't call myself experienced. I just don't do casual. Call me old-fashioned, but sex is too intimate. It's too raw, which maybe makes me almost a romantic?

I can't comprehend how someone could have a one-night stand without getting all kinds of emotional. So, Paul and I had waited a long time before sleeping together, and he hadn't minded waiting at all. Maybe he didn't desire me much because I'm just not that desirable?

Hm. Ryan had desired me. But Ryan desired everything with legs, it turned out. *No more thinking about Ryan!* Left right, left right.

I look out across a grassy square filled with families, dog walkers, Frisbee throwers, and couples. I see one guy leaning over a girl stretched out on a blanket, talking down to her like they're the only two humans on the planet. I feel a tiny stab in my heart.

Matt is like Ryan. I am right, Sam is naïve. Would Matt look down on me that way on a blanket in a park in Brooklyn? Intense, like we were the last two people on the planet? Yes. He probably would. But that's because he's liquid heat. And I don't want to feel that burn.

But do I want a soft cold lump?

Wait, is my relationship a soft cold lump? Just because Sam says so? Maybe I just need to warm things up. Maybe we're just in a rut and need a jump start. Yes. That's it. We just need some rekindling. *After shower, google "How to be a sexpot" and make my grand plan for tomorrow.*

CHAPTER 3

> **Me: Are you alive?**
> Paul: Hey, sorry, got in the zone on this zombie thriller. How was last night?
> **Fun, but I didn't get any dessert after dinner ;)**

He doesn't seem to mind that I didn't come over. But I'll just make him mind. A sexpot is all about innuendo, Google said.

> I didn't have dessert either ;)
> **How about dessert now?**
> Ok, half an hour?
> **Yep**

I smile to myself, feeling warmer toward Paul already. I'm doing the most cliché sexpot thing there is, but Paul will still be surprised, so who cares if it's cliché? Sam has a long, gray lightweight jacket that passes as a trench coat. So, I'm wearing a lacy black bra and lacy matching underwear and the trench and nothing else. I almost went with a thong, but with my luck, I'd slip over a homeless person's dog's leash on my way, flying spread eagle into a busy street. Innocent New York passersby don't need to see my entire eagle in all its glory. So brief-cut underwear it is. I put on my walking sneakers and take my small canvas shoe bag containing scrappy black heels.

Sadie was the one who'd explained that no one wore cute shoes to walk around the city. They wore disgusting comfortable athletic shoes and carried designer shoes in little bags, sometimes canvas or brown paper or even plastic. A woman could be wearing Chanel from head to ankle, but at the ankle, you'd find grungy New Balance. And in the same hand as her three-thousand-dollar clutch, she held a small canvas bag almost the exact same as mine. Those types of sightings always brought me great joy. I try to make eye contact and say, *We're the same underneath, Lillian Vanderbergenstein the Third. The same.* It's really the little things in life.

It would only take me ten minutes to get to Paul's, so I left. I'd dried my hair enough to put it up in an unruly ponytail that I hoped looked messy-sexy. My makeup was normal except for extra eyeliner and mascara. Sexpots had smoky eyes, obviously. I was locked and loaded, and I wanted the element of surprise.

And I was surprised. By how hot I was. The coat had looked sleek and lightweight when Sam handed it to me, but it was like a rain jacket. I was basically walking through the city wrapped in a plastic tarp in late August! *Idiot!* But I was already halfway there by the time I realized my mistake.

I powered on. But getting sweaty made me nervous, because what was happening to my sexy vibe? Was this a dumb idea? My liner was starting to feel smudgy in a bad way, my hair was frizzing from the humidity, and my buttcrack was getting swampier with each step. *How do people not wear thongs? Torture!* And then my nerves did what they always do: made me sweat.

I decided to pick up my pace. The lobby of Paul's apartment building would have air-conditioning. I could just hustle there and then cool down for a minute. I was officially speed walking. But with the sweating and the nerves, I made the stupid mistake of looking at my phone while walking across a crosswalk. This is something you don't do, because crosswalks are primed for puddles. Puddles of varying depths of absolute, unequaled, unimaginable filth. Doesn't matter if it recently rained. This isn't rainwater. Think urine and vomit and day-old pizza sauce and hose water. And then add much more urine and vomit. And a couple mystery substances. That's what was in the puddle that my right foot smashed into, ankle-deep, sure and fast. The mini-pond consumed my entire right foot and splashed hell's gutter runoff all over both of my legs.

So now I'm walking along—*step, squish, step, squish*—refusing to breathe through my nose because I don't want to know how bad it is. Because it's bad. Really bad. My eyes start to water from the smell that I'm not even fully smelling. I keep moving, only a block over from Paul's place. Almost there, he'll still be surprised. *Just get in there already!*

I walk into his apartment building and say a quick thank-you prayer to the Good Lord for air-conditioning. But I'm so close, I just keep going instead of airing out. I have a key, so I let myself on the elevator up to Paul's floor and step-squish-step-squish quickly down the hall. I knock on his door. He doesn't answer. No problem. I'll just quietly let myself in like I have many times.

He lives alone in a nice one-bedroom apartment with zero personality and one million apartment amenities. The place has good light and came with decent modern furniture. I made Paul change out the cheap art prints, so at least the walls have some life. Paul couldn't care less, and I don't stay over enough to mind either. A quick scan tells me he must be in his room. Perfect! I use my left shoe to slip off my soiled shoe and sock and then pull off the other.

Adrenaline has taken me over. I pad to his bedroom and slip on my scrappy black heels. I push open the door and step in. He's in the bathroom with the shower running. Shower sex! Super hot! I'm actually getting excited now. I walk over and fling the door open with my newfound confidence. He's naked but not in the shower yet.

"Hey, big boy, want some dessert?" I say in the sultriest voice I can muster.

Bzzzzzz!

Crunch!

"Ah!" he yells. "What the ffff— owwwww!"

"Ah! Sorry! It's me!"

"Ahhhhh! My . . . I think I'm bleeding!"

"I'm sorry! I was trying to surprise you!"

Oh, dear God.

I surprised him while he was . . . grooming. Wow. This could not be going much worse. He grabs a towel and holds it onto his crotch and then grimaces as he looks back at me, raising a hand to his face.

"Ugh, what is that smell?"

I forgot to rinse off my feet! City-puddle-sludge particles are still all over my legs. He turns to really face me and looks genuinely concerned, not even noticing the trench coat and heels. "Skye, are you okay? What's going on?"

I peer around him to the mirror.

Dear Jesus, return now and take me to glory, please.

This really is too mortifying. Not only did I just puncture my boyfriend's equipment, but I look like the walking opposite of sexy. I am somehow flushed, while also pale and slick with sweat, and my mascara has left my eyes completely. It's halfway down my cheeks. My hair has gone beyond frizz. It looks like I took a 1989 crimper tool to it. And look at that, there's a splash of sludge puddle across my forehead. I look like a goth tween stole her mom's makeup on the way to an '80s party but got run over by a trash truck on the way. *Wow. Just wow.*

"I-I'm fine. Sorry, are *you* okay? Do you need to go to the ER?"

"I think it's okay, but uh, can you give me a minute?" he says, also mortified.

"Yeah, of course."

I make my way out to the kitchen and wet some paper towels to clean off my legs. Talk about a swing and a miss. I'm not sure anyone has swung and missed anything harder ever in their lives. I stare at the beige carpet trying to figure out a way to salvage this situation. After what feels like forever, Paul comes out of his room in his boxers. He joins me on the couch, where I've collapsed in defeat.

"Hey." He bites his lip.

"I'm sorry, I was trying to be a sexpot."

He chuckles. "Sexpot, huh?"

I start giggling too. "Safe to say, I failed."

"I don't know, I didn't actually get to see what you're wearing under there." He nudges me.

"You know what, I should probably shower."

"Okay," he exhales, leaning back to let me get up.

I cock my head. "Want to join me?"

"I think I'm going to need a few hours." His eyes dart down to his new wound.

I nod and head to the bathroom. Instead of disappointment, I feel . . . fine.

I rinse quickly and step out into his room to find some clothes of his to throw on. I attempt an easy-breezy tone as I join him.

"What are you doing the rest of the day?"

"Hm?" He doesn't look up from his desk. "Just editing, you know."

"Want to order some dinner?"

"Sure."

I open the hall closet and throw my shoes and socks into the washer. I flip the washer on and turn to ask him if he wants to watch some garbage Netflix with me. But he's already absorbed back into the zombiepocalypse. I lie on his bed and pull up Instagram on my phone, but I'm not really looking as I scroll.

I think about the day's failure. And about how I'm not all that bummed about it. When was the last time Paul and I really went at it? The last time I wanted jump on him? When was the last time I'd blurted "I love you" or heard something from him other than "Sure" or "Yeah"? Was this just a rough spot in our journey or the end of the road?

48

I look over at Paul, tense, staring at his computer. Bless his focused heart, if I got up and left, he wouldn't notice until hours from now. And even then, he'd probably text just to ask if I made it home okay. But I like all the space he gives me, don't I? Paul is kind and funny (on the rare occasion that he chats), and he gets my need for space. Am I really going to give up on him, on us, to go back to the cruel and unusual punishment that is dating? Ugh.

On my walk home, I decide to call Susan. As much as her mothering and managing drive me insane, she has the right brain for picking in this specific situation.

"Skye? What's wrong? What happened?"

"Everything is fine, Suze."

"No one is dead? Injured? Bleeding?"

My face pulls tight with annoyance. "Very funny. Great reminder of why I just *love* calling you so much."

Susan laughs freely. "All right, all right, sorry. What's up?"

"I, um, need some advice." My admission is as wobbly as my freshly cleaned feet. I wait for her reply as I watch every step at a busy crosswalk.

"Is this about Sam's texts while I was sleeping?"

"Sort of. I just . . . when do you know if, like, the spark of a relationship has totally gone out or if you need to just work harder at it?" She doesn't respond. "Suze?" She sighs on the other end. Which is weird. Normally she'd be well into her second paragraph of advice by now.

"Skye, if Paul ended it tomorrow, would you be sad?"

I slow my pace. That's a good question.

"I mean . . . maybe—" I start, but she cuts me off.

"Would you be devastated, though? Like beyond a couple weeks of Rocky Road and Chardonnay. Would you have trouble functioning?"

"No . . . no, I think I'd be fine."

"Then you have your answer."

My eyes start to sting. "So, the sign of a good relationship is if you're some kind of dumbstruck, weepy codependent? I mean, that's not me, Suze, it's just not."

"No, but if it's real love, it's unbearable to live without," she says. I sniff. She goes on: "And Skye, you deserve that. Real, crazy love." I scoff. "I know, I know, you thought you had that with Ryan, and it turned out he was an ass, and that scared the crap out of you. But maybe you over-corrected a bit?"

"Over-corrected?" I ask, passing back by the park from earlier. The couple on the blanket is long gone.

"Yeah, like you were reeling from Ryan, so you went with the safest, kindest, and if I'm being honest, most vanilla man I've ever met in my life."

"Oh, what, because Adam is a such a Casanova? With his dad jokes and his football obsession. Practically the Dos Equis guy. Soooo fascinating," I snap.

"I asked for that, I guess." She sighs, and I join her, breathing out regret. *Two sisters in one day, look at me go.* I love Adam. He's been my brother-in-law for over a decade. But I did have a point. He could definitely be described as vanilla, and he was *Tulsa vanilla*. At least Paul was *New York* vanilla.

"I'm sorry, Susan. I'm just confused."

"Confused because of this Matt guy?" She smiles as she says it, more as a comment than a question.

"No . . . I mean, yes. But he's just like Ryan. Smooth and hot. Too hot. But I think it just—"

"Made you realize Paul is not even, uh, a little bit warm?"

"Wellll . . ." I wince. I hear her mumbling something to one of the kids as I ponder what she's saying. I try to reel her back in to our conversation. "So, no chance that things with Paul could turn into something I can't live without?"

"Skye. You've been with him forever—"

"Only two years."

"Exactly. Forever. You already know the answer. And listen, you called me because you wanted me to confirm it for you. So don't you go getting pissed at me for doing exactly what you wanted me to do." I don't know what to say. She's right. As always. So unbelievably irritating.

"Listen, I've got to put out a glitter fire happening here. Just a couple weeks till we're there, so then I want to hear more. It's important for you to be there, with us, you know that, right?"

"Yeah, yeah, I know. I'll see you then."

"Hey. One more thing. For what it's worth, Ryan would never have gone to one of your openings."

"Hm."

"K— No! Do *not* open that! Put that down! I really have to go now. Love you, bye."

"Love you."

I stare off at the city in the distance. So many buildings. So many people. Surely somewhere out there is a guy who is hot— who'd be hot to me and *for* me—without the burn? Or is real, deep love a devastating fire that will consume you, no matter who you fall for? And that last bit about my show—is that enough to prove Matt isn't a Ryan? Is it enough for me to get to know Matt and find out? Maybe it is.

At this, my shoulders tense as my stomach drops, but I know what I have to do.

CHAPTER 4

"Well, that was easy," I say as I close the apartment door and set the plastic sack down on the counter.

"I'm . . . sorry? I don't know how to feel. Are we relieved, or are we bummed?" Sam asks as she gets up and walks over. "Holy crap, you really did buy every candy bar they had. Ooo even a Toblerone! Please break up with people more often—those are my favorite!"

"Honestly, if all breakups are that easy, I guess I can keep 'em coming for you," I say, digging out a king-size Snickers.

"So? What did you say? What did he say? Did you cry? Did *he* cry? Tell me everything." Sam hits me with questions in the same way she sends texts. We move to the couch with our chosen chocolates.

"We had dinner, and then I said I thought we'd be better off as just friends."

"K. Classic. And he said?"

"He said, 'Oh, really?' like kind of surprised and sad." Sam stretches her mouth out and down in what can only be described as an "eek face." I go on: "But then he was like, 'Uh, okay,' totally recovered. Didn't argue or ask me anything, and I didn't know what to say next, so we just sat there marinating in awkward. After a few minutes, I just got up to leave and we hugged and said we'd keep in touch and see each other around."

"Thassi?" Sam asks, mouth full of caramel.

"That's it. Like it was no big deal."

"Isn't that good?"

"Yeah."

"K, sooo theeen, why the fifty pounds of chocolate?"

I sigh. "Because it's still sad. In fact, it might be even sadder that it just ended like that—no fight, no crying, no spark. Just like it started . . . two whole years of a limpy, lukewarm blah." My voice gets shaky.

"I'm going to go ahead and get the bag," she says as she gets up to grab the sack and bring it to the coffee table.

"And now I'm single again. And I have to get back 'out there.' You know I hate it 'out there,' Sam, I hate it! Ughhhhhh, kill me slowly with a dull spoon."

"Disturbing. But! You know what it means if you're single?"

"I'll have more time to paint?"

"Pshfff, you'll have more time for Hot Matt!" She squeals with delight as I sigh. But I accidentally let the corner of my mouth kick up the tiniest bit, which sets her off in the worst way. "Yes! I saw that! You like him! Ahhhhh! This is so exciting. I'm dying. I'm literally dying right now. Let's text him!"

I kill my enthusiasm. "I don't even have his number."

"But he follows you on Insta! Eeeeeee, I'm pulling him up right now." The Sam Train has officially left the station.

"He does, but—"

"Found him! Matt James, this is him, right?"

"You're terrifying, you know that?" I scoot closer to her on the couch with a share-size KitKat that I will not be sharing.

"So . . ." She tilts the phone in my direction. "Just message him."

"Absolutely not. Message him and say what? 'Hey, I broke up with my boyfriend for you, even though I don't know you at all. Totally normal. No pressure!'"

She ignores me.

"Hmm, his profile doesn't tell us much. No bio link either. Did you google him?" She pulls up Google before I can save her the trouble. "Oh. Matt James. There are ten million Matt Jameses."

"Exactly." I watch her pull up LinkedIn. "Ew, LinkedIn?"

"Psh, everyone who's not a painter has a LinkedIn. Look! Here! Matt James, New York City . . . President of Engineering, ooooooo, fancy." I take the phone from her. Software engineering degree from University of Texas *(barf)*, worked at a few techy-type companies I've never heard of. Says he's currently a cofounder of one company and the president of another. Well, crap. This all sounds very intimidating. Sam has read right along with me. "Aside from the Texas bit—gross—he looks pretty amazing on paper, er, screen, don't you think?"

"I don't know. What if he's Besos junior, ruining all our lives one wirelessly connected endorphin hit at a time?"

"Okay, *Dad.*"

"On that, Dad and I actually agree. So what if he does sound good on paper? I'm not going to message him on Instagram, and I don't even have a LinkedIn. I just need to be alone for a while, focus on my next series."

"Laaaaaaaame!" She is just so, so loud. "Do you follow him back?"

"Nope."

"Well, that's step one."

"No!" Now I'm getting loud. "Hello, Desperate! Also, following back doesn't exactly tell him I'm single."

She taps a finger to her lips like a detective from a '90s movie. "Does he like your posts?"

"Watches my stories."

"Skye! You little minx. You didn't even hesitate. How long have you been secretly stalking him? Eeeeeee! You're going to fall in love and get married and have such hot little babies."

"Can you take it down like one hundred notches, please? Yes, I notice when his profile pic shows up in my stories. But he doesn't like or comment. I'm not sure he's even still paying much attention after learning about Paul a couple weeks ago."

Sam pauses uncharacteristically. "I've got it. You post a hot selfie, and I'll take care of the rest."

"I'm not posting a hot selfie."

"Okay, forget about Wizard Hands then."

I slump in defeat. She's got me.

———————

I hit Post and immediately take a trip to Splotch City. Because it's embarrassing how long I spent on an image of myself.

Earlier today, I set my phone up on an easel in my studio after waiting until the light was just right, like a cross between an incredibly vain asshat and an incredibly artsy light snob. I decided to put my hair up and leave my hands covered in paint. I put on my nicer brightly stained apron smock (versus my favorite oversize sleeved smock that looks like a muumuu). The cuter smock covered my short shorts and a tank top. *Okay, yes, it looks like I am maybe wearing my smock and nothing else.* It's as thirst trap—an intentionally sexy post aimed at getting a reaction, Sam explained—as I'm willing to get.

I held a medium-size angled brush in my right hand, one of my favorites, and smiled a wide smile at the camera. Then a small smile. Then a toothless smile. Then I tried a sexy grin and reviewed. *Hi, I'm Skye and I'm constipated.* Then I looked away from the camera, then I fake laughed. Yes. I stood alone in my studio and fake laughed while my phone took bursts of images.

I am the lamest of the lame, and now the back of my neck is sweating.

But the result—my smiling wide but looking off to the right of the camera—looks good. Cute. Intriguing. Messy. Which was funny, because I'd strategically planned all the mess and spent an eternity getting the perfect impromptu vibe.

I edited the image to give the colors a faded artsy feel to match the rest of my posts. I went with "Starting something new" as the caption, like Sam and I had agreed upon. I felt like a seventh-grader conspiring with her friends on how to best send her crush a note in fifth period. I was oozing lamesauce.

"Okay, I posted it!" I call to Sam in her room. I'm home and curled up on the couch with Gus, who is purring away. My body curls tighter with nerves. She better know what she's doing. Immediately her comment comes in with a ping.

@SamCHammer: WATCH OUT NEW YORK SHE'S SINGLE AND READY TO MINGLE!!!!! [Five fire emojis]

What!

"Single and ready to mingle!" I screech. Gus tenses. "Are you insane! Oh my gosh, this is so bad. I am the most pathetic. I'm deleting that!"

"No! Trust the process, you wimp! Eye on the prize, Skye!" She rushes in, making some sort of awkward jazz-hands motion I don't understand. "Hot Plane Hands, remember?"

I flop sideways on the couch and throw a pillow over my head. "Ughhhhhh."

Then I have a thought.

A reply to her comment.

I can do this.

@APaintedSkye: Sure, if by mingle you mean chug coffee, sleep, paint, or run.

There. Much better. I am a busy, focused artist. And I'd rather get a colonoscopy than do anything remotely close to "mingling."

"You're already blowing up with likes and comments. So many fire emojis! And what, five guys have already said they want to mingle. I kind of hate you." Sam sighs as she joins me on the couch. She takes Gus and puts him in her lap. I huff at her for taking my cat. She side-eyes me. "I need his emotional support right now. I'm turning green."

"Bob." I use one of her favorite nicknames to make sure she's listening. "If these people could see the real me on the inside, cranky and anal, and then the real you, somehow through their little screens, you would have one million followers and I would have zero."

Her face says she's considering the idea. "You'd have one."

"Who, Matt?"

"No, me, you cranky, anal dummy."

Remember to tell all my followers to follow Sam, who is, in fact, the best.

She pulls out her phone. "So has he liked it yet, can you see?"

"Nope. He never likes my posts."

"Have you ever liked *his* posts?"

"No, like I said, I don't follow him."

"Seriously? Throw the guy a freakin' bone, Skye. You've kind of rejected him twice."

"I haven't rejected him! I had a boyfriend!"

"And now you don't, and unless you get his attention, he'll never know. Just follow him. No liking or commenting—just a follow back."

I suck in my breath nervously as I tap the button. "Okay, followed."

"Good. Okay. Now share your post to your story so he'll see it here. I'm telling you, he's going to message you. Just wait."

I did wait. All afternoon. Nada. Which filled me up with all kinds of questions. Did Matt already move on from me? Why did that disappoint me so much when I hardly know the guy? And why was I already forgetting that what I *did* know of this guy was pure trouble? If he didn't respond, what was I going to do? And why on earth did I start any of this? I could still be with Paul, painting away, oblivious and content. Too many questions. And if my brain wanted to race, then I'd freaking race.

———————

I walk into the apartment, raced out after a hard eight miles, panting and drenched.

"Hey, you need to check your email!" Sam calls to me.

"Why?"

"Susan and Dad are scrambling about a last-minute change for next week, and they need all of us to weigh in asap, but by all of us, they really mean you."

I groan. *Only a few more months, maybe a year or two, max,* I tell myself as I pull out my phone. Then I can quit my role in the business and go out on my own full-time. I don't hate the job, not really. I do have an eye for marketing, and Susan lets me work whatever hours I want under the title of brand consultant. All I have to do is guide the great Canton Cards brand enough to keep us from veering off track with a bad line of stationery or a lame advertising campaign.

We have—not we, Dad—*Dad has* assembled a great marketing team over the years, but every so often they do get complacent. I stay removed enough that I'm able to stay fresh, critical, demanding. The marketing people hate me. And I don't blame them. But it's temporary. As soon as I can cover my expenses with my own painting money, I'm out. Which I've told Dad and Susan—sometimes more the Canton Cards COO than she is my actual sister—one thousand times. He wants all five of his Canton girls in the business. He's never said he wishes he'd had sons, but *I* wish he'd had at least one son to carry the mantle for all of us.

I've put in the work, building my brand completely separate from the Canton name. I haven't asked Dad for any favors in New York, haven't tried to capitalize on Sadie's fame. Dad insisted on paying for my education, which I'm grateful for, and of course he gave me a job. But I insisted Susan check the right salary range for my position, make me work my way up, and earn any bonuses or raises. I'm more of a stickler about it than either of them. And it will be worth it. Only a year or so more.

"This is the most stressed I think I've ever seen them," Sam says as she taps on her phone in the kitchen.

"I know."

"Did you see New Cards on the Block is doing a big app reveal at convention? Dad blew a gasket. Told the whole marketing team we needed an app before next week."

"Oh, I know." I chuckle. "I've seen Dad spout off about competitors before, but this is next level. I bet Suze has got him on blood pressure meds."

"I think he's actually scared. I don't like it."

"Yeah." I sigh. "I don't either." I close the email after putting out the branding fire and open Instagram, yet again.

I have a bunch of notifications, mostly just emoji reactions to my selfie.

But then, there it is.

@MattJames1010: I can chug coffee or run. I can also eat, but that wasn't listed.

"Samantha Louise!" I shout. "You beautiful genius! He sent me a message!"

She bounds into the living room so fast Gus hollers and skids under the couch in a blink.

"Eeeeeee! What's it say? What's it say?" She comes up next to me to see over my phone. "Ew, you are dripping." She moves a foot away, squealing some more. "I told you. You owe me forever! I call maid of honor *and* godmother. Janie can suck it."

I laugh at her. "Maybe first you can tell me what to write back?"

"Tell him you eat. Make him take you to dinner."

"No. Dinner is too much. I'm not ready for dinner. Plus, what if he's a creep? What if he's a serial killer?"

"He went to Texas. He's not a serial killer."

I laugh out loud. "Serial killers can have college degrees, Sam. No dinner. What do I say?"

"Send a coffee emoji? Can you handle coffee?"

"Nope. I can feel the hives forming. I think I'll send a running emoji."

"Running? How can you go on a date running? Also, uh, hello? Look at you, you're disgusting. This is not Sporty Spice. This is Prescription-Strength Antiperspirant Spice. Minus the spice. You want him to go on a date with this?" She motions her hand up and down at my person. I consider her very valid points.

"Running means very little talking. Which is good. And we can just do four or five miles, so no super sweating."

"Skye, I love you, but you super sweat just thinking about having to make a phone call." I grunt. Because she is correct. There would be sweat. I look back at his message as she carries on. "Plus, is he, like, a runner? I mean, could you tell if he was in good shape? What if he's panting and gross? What if he has a heart attack on your first date?" She starts laughing. "Think about it! If there's anyone who's gonna have a guy keel over on their first date, it's you." I start to laugh too. She's not wrong. I tried to be sexy, and Paul almost lost his junk, I remember vividly. Hmm, okay, let's see if he can hang . . .

@PaintedSkye: You can run like you're a runner? Or you can run like you're a dude who sometimes works out and thinks you can automatically keep up with a girl?

"What, what are you typing? What did you say? Please say it was a coffee emoji." Sam comes back over into my sticky personal space. I show her the message. She sighs.

"What?"

She shakes her head. "You're just so . . . *intense.*"

"*I'm* intense? Are you kidding me right now?"

"Intense like serious. Intimidating. I mean, damn! Was your goal to scare his balls up into his bladder?" We're interrupted by a notification.

@MattJames1010: Runner enough that I am confident I can keep up.

"See? He's into it!" My stomach tries to join Gus under the couch. "If he was scared off from one snarky comment, then he's done for anyway."

"Now *that's* the God's honest truth."

I glare at her. She doesn't need to pile on, though she's earned the right. "Just tell me what to reply that will keep his balls firmly outside of his body."

"K . . ." Sam thinks.

"How about, 'I look forward to seeing you try'?"

"Oh, that's hot. Yes, definitely send that!"

"Does it matter that I'm not actually that fast?" I wonder.

"No, he doesn't care about the running, you idiot. He's probably ecstatic that on the first date you're going to be wearing head-to-toe Spandex!"

"Wait, *is this* a date? And why didn't you remind me of the Spandex situation *before* I sent that?" I moaned.

"Just send your sexy reply already."

@PaintedSkye: I look forward to seeing you try.

@MattJames1010: Morning or evening?

@PaintedSkye: Evening

@MattJames1010: Tomorrow? 6? CP?

@PaintedSkye: Meet at General Sherman?

@MattJames1010: Roger.

"You could've made up plans tomorrow, pretended that you actually have a social life," Sam chimes in, even though the messages have flown by already.

"Welp. I didn't. What do I say to 'Roger'?"

"Go back to that *like to see you try* energy. Something flirty." We both stare at my phone. "C'mon, you're the clever one-liner girl, say something. Quick!"

"How about this?"

@PaintedSkye: Don't forget to stretch and hydrate. Longhorns aren't exactly known for their speed. Wouldn't want you to pull something.

"Yes, quick, send it!" Sam says, and I hit the arrow.

@MattJames1010: Arrive warm and fully stretched. Got it.

"Warm and fully stretched? Are you kidding me?" Sam goes full Sam. "I bet he's 'warm and fully stretched' as he typed that. I be he's looking at your selfie and stretching. Holy crap, I cannot. Skye, I cannot with this guy." And I'm feeling on the inside what she's yelling on the outside. All twisty and excited and . . . worried. I quickly lock my phone and set it down like it's on fire.

No. Not fire. Sam was right. Not all smooth talkers are mean, cheating bastards. It's just one date, and not even a real sit-down-and-talk date. I'll feel out if he is truly a jerk and go from there. Maybe I'll feel a lot of things. As long as I don't let myself get carried away again.

CHAPTER 5

I stretch on the subway, more nervous than I can remember being in a long time. More nervous than I was for my last two gallery receptions, and that's saying something. I'm wearing tight, black, biker-length shorts and a slouchy, long-sleeve, neon-pink running shirt. It's mesh, but it'll still be hot. It covers my scars and the hives that are surely on their way, and it shows my black sports bra underneath. I go with the padded sports bra, because duh. I only have a handful up there, and the running that keeps me sane also keeps me lean. Lean used to be good, until the Kardashians changed everything with their amazing butts. *Must check Amazon for butt-padded running shorts!*

I step off the train and put my phone in my side pocket as I hustle up to the street. I'm eight minutes late because I am me, and no matter what, I cannot arrive on time. It's not that I don't care or try. It's a law of the universe. Sometimes I wonder if it's God's way of punishing me for all the snark. The gold General Sherman statue right outside of Central Park is only a few quick steps away, and my heart seems to be starting the run without me.

Oh.

Maybe this wasn't such a bad idea, after all. Because there he is, stretching again, opening up his substantial chest just like he did on the plane. But this time, I get a full view of his built, veiny arms in a white, short-sleeve, dry-fit shirt and dark gray running shorts. Shorts that somehow highlight his firm butt without being tight. Upon further inspection, I can see now: he is clearly a runner. With great calves. He's talking to one of the guys he brought to my opening. He brought someone along on our date?

Someone bumps into me because, whoops, I stopped walking. And he just caught me staring at him. Yet again. *Fantastic.* I remember how to move my feet as he smiles and walks toward me. His hair is mussed like he's had a long Monday of Mondays. His intense brown eyes look me up and down and not in a subtle way.

"Hey, Skye. This is Carter, my cousin."

Carter is not dressed for running, clearly on his way elsewhere. Not tagging along on our date. He gives me a sheepish smile. "Nice to meet you."

"Hi?" It sounds like a question.

"You kids have fun," Carter says, heading back toward the street.

"Hey." Matt smirks at me as I'm about to ask why his cousin was almost our third wheel, but suddenly he's much too close. He puts his right hand on my shoulder. Is he going to hug me? Kiss me? Right here on our first non-date in front of all these randos walking by the statue? Wait, did I have onions at lunch?

He smiles and pulls up his left leg with his left hand to stretch his hamstring, using me for balance. I wobble a tiny bit. Unable to think about anything other than the fireworks happening on my left shoulder. "You ready to go, Usain Bolt?" He switches hands and legs.

"I'm not *that* fast." I backtrack. "Actually, I'm not even fast." He's fast. Crap. Aaand my hives have joined us. "I-I was just giving you a hard time."

"No, no. No going back now." He chuckles. "I fully intend to watch you run ahead of me for what, ten miles?"

I laugh too loud at the number. "How about five miles?"

"Five miles." He motions his hand out wide for me to lead the way. I pull out my headphones, and he gives me a look. Knowing he was hoping to talk to me gives me a weird confidence boost, so I say "Enjoy the view" with a smirk as I take off. *Did I really just say that? With my tiny butt?*

After about twenty minutes, which is two miles for me, I turn to jog backward for a couple steps so I can smile at him. But he is actually way behind me. Which is surprising. He looks relaxed, smiling, has his own headphones in. So, what's he doing way back there? I turn back around and enjoy the AJR song that fits my pace. I turn again just before I hit three miles, curious about what he's doing.

He's running away from me?

Oh, Lord.

He's doubling back.

I'm so slow he's making laps back and forth behind me! I feel my face flush, but I'm already bright pink from running anyway.

He's probably bored out of his mind.

He's probably a retired Olympian.

He probably runs six-minute miles.

I turn up the volume on my headphones and get moving.

That fourth mile I am hauling. And it feels amazing. My nerves have been successfully drilled into the street, and I'm feeling confident in my athleticism. I'm not even sweating that badly. So, I turn back again to see if he's still sprinting three miles to every one of mine. He's not as far and gives me a huge smile.

And my foot catches on a bubbling crack in the asphalt.

Because I am me.

No, no, no, remain upright! Upright! But my leg defies physics, launching up into the sky with abandon.

Why did I think I could run backward? In what universe do I do that without wiping out?

I go down in a crumple. Not gracefully. Not firm and swift like a felled tree. No, I go down like an air-blown Christmas yard snowman that's been unplugged. I think I even heard a sad trombone sound as my tailbone lunged toward the earth's crust.

I try to catch myself with my right arm, scraping my elbow so hard that both my skin and my shirt rip open. Blood again. *Second bloody date in as many weeks. What. Is. Happening?*

Matt's kneeling next to me one second later, having bound over at the speed of light.

"Are you okay?" He's smiling as he says it, because he saw that crumple in all its glory.

I just half laugh, half groan and put my head in my hands in mortification. Then I wince at the pain in my elbow. "I'm fine."

He gently puts his left hand on my shoulder and pulls my hands away from my eyes with his right. "That was"—he starts laughing as we make eye contact, he just can't help it—"the most epic fall I've ever seen in my life!"

"Matt!" I can't help but laugh too.

"I'm sorry, but you should've seen it. How did your leg even do that?" I start to stand, and he takes both of my hands in his. "I'm sorry, I'm sorry," he says, calming his laughter. "Are you sure you're okay? Can you walk?"

"Yeah, it's just my elbow."

He pulls out his phone. "There's a CVS just a couple blocks away."

"It's fine. I can clean it when I get home," I say.

"Nope, can't have you bleeding out on the subway. C'mon." I'm about to protest again, but he grabs my left hand with his right, holding our interlocked fingers tightly as he leads me forward.

He's holding my hand.

He grins down at me as we stop at the crosswalk. "Well, at least I didn't slow you down, right?" He starts laughing again, and I laugh too. I mean, could this get any more embarrassing? Surprisingly, though, it doesn't feel as awkward as it should.

I nod and look out into the street, blushing.

"What do you listen to?" he asks. I look back up at him. "While you're running?"

"AJR today. You?"

"Nice, a couple of their songs popped up for me too." I don't tell him I listened to the same song on repeat for five miles. Gotta save some of my weird for him to discover if we make it past this pharmacy date. *Ughhhh.*

We walk into the busy street. He has to cut in front of me in spots to let people pass, but he keeps a firm grip on my hand, which is making me giddy in a ridiculous way. And also wary in a sobering way. It's hand-holding, it shouldn't feel like such a big deal. We stop at another crosswalk.

"So, single and ready to mingle, huh?" He gives me his signature smolder-smirk.

"Sam's words, not mine," I say, but he just stares. "But y-yes.
Single." He looks away as the light changes.

We go into CVS and get the essentials: water, hydrogen peroxide, paper towels, and a few big Band-Aids. A couple times,
as we walk, he puts his hand lightly on the small of my lower
back. I'm sure it's sweaty, but I kind of don't care because he's
sweaty too. And it feels so nice. I don't think Paul ever put his
hand there, claimed me like that. Ryan did, though. I try to shake
off the thought.

"Hey, should we buy all these and trash them?" He motions at
the large display of fresh flowers as if offended.

"Tempting," I say with a dorky-huge smile as I walk toward
the counter. I can't believe he remembers so much. Way more
than Ryan ever did. *Quit thinking about Ryan!*

Matt ignores the card I hold out and buys everything. He takes
the sack and resumes the hand-holding, causing me to swoon
again and to wonder just how much blood I've lost. We head out
of CVS, and he leads us over to a tree surrounded by bright orange half-wall construction barriers.

"Sit," he says. And I do. He picks up my right arm with both
hands to survey the klutzy damage. "We probably should've
grabbed scissors to cut the sleeve off." I feel a flash of panic. I
don't really want him to see my arms. But I can feel the shreds of
fabric sticking against the wound. There's really no way around
it.

"Just roll it up maybe?" I suggest. He nods and gingerly rolls
the sleeve up to just above my elbow. He's good with his hands.

I can't help but think it. His fingers are long and warm and sure. He leans back to take a look. From what I can tell, the scrape over all my elbow is pretty gnarly, but not deep or gushing blood, thankfully.

"This'll be cold." He pours some of the bottled water down my arm and over the scrape. I barely feel the paper towel as he pats it. His touch is so tender my throat starts to close. I am speechless. Sam is going to lose her mind over this Dr. McDreamy in the Middle of the Upper West Side situation. In fact, I probably shouldn't tell her.

"You doing okay?" His eyes meet mine. I'm caught off guard again because he is stunning, with a sheen on his brow and his hair curling a bit from his run. I nod with a smile. What is speaking? What are words? If I could remember, I'd probably say something about dreamy fingers, so it's best I just breathe.

"Now the stinging." He pours the peroxide over the area, and I wince. "Sorry," he whispers and—

Then.

He.

Blows.

Air.

From his mouth.

Onto my arm.

Everything inside me has suddenly come to its full and upright position, just like when he touched my wrist at thirty-six thousand feet. He gets out the two big Band-Aids, and I realize I've forgotten about my scars. And he hasn't said anything. Maybe he didn't notice because a chunk of my flesh is gone? Hopefully.

"All right, I think you're good now." He gathers up all the trash into the CVS bag. He hands me a water bottle and grabs one for himself.

"Thanks, Matt," I finally manage to say. I mean, he didn't even flinch at the sticky blood-soaked fabric or the bubbling peroxide. The man might be a saint. No. Saints can't be this hot.

"Of course. But now, as your official knight in shining armor, you have to go get something to eat with me." He pulls me up to my feet.

I squint at him. "How do I know you're not a serial killer?"

"C'mon. I can't be a serial killer. I'm from Texas." I smile stupidly as he parroted what Sam had said. We heartlanders definitely have a way about us. I roll my eyes, and he grabs my hand again. "What sounds good?"

"Something light after all this." I hold up my right arm.

"Sushi?"

"Yeah."

We walk a few blocks in silence, but at the crosswalk, his thumb plays absently along my fingers. Which feels . . . intimate. Like, isn't that kind of a boyfriend move? He barely knows me. Or maybe it's a player move. I take a deep breath and think about it. He is sexy, confident, funny. His hand was probably interlocked with someone else's yesterday. And someone else the day before that.

I can't help it. I get lost in a deep, dark how-much-is-Matt-like-Ryan thought forest, until it's time to order.

"Skye?" Matt's staring at me, as is the nice old man behind the counter. I stammer through my order, and again Matt pays, even though I make a fuss about it. We stand at the end of the counter, and I shiver. It's always freezing inside during the summer months. "Want to grab one of the little tables outside? I'll bring it out," Matt says, looking down at me.

"Yeah." I smile. As I wait outside and watch all the people in the evening light, my mind goes back into the forest. I don't want to be cynical and guarded, but I've learned the hard way, if it seems too good to be true, run away. And Matt, who sets our tray down while smiling, seems too good. Way too good.

"So, running, coffee, eating, sleeping, and painting?" He opens up the plastic packaging.

"Pretty much." I watch his fingers at work again. I come to my senses and start to open up my own little rectangle of California rolls.

"So, do you paint full-time?" He takes a bite of his rainbow roll.

"Almost. I do some marketing work too."

"Cool. What kind of marketing?"

"Boring branding stuff for my dad's business." I say it quickly with a shake of my head, eager to skip talking about the Canton Empire and all that goes with it.

"How did the exhibition go? Or is it still going? Orrr?" he says with his mouth full.

"Still going. The collection will stay up for a month. Hopefully the last piece will sell."

His eyebrows shoot up. "So, you sold most of them already?" I nod. "Wow, Skye, that's amazing. Congrats!"

Okay. This is just too much now. I can't.

I scoff at him. "And you? You said ones and zeros. Like you were sitting around writing code. You left out the president and cofounder parts."

He tilts his head with a wide grin. "Been googling me?"

"LinkedIn-ing."

"I do still sit and write code, sometimes, for the record."

I just stare at him as he chews the next bite until he goes on.

"But yeah, over time I took on leading teams, building teams, and Carter and I are always starting or investing in other software ideas."

"Just your everyday tech rockstar," I say. He rolls his eyes. "I'm serious, very impressive, Mr. President." He just chuckles, a bit shy almost, which is the most adorable and sexy thing I've ever seen. "So, what is Input.co exactly?" I ask, remembering his LinkedIn profile, which I may or may not have memorized. The question causes his brown eyes to smolder a bit. I guess paying attention is a turn-on that goes both ways. I try not to reveal that I'm hoping he's not a hoodie-wearing soul-sucker.

"It's a software service that uses artificial intelligence to digest, sort, and summarize massive amounts of information." I fast blink at him with my mouth hanging open to show I understood zero of the words he just said. He laughs. "It's not as boring as it sounds. At least, not to me."

I consider his company. I'm not thrilled. I sigh without meaning to.

"So. You replace human jobs with AI."

He's not scared of my question or my tone. "We replace the absolute worst, most tedious, mundane part of a specific set of humans' jobs, allowing them to work better and faster." I squint at him again. "What? What now?"

"You just don't seem like a numbers nerd, Matt." I pop another bite of sushi into my mouth.

"Oh, yeah? Why's that?" He leans in as he asks it, injecting his unexpected sexiness into what was just a run-of-the-mill conversation. Now I'm sweating again. From a lean. I smile and look out into the street so I don't have to answer. "What do I seem like?"

Aaaand I'm done holding it in.

"Honestly? You seem like a classic player. A too-cool, too-smooth, first-class-flying, woman-pleasing, slick sales executive type." I worry for a second after it's out. Maybe I've gone too rude too fast. Until he breaks into a huge smile.

"Woman-pleasing?" Okay, he has only heard those two words, and is in heaven now. My face is transitioning from pink to purple like a blotchy, sweaty sunset.

"Ughhhhh! I take that back. Woman-annoying! Woman . . . repulsing!"

"Oh, I can't unhear that now." He takes a drink of water and stares at me, positively beaming. I shake my head and look anywhere but at him. Eventually he says, "Okay, you caught me. Total player. I spend all my Friday nights at various art openings all over the city, just to hug ridiculously cool, gorgeous painters who hardly talk to me, and already have boyfriends." I look back to him as my protective shield starts to melt down into the metal patio chair. "You nailed it," he adds. He's gone from beaming back to smoldering. I side-eye him again, but I have to drink water to hide my smile.

"I talk to you," I say weakly.

He uses the opening to ask me a million questions, and I keep my answers short, lest the nerves take over and I spout off something deeply personal or inappropriate. I make sure he answers each of his own questions, which he does with ease. He's from Fort Worth, and his family is still there. Parents still married, one older brother he's close to. He has another roommate, in addition to Carter, and they all work together.

He runs or works out almost every day. He has no pets, but he's considered getting a dog a million times. He watches *all* of the sports and plays tennis once or twice a month. He works in the office every day, even though he can work from home if he wants. I explain to him that that's straight-up insanity, and he laughs.

"I like it. I like our offices, the people, the meetings, the happy hours. Everyone works really hard, so we also keep a stocked bar, nap pods, pool tables, air hockey, shuffleboard. It's fun." I just raise my eyebrows. A software nerd who would rather be in the office. I never would have guessed. "Ready to go?" he says, and I nod.

We take care of our trash and start walking. But I hold my water bottle in my hands to avoid the hand-holding. If I'm not careful, I'm going to be madly in love with this guy in a week; meanwhile, he'll probably be on a date with one of his *fun* coworkers.

"What are you thinking over there?" he asks me with a tentative smile, looking almost shy again, but not quite. I shrug. I'm not about to tell him I'm already worried about all the other women. This is our first date! *Get a grip!* But my grip is lost as he playfully nudges me. "Want to know what I'm thinking then?"

I nod. "I think we've covered running and eating, so next we should get—excuse me, *chug*—coffee."

"Now?" I say it with so much shock he laughs at me.

"Uh, no, definitely not now. Horrible idea. Pff . . . who would even suggest that?" He nudges me again. "Sometime this week?"

"All right." I smile up at him, totally helpless. I didn't even pretend to be busy. *Pathetic!*

"Right now, I really need a shower. Where can I walk you?"

"Oh, thanks. But I'm good. Subway's right there."

"I'll message you my number?"

I smile and nod at him, and he pulls me gently by my elbow over to the side of the sidewalk, out of the crowd. He's clearly coming at me, and I freeze, not sure if he's going for a kiss or a hug, and not sure I'm ready for either of those things. I'm sweaty and bandaged and probably taste like soy sauce. *Must always carry gum from now on!* My knees wobble a bit, and he smiles like he knows my knees are firmly on Team Matt.

He wraps his arms around me, squeezes, and picks me up so my feet leave the ground. He sets me down and pulls back a bit and stares, not letting me go. He's holding his face so close to mine, I hold in my soy breath. He smiles wide and pulls away.

"No looking back, okay? Please, only walk forward all the way home." He chuckles.

"Shut up!" I turn to leave, but he grabs my hand and pulls me back and plants a kiss on my forehead. I'm frozen again. And he knows it. He says "G'night" and releases my hand and turns to head in the other direction. So, I turn away too, smiling like a doofus. I make my way to the subway entrance and do not let myself so much as look over my shoulder.

I am feelings things, all right. Specifically, I feel mostly excited that he was going to kiss me, and now fully disappointed that he didn't.

Why didn't he?

CHAPTER 6

"**H**ave you texted him yet?" Sam pads out of her room, yawning but smiling wide, as if she had the best night of her life last night vicariously. Gus abandons my lap to go and greet her.

"No, I told you, I need a minute."

"It's been many minutes. It's been like ten hours."

I roll my eyes. Last night, after scolding me about my elbow and reminding me I'd have to wear Band-Aids and long sleeves for weeks *(I know, I know),* she'd quickly fallen into a sighing pile of mush over my evening. She whined about how lucky I was, which was ridiculous.

Sam is prettier, happier, more fun, and more lovable than me or probably anyone else in the whole city. She has it all, which is why she is asked out constantly. She just has a habit of throwing it all at every guy she dates on the very first date. It's why I have to be careful with her take on things. She'll be picking out wedding invitations and naming mine and Matt's babies by the end of the week if I don't rein her in. But she helps to balance out my cynicism and . . . crustiness.

Because despite the butterflies in my stomach and the grin on my face, all my internal warning bells were ringing. I'd been surprised Matt had sent me his number last night. It wasn't until around midnight, but still, he hadn't brushed me off or waited for a couple buffer days to pass. Did that mean he was genuinely interested, or did it mean he was used to getting (taking) what he wanted?

And what was up with the hand-holding on our very first date-not-date? Genuine affection, or a tactic he used on all his dates to woo his conquests? Of course, if I really was a conquest, wouldn't he have made more of a move at the end of the night? *Ya think maybe the bloody shirt and sushi breath deterred him?* Couldn't fault him there.

"Please?" Sam, who's apparently been speaking to me from the coffeepot in the kitchen, interrupts my thoughts.

"What?"

"Please come by the office later to help me sort? I know it's not within your normal hours, but all the stuff is coming in for next weekend. Sooooo much stuff."

I roll my eyes, knowing I'm going to say yes even though I don't want to. Setting Sam up at our sales office in Manhattan had been a genius move on Dad's part. He knew I hated to let her down. "C'mooooon, you know next weekend is like do or die, make us or break us. I need your help."

"Fine, but you're feeding me dinner."

"Deal!" She heads back to her room, and I head back into my thoughts. Without thinking, I start to pick at my cuticles, and like she's got bestie spidey sense, Janie texts me.

Janie: Headed to the studio?

Me: Not yet

Eyes on the prize. Turn over the studio first, obsess about Matt after.

I don't wannaaaaaa

You'll feel better once you do.

Psh [Grumpy emoji]

Text me a thank you when you're done.

After I respond to a few more emails, I get ready to head into the city. Because Janie is right. I have work to do. Turning over the studio is a ritual after a series is complete. Beyond a comforting routine, it's just plain necessary. The place is a pit. I always start on new ideas with a clean, organized space, and then as I keep working, I get more focused and stressed. By the time a series is complete, you can really only walk in one small path I've cleared from the door to the easel to the desk.

I smile as I open the heavy metal door to my happy place. Call me touristy, but I love the Flatiron District. It's my favorite spot in the city, the iconic building and the cafés and Madison Square Park. So when a shared studio rental and co-working space popped up a few blocks over, I jumped on a spot. The studio is an overpriced twelve-by-twelve square with concrete floors, metal shelving, and one small fogged-over window. But I've warmed it up with thrift rugs and big floor pillows, all spotted with paint. A few favorite sketches and prints hang on the walls. It's small, but it's perfect. It is my sanctuary.

Headphones blasting Macklemore, I get to work. First, some before photos and video clips for social media. Before and after porn always gets a ton of engagement, especially when you throw in bright colors organized in rainbow order. Next, I reorganize all my paint, palettes, brushes, knives, and cups on the shelves. I fold and stow drop cloths that can be reused, as well as my rags, aprons, and smocks.

As I work, I feel my phone with Matt's unanswered message burning a hole in my back pocket. The amount of excitement I feel, the hope and dread together—it cannot be good. The higher your hopes at the start, the harder your fall at the end. Maybe that's why things had been so easy with Paul. I hadn't had very high expectations, and he hadn't either.

Expectations go two ways, that's what Sadie and Sam don't seem to understand. Was Paul a romantic dream boat? No. But guess what, I wasn't the doting bright-eyed girlfriend. I wasn't waiting for him at home with dinner on the stove. I was a lot more prickly pear than I was delicate flower. *Which Matt will realize, eventually.*

I sigh as I throw away months of napkins, Post-its, scrap papers, and gallery stubs. My desk by the small window is littered with journals, notepads, and sketchbooks, which I close and restack. Next to my desk I dust off my mini fridge and microwave. Wow, so many various food wrappers.

Okay, I'm low-key disgusting. But hey, it's been working for me. I sold another painting yesterday.

I take out the trash, grab cleaning supplies from the shared utility closet, sweep, shine, the whole nine yards. I take a deep breath and smile as I look around. Ready for the next idea . . . whatever it will be.

Anxiety stabs my stomach, quick and lethal. To distract my-self, I post my before and after studio clips on Instagram, avoid-ing my messages. I respond to a few comments and check out what a few galleries have showing. I check my favorite artists' feeds—for inspiration, I tell myself. A text from Sam tells me it's already dinner time, so I turn off my multiple lamps and lock up the space.

On my way over to the office, my stomach twists like a Twiz-zler. I should've gone for a run today. I shouldn't have looked at those Instagram feeds. Because now the clean studio, the lack of ideas, the thought of texting Matt, the thought of him replying, or not replying, plus the stress that waits for me at the office and then next weekend . . . Dad, Susan, it's all catching up to me. Plus, as Janie teased, I really am a creature of routine. And this is not my usual, heading to the offices.

Usual is an early morning when I get my Canton emails out of the way, followed by hours in the studio, an afternoon or eve-ning run, and more studio time if I'm on a roll. Then I head home to decompress with a book and dinner. After dinner, I catch up on social media comments, head to bed by ten, but then stay up a little too late reading. I deviate from my schedule a tiny bit on the weekends, but only to add more studio time and longer runs.

Today, though, I woke up late, dallied at the studio, missed my run, and instead of heading home to learn what happens next in the last epic battle in the amazing fantasy romance Paul sent to me before I ended things, I'm headed to Canton HQ. I regulate my breathing and quicken my pace. *I'll be fine.*

"Reporting for duty," I say loudly as I step off the elevator into the Canton Cards East Coast sales office. It's a small suite of offices in Midtown, but it does pack a punch. The big back-lit purple C mounted on the entry wall behind reception, where Nicole would be sitting if it weren't so late, prepares you for the space's classy white floors, glass walls, sleek furniture, and large windows.

Part of me is proud, of course. Canton is my last name, after all, but a much larger part of me tenses, remembering Ryan's larger-than-life presence here. It was years ago, but I can still see him walking around the space, making jokes, shooting paper balls into people's trash cans. He had been such a big part of our—Dad's—East Coast operations. He had even helped with the remodel of the offices. Everybody loved him. And then he was gone.

A wave of anxiety courses through me and gathers in my fingertips. Absently, I pick at my cuticles to relieve the pressure.

"Back here!" Sam interrupts my habit, calling from one of the conference rooms. The long room is filled with box after box, piled up to my head around the walls, and filling almost every chair at the long table. The tabletop itself is a color-sorted extravaganza of pens, papers, cards, notebooks, and knickknacks. All of which I recognize. This is one of the big projects I help guide at the start, but it's Sam who'll bring it home. "Tacos are on the way," Sam singsongs at me, knowing I hate being here.

"Wow, this all looks amazing. Way to go, guys," I exhale to Sam and Nicole, who are both elbow-deep in boxes. They've done a great job, meaning I won't have to stay too long. Still, looking at the work ahead of us, facing the fact that convention looms in my near future, makes me tense up again.

"Thanks! There's a master list for next weekend on that clipboard there, so just get into the boxes and help me mark what's arrived so far," Sam says.

"One of each out onto the table then?" I ask, picking up on her system.

"Yep. The second conference room and my office are full too."

"Wow. All right." I put down my bag by the door and grab a box cutter off the table.

"Skye. Band-Aid." Sam sighs at me. I look down. I take a deep breath, embarrassed. Guess I am more tense than I realized. I don't say anything as I go to the bathroom, where the first aid kit is. I kick myself again for not running just a couple miles before coming here. I know better.

I bandage my right thumb. When I return to the room, a space has been cleared and tacos are laid out.

"So . . . did you text him!" Sam says with her mouth full.

"Not yet." I pick up a brown box with two tacos and some chips inside.

"Do it right now!" Sam almost yells.

"Yes! You have to!" Nicole chimes in, bobbing her head of thick black curls. She's a lot like Sam, graduated the same year and as sharp as a tack. Her outgoing personality suits her job as an executive assistant, but she'll move up into marketing or sales soon, I have no doubt.

I don't even pretend to be surprised Sam has told Nicole everything. "You think I've waited long enough?" I ask them.

"Yes!" Sam is exasperated. "It's been all day. Plus, you posted to your Stories, so I bet he's wondering if you're blowing him off."

"I doubt it. I was smiling like such an idiot. I was so obvious. I have zero game." I pull up my phone and add Matt to my contacts. I hesitate and then type a quick hello, my nerves turning my face pink, as if texting opens a visual portal where he can see me staring at my phone.

Me: Hey, it's Skye

"Okay, sent."

"What did you say?" Nicole asks, only getting a word in because Sam was swallowing.

"I said, 'Hey, it's Skye.' What was I supposed to say?"

"Oh, okay, that's fine." Sam nods. "Casual, cool, relaxed. I like it."

My heart pounds wildly in my ears, as much as I tell myself a text message isn't a big deal.

"He's writing back! He's writing!" Sam yells in my ear, somehow suddenly right on top of me. His messages come in.

Matt: Hey, Skye
Nice work on the studio.

"What?" Sam asks.

"My Instagram," I tell her as I type a reply.

"I told you!" Sam is beside herself, jumping in her seat. I reply.

Me: Stalker

Sam sighs. "Really, name-calling? That's your go-to?" She's got a point. I wince.

Matt: Exhibitionist

I grin, finding myself slipping right into my element.

Me: Just giving the people what they want.
Matt: I want coffee tomorrow. Morning or afternoon?

I look up to my excited advisors. "Morning or afternoon?"

"Afternoon!" Both Sam and Nicole say in unison. I start to ask why when Sam continues: "Afternoon can turn into dinner, drinks . . . *dessert*, if you know what I mean." She laughs at her own joke. But the idea of metaphorical dessert helps clear my head and write my reply. Not to mention, my anxiety right now should be reminder enough that afternoons are for working or running, not coffee.

Morning
8 am?
OK
[Dropped pin location]
[Liked dropped pin]

"Eight in the morning? That's possibly the least sexy time of day. Ugh, you are the worst, Skye. The *worst!*" Sam rails on, but I smile to myself. Eight in the morning is a solid time, a safe time. No one falls in love—or lust—at eight o'clock on a Wednesday morning, right? Plus, he'll probably have one hour. Then I can head straight to the studio and get an early start on my day.

It'll be a perfect first non-date date.

CHAPTER 7

Matt picked a local café over a chain, scoring him some major points. He also picked a convenient spot close to the subway. I decided, to half-awake Sam's great disappointment, to wear a running outfit like I normally would, though much cuter than my usual attire. The black shirt has long sleeves but with thin moisture-wicking material so I don't totally die on the walk over, and my neon-blue shorts are tight and short. Hopefully Matt is a leg man. I mean, if I even care what kind of man he is, which I don't, because he's likely a playboy heartbreaker, *whom I will never see again after he realizes I'm not going to sleep with him.*

I walk into the warm, trendy café at 8:06. Not bad. I look for Matt and spot him . . . with people. Oh. I am way too disappointed at this realization.

The Hot Hoodie Brigade—Matt, Carter, and I'm guessing his roommate Jimmy—is chatting with a breasty brunette in a sleek power suit. They all laugh, and Breasty playfully punches Matt's arm. I hate her. Whoa, Nelly, cool it. She probably punches all their arms. Also, suddenly, I am hearing Sam's voice in my head warning me to "err on the side of sexy and dressy rather than what's functional and causes you to sweat the least!" I freeze for a moment, debating if I could run home and change. Wait, no, of course not—that'd put me back here over thirty minutes late. Idiot!

And now he's seen me. Frozen at the door like I've never been in a coffee shop before. He leaves his group and comes over. I don't miss that Breasty watches him walk away. I smile and blush involuntarily as he gets close. He looks gorgeous in tight jeans, an olive-green shirt that suits his dark hair and eyes, and his gray zip hoodie.

"Good morning," he says softly. I keep my hands on my backpack straps as a shield between us. I didn't want to let him come in for another hug or forehead kiss. I'd been too weak in the knees last time. I need to keep my wits firmly fastened about me this time.

"Hey," I say.

He takes in my very exposed legs. "Going to brave the pavement again today? Are you sure that's a good idea?"

I blush and roll my eyes. He's just standing there staring down at me as if we're the only two people in the crowded café. As if we shouldn't be getting in line and starting our order. His stare lights me up as if we're under spotlight in a dark empty room. It's so disarming. I look to the menu to get us back on track.

He motions for me to go first but then tugs on my backpack handle, bumping my back to his front for a second. His friends eye us sheepishly as they leave with their drinks. Breasty gives me an obvious once-over with a tight smile. Matt gives them a small wave.

"See you at the all-hands, Matthew," Carter says.

"Matthew?" I smirk at him.

"Family calls me Matthew. Sometimes he slips."

"Ah." I nod as I turn back to the menu.

He tugs on my backpack again, bringing his mouth closer to my ear. "What sounds good?" My toes curl in my sneakers in response to his warm breath on the side of my neck.

I cough out, "Just a latte," wanting him to let go of me and also to never let go of me, ever. *Wits, Skye, your wits!*

"Want to try a couple crepes? They're supposed to be really good here."

"Sure," I say casually. He orders, and when I pull out my card, he puts his hand over mine and pushes my card away. He keeps a vice grip on my hand until he's done paying. His wizard hands are at it again, creating a buzz in my skin as if my hands have never been touched.

"What happened to your thumb?" He holds up my bandaged thumb, and I clench my insides.

"Eh, nothing." He eyes me and takes back his card, letting my hand go as we move down the counter. He keeps a hand on my backpack as we wait, as we get our drinks and crepes, and even still as we head to an open table for two by the windows. Before he sits, he takes off his hoodie and extends it to me, open.

"It's freezing in here," he says. I smile like a fool, yet again, at his thoughtfulness. And at the way he's putting the hoodie on me rather than handing it to me to put on by myself. After both of my arms are in, he gives my shoulders a squeeze before sitting in the seat across from me.

He puts his legs outside of mine under the table, flexing inward so that I feel his jeans along my bare legs on both sides.

As I fill with warmth, all my warning bells ring again. This guy knows exactly what moves he's making. And damn. Because they're working.

"So, what do you have going on today?" He opens up our crepe boxes.

"Emails, work, run," I say. "You?"

"Work—meaning, painting?"

I tilt my head, mentally reviewing what I have going on today. "Maybe." He just stares at me with his brows raised. "Um, I'm not sure yet what my next series will be, so today will probably be more brainstorming than painting."

"Ah." He nods and takes a bite. "Ohmmgr." His eyes grow wide. "This is so good. Here." He cuts a piece of his bacon-and-egg crepe and holds out his fork to me. I gulp my coffee and tilt my head, dismayed that he's actually going to try to feed me. "C'mon, seriously, it's so good," he says, waiting.

In that moment, I have the choice to just take the bite like a normal human being, or to try to be sexy. *I mean, he's feeding me, it's supposed to be sexy!*

I make the wrong choice.

Because as I try to be cute and sexy with my mouth, looking at him from under my lashes, my nerves reach my teeth, which clamp down hard on the end of the metal fork. It flaps right out of Matt's grip and slams me, hard, on the nose. Then, as I react, the fork falls down into my crepe. I just close my eyes and chew, letting my face turn magenta.

Matt tries not to laugh, but I start laughing as I see his shoulders shake, so he lets himself go. "That looked like it hurt . . ." I put my hand to my forehead, marinating in the mortification.

This is what I get for trying to be hot. He says softly, "Can I have my fork back? If I promise not to feed you ever again?"

We continue to laugh, and I hand him his fork, refusing to look at him. It's just unbearable. I am the most awkward of awkward. Maybe I'll get lucky and a grease fire will break out in the kitchen. Or there'll be a drive-by, and I'll get taken out in the spray aimed for a mob boss. *Please tell me mob bosses eat crepes!*

"Skye," he says. But no. I am not looking at him. "Skye, c'mon, it was cute." I glare at him, feeling anything but cute. "Do all of your dates end in injury, or is it just dates with me?" He's still half laughing.

"Oh, you think this is a date?" My snark arrives in time to salvage my last shred of dignity.

"I do."

I shake my head. "This is just coffee."

"And breakfast." He squeezes my legs in his under the table. "Next up is paint."

"What?" I ask, getting lost in his smolder-smirk.

"We've chugged coffee, gone running, eaten—which I should get bonus points for since that wasn't listed as one of your single-and-mingle activities—so next up is paint."

"Oh, you're into painting now?"

"Lately I'm into *painters*," he says, leaning in. I shake my head at him. I'm smiling because I can't help it, but my brain is registering how smooth that line was, how infuriatingly attractive he is. How he's been getting ogled by almost every woman who's walked by since we sat down.

"You didn't say what you were up to today?" I say feebly, trying to change the subject.

"Meetings all day, workout, and then I can bring dinner to your studio."

"Nope." I am back to shaking my head.

"Why not?"

"No one comes to the studio." It's not totally true. Friends have stopped by on occasion, Paul dropped things by a couple times. But painting is a solitary activity. Only Janie has ever hung out with me while I worked, and that's only because she was also working. We can sit in silence and work independently for hours. It's our favorite form of bonding. I'm not ready to have Matt in my sanctuary, not to mention the hazard. I'd probably get nervous, trip, and impale myself on my easel.

He gives an exaggerated sigh. "Well, the last activity on your list was sleep, so I guess we *could* do that." He stares, smug, as I choke my coffee. "Except," he adds, squeezing his legs around mine again, "I mean, call me old-fashioned, but you should probably buy me a real dinner first, an official date."

I scoff. He's just sealed his fate. I'm out. I cannot fall for this guy. Correction: I already fell for this guy before, and I know how it ends. I can't live through that again.

"I don't think so."

"Oh." He looks almost thrilled now. "So no date first?"

"Um, no date, period." I take off his hoodie. I have to get out of here, fast.

His face falls. "Hey, wait, Skye, I was just kidding."

"Pff, sure you were."

He reaches out a hand toward me on the table. "I was, really. C'mon, let me take you out on a real date."

I shoot up from my chair.

"There are at least four women checking you out in here right now," I huff as I put on my backpack. "I'm sure all of them would be happy to take you up on that offer, Matt."

"What?" He twists up his face as if what I said makes no sense. I hand his hoodie to him and head for the door.

I make my way out into the street, choosing a direction and walking, not caring if I'm headed north toward my studio or not. I just have to get moving. I cannot live through this again. But I'm pulled back by the handle on my backpack, and Matt is in front of me.

"I was joking, Skye, really. I'm not like that, please. Let me take you out for real."

"Pretty sure you're *exactly* like that, Matt." I try to step around him, but he blocks me.

"Let me take you out tonight and prove you wrong. C'mon."

"I'm busy." I finally move around him.

"Tomorrow night." He keeps in step with me.

"Also busy."

"Friday night."

I scoff. "I wash my hair Friday nights. Gee, darn."

"Saturday night."

Suddenly my thoughts pour out of my mind, unfiltered. "I'm sure Breasty is free Saturday night, or for you, maybe all of those nights, but *I* am not. Now please just get out of my way."

He laughs out, "What? Who is Breasty?"

"Doesn't matter. Bye, Matt."

He keeps pushing me farther to the right with his body, pinning me to the side of the flow of walkers.

"Sunday lunch."

"No!"

"Sunday night."

"Let me go!"

"Not until you give me another shot."

"Are you serious right now?"

"Yes, and I'm willing to start asking about Monday and go through every single day of next week."

I close my eyes and take in a jagged breath, dismayed at the scene I'm living. His persistence is unbelievable—as in, I shouldn't believe it. But I look up at him. His face is earnest, open, apologetic. Not smug or even playful, which surprises me.

"There's no way you don't have any plans between now and Sunday night," I say, feeling triumphant. He cannot be serious.

"I'll cancel."

I knew it. *Just as I was about to cave!* How many dates does he have every week? I'm not going to find out.

"No, save her the heartbreak," I say, trying to make a break for it again.

"Friday drinks with the guys after work. Their hearts will remain intact." He smiles a little and puts his hands on my forearms below my hands, which are gripping my backpack straps for dear life. "C'mon, Skye, please?" I start to spout that there are four million women for him in the city, something Sam had googled in a moment of dating despair, and then I realize: there are four million women in the city. And he's pinning me on the side of the street, refusing to let me go. I start to smile, which causes him to squeeze my arms in his hands. He smiles. "Tonight?"

I sigh. "I actually do have plans with Sam tonight."

"Tomorrow night?"

"Okay," I grunt, grumpy and annoyed that my smile is betraying me. I try to snuff it out, but he bear-hugs me and picks my feet up off the ground again. He sets me down and keeps his arms around me, pinning me in place, grinning down at me like an idiot. "Now will you move?"

"Can I walk with you?"

"No. Go away!" I am smiling as I say it, but I push him off for emphasis.

"Okay, but only because I'm late for a meeting."

"K bye!" I yell as I make my way into the crowd, jumping as he tries to catch my backpack handle. I evade him and hurry off before he can catch up. After a few blocks, I realize I'm headed in the wrong direction, so I turn and head toward my studio. But I can barely feel my feet on the ground. I sigh. Where are my wits? Because I did not keep them about me. That's for freaking sure. Still, wits or not, I cannot wait for tomorrow night.

CHAPTER 8

WEDNESDAY 1:07 P.M.

Matt: Hey

Me: Shouldn't you be in a meeting?

I am, but I had to ask you a question.

?

Who is Breasty?

The chick who was with you guys this morning.

LOL

Accurate, no?

I hadn't noticed.

Liar.

Well. I didn't notice this morning.

Too busy looking for you.

While you were looking for me, she was trying to climb into your pants.

[Animated GIF Man spit laughing]

I bet she's free Saturday night.

I'm busy Saturday night.

Congrats.

Taking you on our second real date.

Cocky much? What if tomorrow night is a dud?

Yes, and it won't be.

[Animated GIF of woman saying "we'll see"]

8:13 P.M.

Matt: Hey, I saw this and thought maybe you should wear it for our date tomorrow

[Image of Woman wrapped in a suit made from bubble wrap]

Me: Well, whatdya know, turns out I'm busy tomorrow.

Admit it, you laughed.

Any dietary preferences for dinner?

Nope

K. What are you up to?

Helping Sam with a project. You?

Playing Madden with Carter.

Oh no, are you a gamer?

Define gamer.

Do you have one of those spaceship gamer chairs? Special headset?

No and maybe.

[Animated Nerd Alert GIF]

[Animated Gif Woman Running and Falling Down]

Too far?

THURSDAY 8:00 A.M.

Matt: Good morning. Headed to the studio today?

Me: Always.

When?

9ish

Address?

No

I promise not to come by.

No

I'm sending something, just give me the address, woman!

If you come by, I'm calling security.

675 6th Ave., B1

9:30 A.M.

Sam: So????

What did he send? Flowers? Chocolate?

Me: Coffee. With a note that said, "Since you didn't get to finish yours yesterday. Can't wait for tonight."

Ermagerrrrr he's the sweetest! Even I'm in love with him! Think how cute your babies will be. Can I be the godmother? [Five pink heart emojis]

Seek help, Samantha.

2:00 P.M.

Matt: Where am I picking you up?

Me: I'll meet you.

No.

Yes.

Fine. 7:30?

Great, where?

6:00 P.M.

Me: ????

Matt: Still confirming. Stand by.

"**H**e's standing me up. That mother—"

"Nah, I'm sure he's just running late," Sam says as I plot how to kill Matt James. I knew this was too good to be true. Now look at me, all dressed up with nowhere to go like a chump.

"Sam, it's ten after seven, and he still hasn't told me where to go. And what if we're going someplace super fancy? Should I be in a dress? Not that it matters because he's *not* coming."

"You look amazing, even for a fancy place," she says, strangely calm. "Why don't you just call him and ask?"

"Um, I am not calling him just to hear some lame fake excuse as to—" I'm cut off by a knock on our door. Samantha, my soon-to-be-dead younger sister, is staring at me, beaming. "You sneaky little traitor," I say between gritted teeth.

I take a breath and open the door.

"Hello," he says slowly, one hand against the door frame, smiling like the frickin' King of the World. I try to give him a death stare, but my smile betrays me once again. "You look amazing," he says as his eyes take their time going up and down my long, puffed-sleeve black shirt, tucked into very short jean shorts. I debated on sexier wedge sandals, but the odds for tripping were just too high, so instead I chose strappy sandals that I knew would be fine for walking around the city.

"You too," I manage to say. And he does. He looks fresh and crisp and clean, and I suddenly want to hug him. Something about his white polo stretched across his muscular chest, untucked over fitted gray pants and white Adidas tennis shoes, in contrast to his dark features, makes my mouth water.

A giggle behind me makes me realize I've been staring. And he's just been standing there enjoying my staring.

"Let me just grab my phone," I say quickly, letting him know he's not invited in. Not yet.

"Here!" Sam says eagerly.

"Thanks for the address, Sam. I owe you one," he says, looking over my shoulder.

"No problem." She is downright triumphant.

I take Matt's hand, filling up with my own Samantha-esque glee as he links our fingers.

"So, where are we going?"

"Someplace Sam says you've never been." I master my glare this time. "If you're debating between mad and impressed, go with impressed." I huff. I am. I am debating. "C'mon, now your sister loves me. It was a win-win."

"She . . . she would love you if you'd met me at a McDonald's, shown up late, made me pay for my own cheeseburger meal, and left before I was even done eating." He squints at me as he gets us an Uber. "She's a romantic. The fact that we met on the plane? Then you came to my show? Psh. Put a fork in her 'cause she's done."

"Ohhh, so I can just coast now."

"You could if you were dating Sam. But unfortunately for you—" I stop myself.

"Skye, did you just admit that you are, in fact, dating me?" he says with fake shock.

"Yet to be determined, Matthew." Something flashes in his eyes that I can't quite place as he squeezes my hand.

"This is us, the Ford," he says as our Uber arrives.

"Wait, Spire? Are you serious? I have wanted to do this for months!" I say after we climb out of what was a very loud techno-disco-inspired Uber ride complete with a bowl of questionable candy.

"So I heard," Matt says softly as he grabs my hand again. He held my hand throughout the whole ride, which should not have affected me the way it did.

"Have you been?"

"Nope," he says, smiling wide. And I get why he is smiling. The man has hit a home run. Spire is a new immersive experience in the top four floors of one of the newest, tallest buildings in the city. It's not just an observatory—it's the view plus strategic use of light, sculpture, glass, sound, and even smell. It's art. And he got us the most expensive ticket option, which includes champagne and access to the fourth-floor outdoor deck.

I am a kid in a candy store. I am oohing and aahing, and at one point, I tear up with how beautiful the reflective sculpture work is. It takes the city lights and bends them back onto themselves in such a way that you can't even be sure which lights are real and which are reflected. If I stand here for a while, I am sure I'll lose my sense of gravity.

Matt enjoys himself, but I know this is not really his bag. And I don't care. I'm so excited to be experiencing it, and so happy to have my hand in his, and feeling so warm and fuzzy from the champagne—he can hate it if he wants. But he doesn't seem to, since every time I look at him, he's grinning. He even took photos for me and with me, without rolling his eyes.

"Oh, man, that is not a very tall railing," I say as we step out onto the fourth-floor deck. I am not afraid of heights, but I'm not *not* afraid of heights.

"Come on," Matt says, leading me. You're supposed to take in the view from the edge to get the full experience. I know, because we just discussed it on the stairs up. I was so full of confidence then, inside, on the steps that were not made of glass.

I take a deep breath and follow Matt out to the edge of the deck. He leads my hand to the rail and stands behind me. Somewhere he ditched his champagne, allowing him to put one hand on either side of me on the railing, pinning me in. The city sprawls out in front of us in all its twinkling glory, and Matt's firm chest is behind my back, warm and stony. Then he takes one hand and wraps it around my waist and plants a soft kiss on the left side of my neck, which is accessible because I went with a high ponytail.

And.

I mean.

It's maybe the most romantic *and* hottest moment that I've ever experienced. And I know he hasn't been here before, hasn't done this with anyone else. Just me. One brush of his soft full lips on the side of my neck, and I have to cross my legs. It's as if fire is going to shoot out of my hoo-ha and burn us both up—that's how hot that one short kiss made me. Unsure of what to do, but sure I'm not turning around to face him, I just put my hand on his at my waist and focus on breathing.

He talks softly into my ear. "Still determining?"

It's the soft talking in my ear that pulls me back to reality. I don't want to think about Ryan. I don't want to feel the scars on my heart. I don't. But I do. Ryan used to do the sexy ear talk all the time, and each time he did, I melted. Just like I'm melting tonight.

I pull out of Matt's arms and turn back to answer him with a flirty smile, hoping he doesn't notice the fear gripping me. "Yep, let's see how dinner goes."

As we make our way down the exhibit space's big central staircase, a couple guys walking past give Matt a wave. He nods back with a "Hey, guys, good to see you." But they don't slow. He still has my hand, guiding me out into the street.

"Italian okay?" he asks me when we're outside.

"Sure," I say.

"I feel like congratulations are in order," he says as we walk with the crowd toward the corner.

"What?" I look up at him.

"We made it through the entire fourth-floor exhibit without any injury." He's laughing before he even finishes his sentence.

I pull my hand from him. "I fell *one time*! While running! You are such a jerk."

He grabs my hand back. "And your thumbs, and the attack of the crepe fork." He kisses the back of my hand, and I forget to be mad at his teasing. And he's right. I am a total mess. I forgot about my thumbs, both donning Band-Aids. Band-Aids I'm glad I left on, because I absently picked at my cuticles a million times tonight, but couldn't do any further damage. So embarrassing.

"For someone who wants to achieve the title of dating, you sure have a strange approach," I say, not looking at him.

He squeezes my hand. "I stand by my methods."

I'll bet you do.

CHAPTER 9

After crossing a couple busy crosswalks, Matt leads me into a hole-in-the-wall café. It's like going back in time. The furniture is outdated, the wallpaper is hideous, and the candlesticks on the tables are melted blobs of accumulated candle after candle filling the same brass candle holder. Old-timey accordion music plays softly, and the smell of garlic bread almost knocks me over. I'm surprised and not at all surprised that the place is packed. It's got to be on the top of some "Hidden New York Gem Restaurants" list.

"Reservation for James," Matt says, and I'm swoony that he made a reservation for us like a real grown-up. Paul never once made reservations in our two years together—that was always my job. Not that we ate out much. I don't think Ryan ever did either.

Shortly after we're seated, a couple on their way out spots Matt and comes over to say hello. The guy, a previous coworker, talks to Matt about his new job, but the girl, a tall blond wisp in a gorgeous little black dress, looks at my date as if he's a plate of pasta she hopes to slurp into her mouth sans fork. Matt introduces me, but I don't pay attention to their names and they're gone after a couple sentences. Still, it rattles me. The man is a magnet, drawing people to him wherever he goes.

"So popular," I say after the couple has left earshot, keeping my eyes on the menu.

"Says the Instagram celebrity," he says back, totally at ease. I blush a bit and tilt my head, with no comeback to be had.

We talk easily all throughout dinner. Well, mostly Matt talks, but I do my best to contribute words regularly. We talk about things we miss from back home. About how underrated OneRepublic is. About how dismal the ending of *Game of Thrones* was. About all epics, which I love: *Star Wars*, *Lord of the Rings*, *Harry Potter*, *Wheel of Time*, and anything Marvel. And so many books, none of which he's read. Of course I try to explain *Stories of Loya* to him, but he's skeptical. It is a romance first, yes, but c'mon, what about Han and Leia? Ron and Hermione? All the words start to pour out, and I feel myself getting overly passionate about books. *You're nerding out! Pivot!* I change the subject.

He explains some of his work, which is all very technical and intimidating. He teases me about being from Oklahoma, and I throw back some anti-Texas smack. He teases me about a lot of things, book obsession included, but I haven't laughed so hard in ages. He was right to stand by his methods—I am having a blast.

And I take no prisoners. Some of the things he says reveals the true dork under those well-dressed muscles. The man has a gaming headset at the age of thirty. Ridiculous. After loading up on the best garlic bread I've ever had, I let myself have a glass of wine. After our entrées arrive with a third glass, I'm feeling loose and he knows it.

"So, did Paul get you the CVS flowers?"

I shake my head. "Paul gave me the succulent."

He raises his eyebrows. "Wow, okay. Good for Paul. So, what happened?"

It's the wine that answers. "I met a hot guy on the plane." He juts his chin out in surprise, and I realize what I've accidentally said. "No! Not that I broke up with Paul for you, because I didn't. It was just Sam, I mean, after the show. She said all this confusing stuff about heat and feelings, and it wasn't about you, really, it was about Paul. Me and Paul. So then I tried to be sexy in a trench coat and make heat happen and then I made poor Paul almost cut his penis off and then I was mortified and it was just so awkward and it was obvious any heat was gone and we just both agreed it was for the best and dear God I said penis and I'm going to stop talking now." I close my eyes and chug my water.

"I have so. Many. Questions." Matt is grinning, enjoying my pain.

"Ughhhhh, can we just move on to a different topic?"

"Absolutely not." He leans in, whispering, "Did you just say you tried to cut your ex-boyfriend's dick off?"

"No!" I roll my eyes and tell him the story in vivid detail. By the end, he is laughing so hard, his eyes water. We are getting side-eyes from the people around us because we're so loud. And while I'm embarrassed, I also know I'm a really good storyteller, and I love that I can make him laugh so hard. "There, now you know my most embarrassing moment ever."

"That is just . . . wow. I can't remember the last time I laughed this hard." He takes a sip of wine. "So. Who *did* get you the CVS flowers?"

"No. I'm not talking again until you tell me something embarrassing."

"Easy." He sets his glass down. "In college, I shit myself on a run in the middle of campus."

I choke on my wine in surprise, especially the way he just says it as if it's no big deal. "What!"

"Yeah, I ate like crap and drank like ten Cokes a day and had uh, digestive issues, all the time. One afternoon, I was a few miles in and thought it was gas. It wasn't gas."

I lean in to beg for the details. "Were you wearing shorts? Did people see? What did you do?"

"Yep. And oh yeah. People saw. It was, um, everywhere. And two friends were running with me, and of course I was showing off trying to be the fastest."

"No!"

"Yep." He motions over his shoulder, reliving the memory. "They were behind me. Saw the whole thing. I ducked into the next open building I could find for a bathroom, but it was too late. The damage had been done."

I am dying laughing now. He is so nonchalant as he tells the story, as if it's not the most mortifying thing that could ever happen to a person. His confidence is completely unaffected. It's maddening and sexy at the same time.

"They still call me . . . names."

"Oh!" I think. "Squirt?" He shakes his head. "Soggy Bottom Boy. Matt McShitter. Poops McGee. Chocolate Thunder? Foxtrots!"

"Your mind is terrifying," Matt says.

"C'mon, tell me."

"Nope, time to move on."

I am loving this tiny chink in his unflappable armor. "Aw, c'moooon."

"Are you up for some dessert?"

I didn't even realize he'd already paid.

"Sure . . . Streaker?"

"I would like to go find something chocolate for dessert, so can we not?" He stands and quickly comes to pull out my chair for me, just like he did when we arrived, like it's 1945 or something. His heartland roots are showing and . . . I don't hate it. *Mark one in the Not Ryan column.*

We walk slowly toward an ice-cream shop Matt loves. He tugs on my hand so my side crashes into his. Luckily, and surprisingly, I do not trip.

"You're not getting out of answering the question, Skye."

"What?" I play dumb. I don't want to talk about this.

He sighs. "I'm willing to withhold dessert."

"Uh, well, I can just go get dessert for myself," I say, starting to stomp off, but his hold on my hand tightens to be almost painful. "Okay, jeez." He stares down at me as we wait to cross the street. I take a deep breath and exhale in defeat. "His name is Ryan."

"Ugh. Total douchebag name," he says after a beat. I don't offer any more information, and after a few steps, he says, "Well, thanks for telling me the story. I totally understand now."

I roll my eyes and blurt the rest out as fast as possible. "Not much of a story. He cheated on me. For a long time. I had no idea. And he got *her* big gorgeous expensive flowers from a florist. So." I shrug.

Matt stops walking. "Crap, Skye, I'm sorry." He peers down at me in a way that makes me feel somehow small and fragile, and also important and powerful, simultaneously. "He's an idiot, obviously."

I shrug and get us walking again. Both of us are about to speak again, but we reach the creamery. I tell Matt I'm full, but he can tell I'm going to ask for a bite of his chocolate-and-Oreo concrete, which he promptly promises not to try to spoon-feed me. We sit outside at a small café table with the big cup between us, each with our own spoon.

"Your turn," I say, as he tightens his legs around mine under the table. Matt looks up at me, confused. "Your turn to talk about a serious ex."

"Serious, huh?" He swallows his bite of ice cream. I just nod. "Lauren. College girlfriend, we moved out here together. But then after a few years, she was done with New York, and I wasn't."

For the first time in the whole evening, silence settles in and things feel a bit awkward. I want to know everything about her. *Stupid Lauren.* But I don't want to talk anymore about my own baggage, so it doesn't feel right to push him. Matt, of course, saves us. "Your paintings—you get an idea like that, and then do you sketch it out first? And the title too? Or, like, how does it go from your brain to the show I saw?"

It's such a sweet, genuine question from him. We talk about my work until the ice cream is gone, and he seems truly appreciative, interested. If he's faking it to be a good date, well then, five stars, brava, and get this man an Oscar. I ask him more about his work too, but he doesn't dive in, fearing I'll get bored. He's probably right.

We start to walk toward my side of town after he tosses our trash. I stop him.

"You can't walk me all the way home," I say.

"I can't?"

"No. Your apartment is in the other direction, for one, and two, Sam just won't be able to handle it."

"*Sam* can't handle it, huh?" He pulls us to the side of the sidewalk under a big potted tree.

"Nope. She'll invite you in, you'll have to stay forever." He lets go of my hand and moves his hands to my hips. "She'll just talk and talk and talk and—" His hands cradle my face as he grins at me, feeling my nerves exploding, singeing my cheeks bright red. "She'll tell you embarrassing stories until three a.m., and then you'll be totally exhausted for work tomorrow and—"

"Skye," he says, and I shut up. Because his thumb is on my bottom lip and my knees are about to give out. I lean into his hands and tilt my head just barely, ready for him to put his gorgeous full mouth on mine. And he does. I close my eyes as his soft lips press firmly on mine—once, twice, then he just barely opens his lips over mine, wet and cold from the ice cream. I shift my weight into him, and he pulls away long enough to lean his head the other direction. He guides my head with one hand as the other goes around my back. Again, he gives me the same barely open kiss that makes me start to open up just as he pulls back.

And I have never wanted a man to not pull away more in my life. Talk about leaving me wanting more. I'm desperate for more. I'm dying. Deceased.

"Okay," he whispers.

"Wha?"

"Okay, I won't walk you all the way home this time."

I blink, trying to remember where I am, who I am, what he's talking about. He's still holding my body into his, smiling down at my clear lack of consciousness. He kisses me on the forehead and pulls his body back from mine.

"Come out with us tomorrow," he says.

"Um, what?" I am having trouble standing, and he knows it. *Woman! At least attempt to play it cool for crying out loud!*

"Meet me and the guys at the bar tomorrow after work. Bring Sam. And Janie, if you want."

"Oh, I'm supposed to help Sam again after work," I say, finally finding my wits again.

"Well, I'll text you when we're there, and you can swing by if it works out, okay?"

"Okay." I smile, because he wants to see me tomorrow. No hinting, no games, no waiting period. It feels nice.

His hand goes up to my cheek again like he's going to kiss me, but instead his thumb finds my lip again. "Text me when you get home, k?"

"K."

Then he turns and heads the other direction toward his apartment. I turn away as fast as I can, not really able to think or move past that, but knowing I don't want to be frozen staring after him if he turns around. I head back to my apartment, but I don't walk there.

Despite knowing I should try to stay grounded, the whole way home, I float.

CHAPTER 10

FRIDAY 10:01 A.M.

Me: Brown Wonder?

Matt: No

Skid Mark Matt?

Please stop.

Trots"R"Us? Shits"R"Us?

I am not above teasing you about the Great Trench Coat Fail.

Thinking about my trench coat outfit, huh?

Yes

2:21 P.M.

Why did I even bring that up? I'm dying over here.

4:03 P.M.

This was your master plan, wasn't it. I bet that whole story wasn't even real.

I try to hide my glee as I slip my phone into my pocket. I tried to distance myself and stay busy all day, but crap if I didn't kind of love that he was still thinking about me and messaging me hours later. I bite down on my smile to keep Sam from pouncing on it with a million questions about said goofy smile.

She breezes into the conference room where we're still sorting supplies. "What are we missing?"

I double-check her clipboard in my hand. "Looks like ten boxes are missing, but tracking says they'll be here by Wednesday, and the huge stuff goes straight to the convention center."

"Is the video done yet?" She takes the checklist from me.

"I had more changes, they're sending me another draft tomorrow, but you know that's something that can be changed right up until the last minute."

"And the artists? They know to bring their own stuff?"

"Yep."

"It's still super weird that you're not going to be one of the artists."

Here we go. "No, it's not."

"And it's really dumb, Skye. Sadie has a section, so why can't you have one?"

"You know I don't want one, and can we please not go around and around about it? I am going to get enough from Dad and Susan when they get here. Which is when, again?"

"Lunchtime Monday. We're all meeting here. I sent you an invite."

"Ughhhhhh." She just doesn't understand.

"C'mon, some of it will be really fun!" Her face is pleading, so I let it go. I know it will be fun for her. And our sisters. But it will not be fun for me. And for both of us, the stress is mounting.

I make a lot of the creative decisions for what is essentially our family's industry Super Bowl, which is next weekend. But

THINGS I SHOULD HAVE SAID

once the event actually starts, it's Sam's show. She works the room and talks and smiles and laughs for days straight. I can't comprehend how she does it. And the stress is a bit different. While I guide the Canton brand from a safe distance, she works in the business full-time. I'm glad I convinced her to go for drinks later because she needs it.

5:55 P.M.

Matt: So are you guys coming tonight?

"Did you tell the man we're coming?" Sam yells from our tiny, shared bathroom.

"Not yet," I say, as I finish the last of my hair's beachy waves.

It's possible I'm overdoing it for after-work drinks, but with Sam coming along, I'm nervous. She would never knowingly go after Matt, but the girl is a flirt. She can't help herself. And she's got bigger boobs and better hair and a prettier face, and even if she didn't have all that on me, she's captivating. Easy to talk to, fun, relaxed, comfortable. All the things I am not.

"Holy Toledo Batman and Robin and the Joker too!" Sam says, taking in my outfit. It's cooler out, so I went with high-waisted light-wash jeans and a tight, black crop top, with a high neck and long sleeves, of course. I've run hard to get such a lean midriff, so I might as well let her out to play. Maybe she'll distract from my barely there boobs and the fact that I only ever wear long sleeves.

"It's not too much for happy hour?" I scratch at my elbow without thinking.

She's suddenly serious. "Stop scratching! Do you have the bandage on still?"

"No, it made a big lump under my sleeve."

"Did you Neosporin the crap out of it?"

I wince but head toward the bathroom. "Not yet. Good call."

"If I see you scratching while we're out, I'm full out tackling you like a linebacker. You've been warned, Skye!"

I roll my eyes, but I know Sam is just looking out for me. But. I ran today, I didn't have any afternoon coffee, I exchanged a couple good texts with my therapist, and now with the Neosporin, I'll be fine.

"You look hot too, by the way," I tell her. She's got on a low-cut hot-pink tee over a push-up bra (that knows what it's doing) and black jeans with sexy open-toe black booties. Her long, thick blond hair is down, straight and sleek. She is a freaking Barbie.

"Thank youuuuuu," she squeals. "Watch out, New York, here come the Cantons!"

6:45 P.M.

Matt: We'll be here for a while.

[Dropped pin location]

Me: See you soon.

[Liked "See you soon."]

Landry's is a classic guy's-night-out bar, complete with dark wood, a million beers on tap, and multiple TVs that are too large for the tight space. We easily spot the Hot Hoodie Brigade in the back corner. In addition to Matt, Jimmy, and Carter, there's another guy and two women. They're laughing when we enter, the music is blaring, two men in suits are yelling at one of the screens, and I immediately wish Janie had been able to come along. Instead, Nicole has joined us, who is even hotter than Sam or myself, with her absolutely perfect olive skin and amazing natural curls and bright white smile. I grab at my itching elbow without thinking, then catch myself.

Matt has his back to us, but Carter sees us approaching. Matt turns and just . . . ugh. He looks downright yummy. Same tight gray pants and white sneaks but with a black button-up un-tucked and rolled up above his elbow.

I'm sorry, when did the male forearm become so erotic? I don't remember noticing men's arms in college. Of course, those weren't men. And this smiling, broad-shouldered specimen walking toward me is all man. He doesn't seem to notice Sam or Nicole at all, and he doesn't hesitate walking right up and bar-reling into me like I didn't just see him yesterday. Which leaves me light-headed.

"You look so hot," he says in my ear as he bear-hugs me.

"Thanks," I say, feeling myself blush already. He doesn't let me go until after planting a quick, firm peck on my lips. Suddenly this tiny, loud bar is not so bad.

We join the others, and introductions are made all around, in-cluding Navid, Cara, and Elizabeth. Navid is a taller, darker Matt but with less natural magnetism. Cara and Elizabeth are both pretty and professional and perky in pencil skirts and heels. What, is everyone who works with Matt hot? Is it part of the application process?

Cara is cute, redheaded, and curvy with large quirky glass-es. Elizabeth is gorgeous, taller, and also curvy, with tanned skin and sleek dark brown hair. She's rocking a vintage tee and lay-ered necklaces, clearly too cool for her project manager job. I dig her vibe while also hating her . . . because I'm a petty, jealous wench, apparently.

Matt gets us all a drink, and everyone does the usual chitchat about what they do. Sam just says sales, and Nicole says she's working her way up in a media company. She knows not to drop the Canton name when she's out with us. If she was alone with strangers, she could speak freely, but Sam and I don't want the hassle. Not like everyone knows our name and brand, but once we launched the partnership with Target a few years back, our visibility went up a notch. Many, many notches. And Canton as a last name is not common, so if they've heard of the stationery, publishing, or retail stores, well, then, they're going to ask. Luck-ily, no one cares about what the Canton family faces look like other than Dad's and Sadie's and occasionally Susan's. Sam, Sal-ly, and I each have our own reasons for keeping it that way.

My love affair with Landry's pub lasted an hour.

Then, as always happens, my younger sister has become the flame, with everyone around her like a moth. Except this time, she's co-flaming with Matt. Even though he's next to me, hand on my back or tracing my shirt or squeezing my thigh, always touching me—which I like, very much—he is somehow also in the center of the circle, as is Sam.

They started with Oklahoma versus Texas banter, then en-gaged Jimmy, a true New Yorker, in tales of "The Heartland" and "flyover states" and "also known as God's Country!"

Then I heard sweet Sam, whom I once loved, say to Matt, "I heard she told you about the trench coat story?" They all die laughing. She turns to me and begs to tell the tale.

"Sure, laugh at my pain," I joke. Then before I know it, they're both telling my nightmare with such animation and horror and hilarious commentary that I'm almost not mad. Honestly, I tell a better story than Sam, but she's just so adorably excited. She laughs before she can get to the punch line, and everyone is laughing with her. But when the good-looking guy behind the bar makes eye contact with me, I lean away from Matt and go straight for the Long Island iced tea. Because that's what I'm going to need to survive this.

I nurse my LIT and enjoy Matt's many touches, but I don't say much. Instead, I watch. Never assume a wallflower isn't having fun. Wallflowers may not be seen and heard, but we're out in these streets seeing and hearing, that's for damn sure. *Out in these streets? Maybe I shouldn't have ordered a second tea.*

So far, I've seen and heard that Cara wants Carter badly because she's laughing entirely too hard at his jokes. Carter doesn't hate it. Elizabeth wants Matt, and she's not subtle about it. She keeps touching him even though *hello, I'm right here!* Jimmy seems to be into Sam based on how his body is always rotated toward her. Sam is into Jimmy, barely looking at anyone else while she talks. Nicole is also into Jimmy by the way she keeps accidentally brushing into him. Navid is into the hot bartender. Or they're all just super flirts who have also had too much to drink. *Food! I need food!*

8:03 P.M.

Me: Guess how many times girls who are not me have managed to touch Matt's arm tonight?

Janie: Why are you doing this to yourself

Because bitches be cray, man. Bitches be cray

Oh no. What are you drinking?

L. I. spill the Teaaaaaaaa

WTF! Get out of there. You're going to drive yourself insane.

The answer was twelve, so far.

Guess how many times a guy has checked out Sam's ass.

I'm never not coming out with you ever again. You're a menace to yourself and society.

Seven that I caught, and one of those was Matt. =(

Speaking of, where is he? Why are you texting me and not fondling him after the most epic tease kiss of all tease kisses?

He's playing pool. He's so hot.

Hotttttttt you gotta add the ts

[Fifteen fire emojis]

Wait. Why aren't you playing with him?

Cara and Elizabeth begged to play with him. It was desperate.

Gross.

Who?

Plus, I've had too much tea.

You can play schwasted. Take all their money.

You think?

Definitely. AND NO MORE ALCOHOL!

"Are those custom Jordans?"

THINGS I SHOULD HAVE SAID

His question pulls my attention away from the riveting text thread.

"No. Well, kinda," I say to Jimmy, who's wearing some killer Prada sneakers.

Sam cuts in. "Crazy here searched forever to find an all-white pair in her size just so she could dub them her studio shoes."

Jimmy's face goes from resting confused face to truly puzzled. "Studio shoes?"

"The paint on them isn't a custom print." Sam is animated with how proud she is of me. "It's actual paint from her studio. Like from her painting. Because she makes a mess."

"He gets it," I say.

"For real, bro? Let me see."

I put my foot up on the rung of Jimmy's stool. And I do this hoping like the childish idiot schoolgirl I am that Matt will see. He's playing pool with stupid Cara, whose shirt is low-cut over her amazing chest, which we all know is why she wanted to play. "They look like you ordered them this way. That is so dope, man." Jimmy manhandles my foot.

"Please never say dope again, Jimmy."

He scoffs at me, secure in his verbose use of the English language.

I nod down at his feet. "Those are nice Pradas, though."

"You a sneak head too?"

This guy. I can't help but laugh. "Only if you promise to never, ever say sneak head again."

He smiles, ignoring my jabs. "Favorite pair?"

I let out a low whistle as I consider his question. "Hard to pick a favorite child, but I had to wait forrrrever for some purple New

Balance Classic 574s in my size. And the pink dunk high-tops too, and some all-black leather AF1s. Platforms. Almost wore those tonight but wanted some color."

"Matt!" Jimmy yells out, much to my delight. "This girl is way too cool for you, man."

"I'm aware," Matt says from the pool table. I give him a small smile and then make an obvious display of turning back to talk to his friend. After all, Matt and his warm, roaming hands left me to play pool. I'm about to try to find a reason to touch Jimmy's arm, or some other flirty move, but Sam whacks me hard on the elbow, which I'd been absently scratching at through my sleeve.

"Thanks," I tell her, then I ask Jimmy, "How about you?" And I bat my eyelashes like an idiot. I also motion to the bartender for some water. Because, Watson, the game is afoot. Get it? Because we're talking about shoes. I'm so hilarious.

"I can't pick a favorite either. I have thirty-three pairs."

"Thirty-three! Jimmy, that's, like, goals! You're living the damn dream!" I cry, as if Jimmy is the most interesting man in the world.

His chest inflates. "I know, right? I got a guy who gives me first dibs."

"You should play him for a pair, Skye," Sam pipes in, clearly trying to make up for stealing all my trench coat thunder earlier.

I fake like I'm insecure. "I don't know."

"Pool? For a pair of what?" Jimmy is cute, but wow, he is not the brightest.

"Winner buys a new pair of sneaks," Sam says. She's definitely working her way off my hit list.

"Nah, I don't wanna rob a fellow sneaker head—that's just mean."

"I'm good for it. I know how to play a little, and you can go easy on me. It'll be fun," I say, hopping off my stool. Sucking down water.

"You scared, Jimmy?" Sam seals the deal.

We head to the only pool table as the others wrap up, with Carter and Cara claiming the win. Matt gives Jimmy a chilling glare as we approach. *It worked! Cheers to acting like a fifteen-year-old!* He also comes around the table when I don't go to him and gives me another bear hug, this time with his hands venturing lower down on my back.

"Hey."

"Hey," I say back to him.

He smiles at me. "You want to play?"

"James and I made a little wager," I say.

His head snaps to Jimmy.

"It was Sam's idea. I'll go easy on her," Jimmy explains.

"*James?* What wager?" he says, still glaring as if Jimmy is about to die via pointed line of sight.

"New pair of kicks. Your girl has good taste." Jimmy racks the balls.

"She does." He looks down at me, still holding me firm around the waist.

Does my chest get all warm at the fact that Jimmy said I'm Matt's girl? And that Matt didn't correct him? And that Elizabeth looks like she might cry? Yes, yes, it does. But I've got shoes to win. I give him a quick, firm peck on the lips, like the one he gave me earlier, and move out of his grip.

"You know we have tables at the office," Matt says to me. Then he turns to Jimmy. "She's not actually buying you any shoes, dipshit."

I smile shyly. This is one thing I actually thank Ryan for. He had a pool table in his apartment and taught me how to play. We played all the time. Naked, tipsy, sober, angry. We settled fights at his pool table. Now, it was a favorite trick of mine and Sam's. Nothing feels quite like being sorely underestimated, knowing you're about to blow everyone away.

Just ask a wallflower.

CHAPTER 11

"I was conned, bro! Not cool!" Jimmy yells, as all of us die laughing, ripping into the poor guy, Sam most of all. Carter shushes him, and I tell him he doesn't have to make good, since it was a setup.

Matt walks around the table and pulls me in again, this time putting a hand in my jeans back pocket. "You are the sexiest girl in New York," he says low in my ear. Then he kisses just behind my ear and down my neck three times, torching every spot his lips touch. I sway a little bit in his arms, still needing to eat. He pulls away to look down. "You ready to go?" I nod. He calls out, "We're out of here. Jimmy, you're buying the shoes."

"You guys good?" I ask Sam and look to Nicole as Matt pulls me past the group.

"Yep, you kids have fun!" Sam says with the biggest smile on her face, raising her eyebrows with innuendo.

My drinks catch up to me as we leave the bar, distracting my feet from their job of walking. Matt catches me and realizes it's time to get some dinner. It was only an hour and a half or so, but I put away a lot of alcohol. More than anyone else and more than what would probably be considered, uh, healthy. But everyone else seemed so relaxed and fun and I was twisty and awkward. I knew better, though. This is an old habit I broke a long time ago.

Until Matt...

He gets us each a huge slice of pizza and bottled water, and we find a bench outside Gramercy Park.

"Hey, you should text your boys about Sam," I say, realizing I've left her out in the wilderness with only Nicole, who is too easily steamrolled. Matt asks me why with his eyes. "Anything past heavy petting, and she'll be planning their wedding tomorrow."

Matt chokes, "Did you just say heavy petting?" We both laugh. "How much did you have to drink exactly?"

I shrug. "I was nervous."

He stares down at me, and I tense, mouth full of pepperoni and grease all over my lips and hands. This is not hot. I mean, his thigh is burning on the bench next to mine and his eyes are making my toes grip the soles of my shoes, but I really don't think this is a good time to—

"You make me nervous too," he says softly.

Okay, kiss me with pizza lips, I don't care!

But he doesn't. And instead, we talk about getting an Uber, which launches us into another discussion about the impending AI apocalypse and his role in humanity's demise. He has strong counterarguments and some convicting points, since I *am* slightly addicted to my smartphone, smart watch, running app, Instagram, and the list goes on. And he's just so dreamy to look at when he's passionate, which he is.

He loves his work, his teams. He takes time and care explaining technical pieces to me so I understand. He's also so optimistic about technology and the future. I wonder for a moment what

Dad would think of his take, and then shake off the thought. *We are nowhere near meeting Dad territory. Wits, Skye! Wits!* Our debate is friendly but spirited, fun. And it lasts all the way through the Uber ride to my apartment building.

We step out onto the sidewalk, but my stomach remains in the car, zooming off down the street.

Because he's clearly coming up.

Which is fine. Good. Great. Sam and I picked up and deep cleaned, just in case.

I start to lead the way to the door as he walks up behind me, but he pulls me back with some kind of ninja spin move. His hands are on my neck and his mouth is on mine before I can think. He moves one hand to my back jean pocket and tugs me into him. I am putty for molding.

His arms feel big and firm around me, his fingers ask no questions. He's holding me up, pulling me in. He smells fresh and woody and not at all like pizza, and I feel his strong chest breathing against my padded bra, which suddenly feels thick and bothersome. Again, he teases me with those strong full lips, not opening all the way. I let out an involuntary moan as he pulls away almost as soon as he starts.

"I don't have to come up," he says, wiping away all the hesitation I had.

"There are brownies," I blurt. He smiles and runs his right thumb along the edge of my shirt, warming a horizontal line across my back.

"Oh, really?" His voice is low, and he's grinning.

"Yeah, you should definitely try them. They're Ghirardelli. I mean, it's just a box mix, but they have mini chocolate chips in them, which really takes the boxed brownie thing to the—"

"Skye." His left thumb is on my bottom lip again, and I'm having trouble not latching on to it with my teeth. "Brownies sound great."

"But," I say, suddenly filled with so much anxiety and lust and feelings, "I'm not having sex with you."

Matt lights up in a fake scoff. "Wow, now who's cocky? I just wanted some Ghirardelli, jeez." His eyes sparkle at me.

"Shut up, I'm serious. I-I like to take things slowly," I say.

"Hey, I don't need to come up, Skye, I can—"

But I turn and pull his hand hard and lead us into my building. At my door, I pull out my key but don't manage to get it in the lock, because Matt has gently moved all my hair to my left shoulder, brushing his fingertips along my skin. The move allows him to plant soft, partially open-mouthed kisses along the right side of my neck. He stops.

"Are we going in?" he asks on my skin.

I cough—apparently my body's awesome go-to response to embarrassment and arousal—and nod and get the door open. I flip on the light to reveal the happy little space.

The door opens into the small kitchen, with old cabinets and appliances, but all bright white and in good condition. To the left is a hall that leads to our two bedrooms and one shared bathroom. Off the kitchen is the small living space with its glorious windows, beyond which the Manhattan skyline shines and twinkles as if just for us.

"Wow, this is awesome," Matt says as he heads for the windows.

"This is pretty much it—bathroom and our two tiny rooms down the hall," I say, feeling confident. Our apartment is cool and homey. The furniture is a mix of antiques from Craigslist, a few necessities from Ikea, and then some nicer pieces, like our comfy couch and cute side chairs. The space is mostly white and beige, but bright throws and pillows add color, along with some amazing art. Some of it is my own, some from friends, and some I saved up for and purchased at shows because I couldn't *not* have them. Matt takes it all in as I move around to turn on lamps.

Gus greets us, weaving through our legs.

"Hey, buddy." Matt gives Gus one long stroke that results in immediate purring.

"That's Gus, who is not normally so social." I give Gus the stink eye. Gus, like myself, needs to at least attempt to play hard to get.

"I'm a bit of an animal whisperer," Matt says, and I believe him, as Gus follows his ankles around, using his legs as scratch posts. Matt eventually stops at the shelf that's hard to miss, in between two windows on the far wall. I brace myself. The top three shelves are Sam's collection of every single one of Sadie's books and movies, with more Canton books and knickknacks on the bottom two shelves.

"Wow." He lifts his eyebrows at me. "Big Sadie Canton fans?"

I groan. "Ugh. Sam is."

He hitches one shoulder. "Some of the movies were pretty good."

"Gag me! Do not tell me you're a fan of cheesy rom-coms," I blurt, a little too passionately.

"Well, damn." He turns from the bookshelf to me. "What did Ryan Gosling ever do to you?"

"Ryan Gosling is faultless and can do no wrong, obviously. But the whole genre is *so* unrealistic."

He cocks his head. "This from the girl who loves fantasies?"

"Epics, fantasies, sci-fi—they create other worlds, huge stories you can get lost in. Romantic comedies paint a shallow, formulaic, wide stroke over all of love and romance, with the meet-cutes and the copycat story arcs and big, fake, fall-out seventy percent through the story every. Single. Time. I just can't. I cannot."

He takes a small step toward me. "I mean, we actually did have a pretty unbelievable meet-cute, you have to admit."

I shrug. "The odds of us ending up together on a flight here from Dallas are pretty believable, actually."

"But look, I'm the left-brained nerd, you're the gorgeous right-brained creative genius." I bite my bottom lip at his choice of words, but I still shake my head. He motions his hand between us. "C'mon, Sadie Canton could write her next book about you and me."

"Here's the thing about that tired storyline. They always show the, ahem, creative genius, as like a Zooey Deschanel or an Emma Stone, let's say. And she's this lovable, ditzy, artsy-fartsy, easy-breezy hot mess. 'Oh, she's so cute! She paints daisies on her jeans and fell off her bike and always runs late, oh ha ha ha, so adorable!'"

"Or maybe 'bites it hard on her ass while trying to sprin' backward' adorable?" He's chuckling again as he says it. I let ou' a small laugh too. But my tone turns less playful, even as I try to keep things light.

"Right. Gashes her whole arm open. Super cute. And it's just . . . people expect artsy-fartsy easy-breezy whennn that is *not* the reality."

"What's the reality then?" He says it so low, I somehow feel his voice in my abdomen. He has walked right back up to me, so close I can smell his heavenly scent again.

"Well." I clear my throat. "Instead of artsy-fartsy easy-breezy, it's a lot more, um, artsy-anxious uptight-neurotic." He squints down at me in disbelief as he puts his hands on my hips. I add, "The running-late, hot-mess part is accurate."

He puts his hands into my back pockets and tugs me into him. "Definitely the hot part." He leans his face in so close to mine, I start to close my eyes. Then he whispers, "Where are the brownies?"

The what? I manage to point to the kitchen counter.

In two long strides, he crosses from the living space to the kitchen and grabs one brownie out from under the cellophane wrap. He's back in my personal space in a second, breaking the brownie in half. He hands half to me. He sticks the entire half in his mouth and watches me for a second, then turns and pulls me into the little kitchen. I am confused as I chew but also still slightly buzzed from the drinks . . . and the smell of him and the lingering touch of his hands in my pocket.

"Tho are real goo," he says through his chewing. He is still holding my hand until he opens our fridge like he owns the place and takes out a bottled water. He takes a few gulps and hands it to me, and I take a sip, feeling his eyes watching my mouth.

For a second, I think about trying to be sexy with the water bottle, but I refrain. I have learned my lesson, finally. And I'm having trouble even swallowing with the way his gaze is piercing me, straight through to my lungs, which seem to be having trouble finding oxygen.

He takes the water bottle from me and sets it on the counter, not looking away as he does it. I feel his large warm hands on my exposed sides. *Must wear this shirt every day from now on!* His right hand goes to hold my face, and both hands pull me into him, my mouth to his.

First, he teases me with his cold, barely open mouth, and I involuntarily squeeze my hands on his arms where my hands landed, one on his smooth forearm, the other on his bicep, which is hard and round and fighting the fabric of his fitted shirt.

Finally, mercifully, his tongue pushes into my mouth and I open up quickly, tasting sweet chocolate. My whole body squeezes at the rich sensation of the sweet brownie on his cold tongue. The man is a genius. No, his tongue is a genius. No, his hand is a genius, as it moves up into my hair and pulls my head back slightly so he can deepen the kiss. And he does, and I feel it in my thighs and my toes and my brain, spinning inside my head. His left hand has moved to my back, his fingertips just barely under the hem of my shirt. More. I need more. *Now.*

I break away with a groan, opening my eyes to see him grinning at me, his eyes dark. I move backward out of the kitchen to the couch and pull him down to sit with me. I move closer and reach up to put my hands into his hair, but Gus hops up, purring loudly, deciding to make camp next to Matt's firm thigh. Matt chuckles and gently picks up my cat and sets him on the floor.

"Told you," he says. I manage to get out an uh-huh as I lie back on the couch and pull on Matt's shirt to bring him down too. I need this hot, kind, funny, considerate, hard man on top of me. He obliges, kissing my neck with his magician mouth.

"Matthew," I whisper, without thinking, just enjoying whatever his lips are doing on my collarbone. He smiles on my skin and uses one hand to shift me up to the far edge of the couch. I shove up a bit more and put my head on the small throw pillow there and quickly move my mass of hair out from under my neck to splay over the pillow. I do this because my hair makes my neck sweaty, but I also spread it out, thinking maybe it'll look hot to have my hair all mussed out on the pillow like a mermaid.

So, I have not, in fact, learned my lesson.

Because I am me.

And I am not a sexy mermaid.

And I let my cat play on the furniture.

So, without realizing it, I've tangled my hair into one of Gus's favorite toys, the little stick wand attached to a short string with a feather on the end. A feather that is now dancing in my hair, by the crease of the couch, as Matthew kisses back up my neck to my mouth. Just as his tongue finds mine, Gus finds the feather, quickly mounting himself on the arm of the couch. I don't notice him at all, until he pounces, as only cats can, with total abandon onto the feather near my head. One paw lands in my eye, three tangle in my hair.

"Ow!" My arms shoot up to protect my mane, smacking Matthew, hard, in the ear. "Doh!" I hear from him as he sits back, but I can't focus because I'm trying to get Gus off my hair. But his little paw beans are grasped tightly into my frizz. As I pull Gus off, he screams in protest and I swear he takes a whole section of my hair with him. "Ahhh!" I lift a hand to my head and sit up, and Matthew is shaking. With laughter.

"Am I freaking bald?" I cry as Matthew—realizing that's his name to me now—lets out his laughter. He can't hold it in any longer. "See!" I say, starting to giggle myself. "This is real life! Not effing meet-cutes and mind-blowing brownie kisses! Stupid cat toys and crazy hair and holy crap that hurt so bad!"

"Here I was thinking we were finally going to make it through one date." He can barely get the words out, he's laughing so hard. So, I laugh too, turning purple and feeling my neck turn splotchy.

"Quit laughing!" I cry, but I'm laughing too.

"Look how much of your hair is in his paws! It's like he's dragging a wig!" He's actually wiping a tear from his eyes as he says it.

"Bad kitty!" I yell at Gus. "That toy is going in the trash!" I start to stand up, but Matthew pulls me in and cradles me in his arms on the couch, smoothing my hair back.

"I don't see any bald spots," he says, still chuckling. I put my face in my hands, shaking my head. Only me. Unbelievable. "Mind-blowing brownie kisses, huh?"

"Ughhhh! You're unbearable," I say as he pulls my hands down.

"Uh-huh." He smiles at my collarbone again, kissing his way up my neck. And then we make out, for ages. We kiss like high schoolers. At one point, I moved to straddle his lap and his hands went up my back under my shirt. There was some butt-grabbing and hair-pulling, but mostly we just learned each other's mouths and necks. He's the best kisser I've ever kissed. Anyone's ever kissed. And it almost did me in. I found myself about to pull off my shirt, but thankfully all my insecurities and doubts and fears won out over my baser instincts.

I dismount the sexy, rock-hard stack of muscles and charm sitting on my couch and sit beside him to catch my breath.

"It's late, I should check on Sam," I manage to say.

"K," he says, spreading his hand across my thigh and barely giving me a squeeze.

I find my phone and send her a text asking for an update. Neither of us drink very much, so when we do go out, we can easily get carried away, obviously.

"Nicole ditched them, but Jimmy is with her."

"He'll make sure she gets home okay." He stands up and crosses to the kitchen, where he drinks some more from the water bottle we left out. "I'll text him to make sure. Or I can meet up with them if he's had too many."

I smile and cross over to him. "Very knight in shining armor of you." I hug him from behind.

"How's your elbow, by the way?" He begins to grab my arm as he asks it.

"It's fine," I say too quickly, then pull my arms away. Good thing I didn't whip my shirt off—I am clearly not ready for that.

"Well. I gotta be honest with you." He smirks down at me with his hands back on my bare sides. "I can't wait to see what happens to us tomorrow." He cracks up again.

"Oh, you think I'm seeing you tomorrow?" I try to pull away, but he holds me in place.

"You tell me," he says, barely above a whisper, right before he puts his lips on mine for another barely there, barely open kiss. "Hm?" He teases me with his soft mouth again.

"Maybe," I manage to get out. He pulls away.

"All right, I mean, if you want to stay here with your hangover and your attack cat, I guess that's your choice." He goes to the door but pauses with his hand on the knob. "Do I need to go rescue your sister?"

I glance at my phone. "No, she's on her way here in an Uber."

"K. Good night," he says before planting a quick peck on my mouth, and then he's out the door.

Gus bellows out, feeling Matthew's absence as much as I do.

"Shut your trap, devil spawn." But I smile as I say it. What a night.

CHAPTER 12

8:07 A.M.

Janie: I just cannot believe your luck. I mean, I can. But wow. LOL

Me: Yep, looking for a new home for Gus if you're interested.

Headed to the studio?

M wants to meet up for brunch.

Wow, he's persistent.

I know, weird, right?

Not weird. Interesting. But just a reminder your new series is supposed to be done in about 70 days.

Ugh. And I got nothin. And Sam needs help at the office today too.

So maybe no brunch then.

Ya. No brunch.

8:44 A.M.

Matt: Good morning

[Animated GIF Cat drinking coffee]

Me: LOL that looks just like him!

How are you guys feeling this morning? This is our favorite hangover place, headed there soon, Jimmy says he's dying.

[Dropped pin location]

Feeling okay. Can't do breakfast today. Need to paint, I'm behind.

[Animated GIF Sad orange tabby kitten]

I will not give in to kitten memes . . . I will not give in to kitten memes...

[Animated GIF Sad white long-haired kitten]

I am only swinging by to get a coffee on my way to the studio. Even though the diner is definitely out of my way, which he'll know, since he knows my studio address. Still, it's just coffee. Then I will get to work.

There are a few outdoor tables in front of the diner, and I spot the back of Matthew's head as I approach. I slow. There's a woman next to him, with perfect blond waves, laughing and touching his arm. I am filled with an irrational amount of rage at the sight, especially since Jimmy and Carter sit across from him. But seriously. What is with the women of New York and Matthew's biceps?

Jimmy starts to look in my direction, so like a ninja, I drop to a deep squat to hide behind the makeshift partition that encloses the diner's outdoor seating. Except I am not a ninja, so I end up falling into the partition, hard. I hit my head, and the partition leaves a huge smudge of black across my purple shirt across my chest. And because that's not enough, my backpack manages to trip a guy walking by. He promptly cusses me out, which I hope is not enough to cause people to look over. This is New York, so it's probably not.

THINGS I SHOULD HAVE SAID

Slow and steady, I turn my body in a squat position, again gaining more colorful commentary from those walking around me. Once I'm fully facing the opposite direction, I put up the hood on my shirt. It's a hooded yoga shirt that has cutouts and little thumb holes. It was cute. Before the big black smudge. I stand and walk away from the diner.

Clearly, I need to get my head right. The man is not mine. He can date whomever he wants, and they can touch him all they want. We've only been on a few dates, so what's my problem? I am suddenly dying to text Matthew and ask him who went to breakfast. But that's a manipulation tactic that I am better than. That is what a psycho possessive girlfriend would do. *Would she also dive-bomb into a metal partition so as not to be seen? You're losing it!* I know all of this, logically. But still, I pull out my phone.

9:50 A.M.

Me: I went by the diner.

Janie: [Facepalm emoji]

Gets worse.

Of course it does.

I walked up and saw a blonde with him, touching and laughing.

Like a date?

Well, Jimmy and Carter were there, so probably not.

Who was she?

Don't know, I turned and bolted and fell. Like a real winner.

I don't even feel bad for you at this point.

Let it go, S. You guys aren't exclusive. Don't drive yourself nuts over what's probably nothing. Ask him about it directly, or forget about it.

Ugh, Janie, you're entirely too mature.

9:51 A.M.

Me: I went by the diner, and Matt was with some blonde

Sam: I WILL KILL HIM!

WHO WAS SHE?!!!

Was Jimmy there?

Was Jimmy with a girl too?

Jimmy and Carter and Matt and the girl next to him. She was all over him. I didn't go talk to them. I just left.

What kind of blonde we talking?

Wavy, long. She was petite.

10:02 A.M.

[Instagram profile link]

Wow. Yep, that looks like her.

Coworker.

Lame. Boring. Vanilla.

Posts way too many bikini pics. Thirsty.

Not into it! Not his type!

Allison Johnston, the coworker, is really cute. Very short with a perfect figure, as seen in her many beach pics from this summer. LinkedIn says she's an engineer. So probably in his department. Great. I don't see any posts with Matthew, but she did post a Story of her egg white omelet and mimosa this morning. *Who goes to a greasy diner and gets an egg white omelet? Gag me.*

Since I'm already torturing myself, I go through Matthew's Instagram follows to find Lauren, the serious ex. It doesn't take long since Matthew doesn't follow many people.

Lauren Bines. Also very short. Interesting. Her face is beautiful in a way that says she never wears makeup and always looks dewy. She has shining, long dark hair and bright blue eyes. She is an operations manager for one of the million Texas gas companies. I'm not sure what that means, but her LinkedIn says she's very organized.

11:12 A.M.

Janie: . . . you texted Sam instead, didn't you

Me: Matt's ex is tiny, naturally beautiful, and an organizational wizard. The chick he's with today is tiny, adorable, and an engineer.

YOU SHOULD BE PAINTING, NOT SPIRALING.

Wow, no need to yell.

YES, NEED.

He seems like a great guy, but I'm not going to let you do this. If you're feeling some type of way, paint it out.

Can't you just let me wallow? Come over with ice cream? Help me talk out all the feels I'm feeling?

No. Put the feels on the canvas, sister.

She's right. She was there to pick up the pieces after Ryan. She helped me find all the bits of myself I lost in him. I'm not going to lose them again. I put my phone on silent and grab my sketchbook.

Hours later, I have pages of thumbnail studies and am feeing pretty good about some of them. I might even see a theme forming, which is what I need, and fast. But unfortunately, I can't rush the process if I want the work to be any good. With Janie's words still rolling around in my head, I get ready for a long run. First, I check my phone. There are texts from Susan, Sam, Janie, and even Matthew. But before I let myself open his message, I tap the Twitter notification. One of our interns sent me the latest burn.

@CantonCards: Who will be at ISC next weekend? We can't wait to see you there!
[Image of last year's Canton Cards displays]

Reply @NewCardsOnTheBlock: 2002 called, they'd like their tradeshow booth back.

Are you kidding me with this? Our tradeshow booths are always beyond cool. Way bigger and better than any other exhibitor there. *Oh, they can just step right off.*

Our team crafted a few responses about being older and wiser, but they are all trash. No one wants old and wise, at least not on Twitter. The Twitter crowd wants all things young, weird, cool, quirky.

I sit and think. Finally, it comes to me.

Reply @CantonCards: You probably can't handle an actual phone call, so you can just text them back for us: This year's booth will feature a collab w/ twelve indie artists who will be painting, drawing, crafting, and sculpting live, in person. #wherestheappforthat #supportindieartists

I send it off with instructions for the team to shout out each artist in the same conversation thread. I smile to myself. Hi their introverted socially awkward selves where it hurts (take one to know one) and support our twelve artists at the same time? So much win.

As much as I want to open Matthew's message, I make myself post some behind-the-scenes shots of my brainstorming process to Instagram and TikTok. It takes longer than I want and drains me more than it should. But immediately the notifications pour in, and as much as I hate to admit it, I am thankful for the power of social media.

Okay, done working, let's see what the Petite-Lady Magnet has to say.

> Matt: Can I bring you lunch?

> Matt: OK, not bringing you lunch because I fear you will call security.
> [Animated GIF "Securrity" Anjelah Johnson]
> I'm going for a long run East River Greenway, come find me?

Something about the hopeful "come find me" makes me melt. I was going to run anyway—what's the harm in another non-date? And maybe I'll just be direct and ask him about the blonde. Direct and honest. Janie will be so proud.

———————————

After a few texts to find each other, I see him running toward me, with Navid. Good Lord, is this man ever alone? But he spots me, and his face erupts into a huge smile that's absolutely devastating. I stop in my tracks like a dork. He's already sweaty, and his shirt hugs his pecs and shoulders in the best way, leaving me wondering if I'll even be able to move, let alone run a few miles.

He runs straight to me and stops just in time to grab my face and kiss me like we've been apart for months. He doesn't hold back with his tongue, which is salty, not that he cares, clearly. It's so strong and sweet at the same time. It takes a second for me to get over the shock of such an unexpected display and melt into him. The moment I do, he pulls away, smiling.

"Hey," he says.

After a couple seconds, I manage to get out, "Has anyone ever told you you're a tease?"

"Me? I don't know what you're talking about." His tone is dripping with sarcasm. "What happened to your shirt?"

"I'm not telling you." I can't help but smile because he is already beyond amused.

"Skye."

"Nope. Less talking, more running," I say as I turn, put my headphones back in, and get going. This time, he charges out ahead of me and circles back as we go. Of course, he sees two women and one guy he knows. He waves but doesn't stop to talk. Whenever he's running toward me, he smiles like a little kid every time we make eye contact. There's also some enthusiastic butt-slapping by both of us when he circles me.

After seven miles, I'm done. And I am disgusting. He is also very sweaty, but somehow not disgusting. Ugh. Men. He gets us each a water bottle from a cart on the side of the waterfront. We walk along the edge out of the path, slowly.

"How was it?" He's panting.

"Good, but slow. Definitely feeling the LITs," I manage to say in between chugs.

He nods. "So where did you fall down tits-first?" He motions toward the big smudge.

I look away with a grin. "Maybe I didn't fall, maybe I was doing some erotic painting."

"Erotic painting with your clothes on?" I growl in frustration, but he adds, "Whatever we do tonight can be indoors, seated, no sharp objects."

I shake my head. "I gotta help Sam again."

"What's the big project?"

I still haven't caught my breath. "Family thing. They're all coming into town this week."

"Oh, yeah?" He looks very interested, surprised, possibly scared.

"Don't worry. You're not going to meet them," I say quickly. He gives a tight nod. "But it's going to be a looooong week."

His big brown eyes study me. "You guys don't get along then?"

I inhale deeply, trying to figure out how best to describe it.

He pushes. "You don't talk about them at all, other than Sam."

"It's not that we don't get along, they're just . . . a lot. My dad is intense. My sisters are intense. I'm intense."

He chuckles. "Sounds like a blast."

"Exactly." I'm eager to change the subject and gather my courage. "So, how was breakfast?"

"It was fine," he says.

I wait, wondering if he'll sense what I'm really asking. I want to blurt out "Who was that hoe next to you?" But I refrain. Instead, I go into Spanish Inquisition mode. "And what are you going to do tonight?"

"I guess just eat at home, probably watch some football."

"And tomorrow night?"

"Whateverrr you . . . want?" He smiles but also looks at me like I'm crazy, which I am. And right then, I have the opening to come clean. Tell him I stalked him at the diner, don't want him dating petite blondes, don't want to obsess about who else he's teasing with his insane kissing skills.

But I don't. Instead, I avoid eye contact and take a breath. And with how crazy I feel—*hello, we're barely dating, let the man live!*—I decide what I need is space. I'm being weird. I can feel it. Matthew stops walking and puts his hands on my hips.

"Sorry, just, uh, thinking I probably won't have much free time all week." I wince.

"I actually have a crazy week too, which is why we should definitely hang out tomorrow." He gives me a squeeze, so I finally look up at him.

"Yeah?"

"Yeah." He pulls my hips into him, wrapping his arms around me.

"No, I'm all gross!" I cry, trying to push him off, but he holds me to him.

"Tell me you'll hang out with me tomorrow!" He laughs and grabs my butt, which is in thin shorts that are thoroughly—no, beyond thoroughly—soaked.

"Ahhh Matthew! Don't!"

He laughs. "Tomorrow! Say it!"

I laugh too, but from straight-up mortification. "All right, fine! Let go, you sicko!" He plants a firm peck on my mouth and then releases me, smiling wide. I just stand frozen. This sexy, infectious, magnetic dream of a man just put his gorgeous hands on my butt sweat!

I. Am. Not. Okay.

"You should see your face," he says as he takes my hand, then we resume walking.

"Does it look traumatized? Because I am traumatized."

"C'mon, it's not the first time we've been sweaty." Then his voice changes, and he leans closer to me. "Hopefully won't be the last." I bite my lip and look away. We pause at a crosswalk, where it's time to go in opposite directions. "I'll see you tomorrow." He gives my hand a squeeze.

"I said that under duress!" I joke.

"Oh, do I need to grab you again?" His face goes dead serious, but playfully.

"Okay! Okay. Bye." I turn and start walking before he can affect me even more. But who am I kidding. I couldn't possibly be more affected. I am walking, talking affection for Matthew James. And it's terrifying.

CHAPTER 13

SUNDAY 9:03 A.M.

Matthew: Good morning, gorgeous.

Me: Morning yourself.

What are you up to?

Sam is subjecting me to an online sermon.

LOL which preacher?

I don't know. You can take the girl out of the Bible Belt . . .

[Dancing church meme]

I listen to a few sermon podcasts. Don't tell anyone.

The tech community would—wait for it—crucify you.

Nice one. So are you coming over after church?

Studio and run first. Janie's orders.

I thought Maud was your manager?

Maud is the brains, Janie is the brawn.

Pretty sure I can take Janie.

She takes self-defense classes. Late lunch?

K, we can order something over here.

[Dropped pin location]

[Liked dropped pin location]

Matthew's apartment is basically a very, very nice bachelor pad for three very nerdy dudes. The fixtures and finishings that clearly came with the luxury apartment are gorgeous, but they've filled the space with big leather couches, a golf putting thing, a basketball hoop, and a wall-length desk set up with three workstations. The light is great even if there's only a street view. The kitchen, dining nook, and bedrooms are sparse.

Jimmy and Carter are home, and I enjoy teasing them all about their gamer chairs. (Matthew doesn't have one of his own—he just steals Jimmy's, according to Jimmy.) I also don't hold back about their manly furniture and cheesy T.J. Maxx wall art. They retort with klutz jokes and now call me "Dick Wacker." But I've been embarrassed about that story so many times, it's lost its hive-launching abilities.

My favorite thing about Matthew's apartment is how handsy he is in it. While we eat and chat, he either touches my leg or tucks me into him from behind, or positions me in between his legs, or sets me firmly on his lap. All of which make me woozy in the best way. I find myself starting to touch him first, rubbing his hard arms around me, or linking my hands into his. He seems to like it. A lot.

After our late lunch, I am initiated into the world of Call of Duty, headset included. I'm terrible, but it's fun. The guys are loud and competitive and honestly a bit ridiculous. But I find myself laughing and smiling so much, my cheeks hurt. I also—shocker—work up a sweat. Matt catches me fanning myself with the open zip hoodie I'm wearing over a cap-sleeve tee and leggings. I didn't think this through.

"Why don't you just take that off?" Matthew finally says.

"I'm fine," I say, clearly melting.

Suddenly Matthew picks me up, throws me over his shoulder, and charges into his room.

He throws me down on his bed and turns to close his door. His room is plain, with a navy bedding set on a soft queen bed, a desk by the window, and some shelves with Texas memorabilia and a few family photos. But I'm not looking around. I sit up on the edge of the bed, suddenly beyond nervous.

He sits next to me, as close as he can get. He clears his throat. "I already saw your scars," he says, barely above a whisper. I look down and absently pick at my thumb cuticles as splotches spread up my neck. He grabs my right hand in both of his, breaking me out of my bad habit. "You don't have to talk about it, but you also don't have to cover them up." I smile a little bit, so he adds, "I don't want you passing out, though. We can't break our incident-free streak." I shove him, so he puts his left arm around my shoulder.

"It's not a cool story," I finally say. He kisses the side of my forehead. "I have eczema, which is like a totally normal thing that shouldn't leave scars like that. But I have pretty bad anxiety, and one of the coping habits I formed is to rip the eczema off." My voice gets shaky. "It . . ." He picks me up into his lap, which is the comfort I need to keep going. "It got much worse after my mom died and after . . . after the shock, there was so much grief and stress. My skin got even more irritated, then I scratched at it even more. Harder and harder, really deep scrapes. So yeah. I did it to myself. Didn't even notice I was doing it and then couldn't stop."

"I'm so sorry about your mom, Skye." He squeezes me tight as he says it.

"It was eight years ago. Drunk driver. It . . . wrecked us, my whole family." He kisses my forehead again. I blink the tears back so they don't fall. "Things have gotten a lot better now. I have a routine, I run, I go to therapy. I tried meds, but they made me feel too weird." I take a deep breath. "So now you know why I always wear long sleeves. And my thumbs, you saw I scratch at my cuticles without even noticing it. And every time I fall, it becomes a thing, because as it heals, I have to stop myself from . . ." I can't bear to say "picking at it." It's just so gross and stupid, like I'm a five-year-old with no self-control. Ugh. "So anyway! I warned you that I was neurotic."

"Hey." He tilts my chin up to look at him. "Lots of people struggle with anxiety. Tons." He gently starts to take my hoodie off, and I help him. It's a relief, since sitting in his lap makes me even hotter than I was in the living room. "They're not even that noticeable, but I think they're actually pretty cool." I scoff at him. "Really. They look like tiger stripes. Like a tattoo, actually."

"If you're just trying to get some action"—I move to straddle him—"it's working." I kiss him this time, soft and small and torturous like he's done to me so many times. Then I kiss down his neck, earning me a sexy sigh as he squeezes his hands where they sit on my hips. I kiss back up to his mouth, and he takes over, hungry, starving. I take his face in my hands and match his tongue sweep for sweep, his lips suck for suck.

Again, we kiss for what feels like forever, until desire takes over and I find myself rocking into him. I feel his own desire beneath me, obvious through his thin athletic shorts. He lets out a groan that makes me feel like some kind of sex goddess.

But I stop us, stop myself. I am not ready for more than this.

I remember Allison from breakfast yesterday, Elizabeth from the bar on Friday, the pretty face after pretty face on his Instagram, and who knows how many other girls in Matthew's life. Someone else could've been sitting right here, on him, earlier this week. There are at least two hoping to sit on him at his office.

"I should go," I say, panting, eyes still closed.

"Okay," he says on my neck in between kisses.

I pull away and stand in between his legs, and he holds me tight, his head on my chest. "Maybe we can run together this week?" I say as I stroke that spot on his neck where his hair ends. It's everything I hoped it would be back on the plane months ago.

"I'm going to have to do morning runs this week," he says, still holding me.

"Oh, okay."

"But we have to eat, right?" He looks up at me. "Let's try for a few meals?"

I smile and nod down at him. I pull away, but he holds me. "Thanks for telling me that, Skye." He stands and kisses me again, but it's soft and slow. It's so sweet, my eyes start to sting, which shocks me back to reality. I am not going to cry from a kiss with this man who is not even officially my boyfriend! *Mayday! Abort!*

I pull away and turn, and he lets me, then he walks me out. Again, at the door he kisses me like he wants me to remember him all week long. Like we are about to be separated for months. Like he . . . *no.* Not like he really likes me or cares for me. Not like he needs me. Nope. It's like he really knows what he's doing. That's all it is.

9:55 P.M.

Matthew: [Article 25 Amazing Tiger Facts]

Good night

[Animated GIF Tiger lying down to sleep]

Me: Night

[Loved Article 25 Amazing Tiger Facts]

[Loved Animated GIF Tiger lying down to sleep]

CHAPTER 14

MONDAY 8:42 A.M.

Matthew: [Link "Eye of the Tiger" on Spotify]

Me: LOL Good morning

The thoughtfulness of the song almost makes me forget how much I'll need it, and the rest of my pump-up playlist, this week. What is it about family? How can a group of people be your absolute favorite while also making you want to jump in front of a Mack truck? Is it just me and my family, or all families? And is it every member of my whole family, or just me? *Well, who's the common denominator there, genius?*

Still, along with the dread in my gut, I'm excited and hopeful. We're only all together a few times a year, and even with the repeated arguments, strained side-eyes, and too-far teasing, we do have a lot of fun.

"Sweetheart!" Dad's warm voice greets me as I enter the conference room. He's an attractive man, average height but built from years of playing football—and then working out as if he were still playing. He's energetic and magnetic, like Samantha, but fierce in a way that's honestly more like me. He doesn't take any crap, not in business, but especially not when it comes to his girls.

"Hey, Dad." We hug, and I take in the scent of him, his cologne and detergent and a million childhood memories. Before either of us can say anything else, Sally has joined our hug.

"Skye!" I smile at her little voice that's not so little anymore. While Samantha is the sunshine in our family, Sally is the darling. She's only twenty, and even though she could get away with anything, she doesn't try. She's a lot like Susan in that way, strait-laced, smart, kind, deliberate. I keep nudging her to sow some wild oats during her last couple years at college, but she claims to be oat-less.

I shift to hug just her. "I can't believe Dad let you miss classes for this."

She laughs. "I know, I know."

"Only you, Sally," Sam, Sadie, Susan, and I say in unison. Dad chuckles.

"Everything looks amazing, Skye." It's Susan's turn for a hug. "You and Samantha have really nailed it this year."

"Agreed!" Sadie cheers, close behind Susan.

"Sam's done all the heavy lifting." I motion toward her as I grab one of the salads.

Samantha and Dad get us chatting away, catching up, mostly pestering Sally about college life and hearing Susan share all the new goings-on with her kids. Dad fills us in on some family friends and his recent golf tournaments and his take on the Sooners football team this season.

Of course, we breeze over that none of the younger four of us have serious boyfriends, much to Susan's dismay, and Sam brings up Matthew. But I shrug it off as new with not much to share. Prompting Sam to share away on my behalf. And I must admit, Matthew is sounding pretty amazing.

"Sending you Tiger facts? I mean, I couldn't have written something sweeter for you." Sadie points at me, and I feel the tide of the table turning.

"Maybe you could do tigers in your next series!" Sally says. I refrain from shooting death rays down the table at her. She doesn't know she's taken the conversation straight into an active minefield.

"Oh, *love* that idea! Did she tell you she already sold all but one from Inside?" Samantha says proudly. But she, in fact, should know better. Death stare activated.

"Of course she did. That's great, Skye." Dad clears his throat, and I steel myself. "Have you seen the numbers on our feature artists? The collaborations have been incredibly lucrative for them," he says, not looking directly at me.

"I know, it's great," I manage to squeak out, using all my available self-control.

"They're all growing on social media too—'blowing up' as you kids say," he adds. "In fact, our Maria—she does those watercolor prints for us—just landed her own deal at Magnolia Farms, thanks to how well her line with us is performing."

Sadie is frozen. Susan sighs. Samantha braces herself.

And I break. "Well, yeah, it's amazing how well things perform once you totally sell out."

"Really? That same old shit? Come down from your high horse and give us all a damn break, Skye, seriously," Sadie snaps.

"Hey, anything to sell more books, right?" I sneer at my older sister.

"Maybe we should focus on convention?" Sam tries to reel us in, unsuccessfully. Sally's face falls beside her.

"I *do* sell more books." Sadie stands. "Which means more people read the work, all over the world, rather than a few self-righteous yuppies in one measly shop on the Upper East Side."

I stand too. "Holy shit, we get it already, Sadie—you're very famous! Wow, we're so lucky to be sitting here at this table with you, the author who, how'd the *Times* put it? *Regurgitates* the same fairytale trope over and over for bored housewives?"

"Hey," Samantha chimes in, "that's not true, and you would know if you ever read them!"

"She's too busy on TikTok," Sadie mutters under her breath.

"Great, Skye, you lasted what, an hour? New record, I think," Susan finally adds with such disappointment, my eyes sting.

"Enough, girls!" Dad barks. He gathers himself. "I'm just glad your mother isn't here to see this."

And that's it.

That's all he has to say to stop all of us in our selfish mental tracks. "Sadie, Skye." His voice is tight but commanding. "You two can go find something else to do while the rest of us go over this week's itinerary."

I'm out of the room before he finishes his sentence. I say nothing, aware I've said too much already. I head home and change and then work out my frustration on the pavement.

For the people in the world who know me the absolute best, my family seems to understand me the least. It's not entirely their fault. I haven't told them everything. But some of it should be obvious. I need to make a name for myself. *By myself.* I want to make statements and create connection with my paintbrush, not create doodles to fill the overstuffed gift aisles at Target.

I want to make real work, meaningful work. Which I know seems odd to someone more practical like Susan, especially when my last collection included the nipple lights and a dentist's chair. But the chair piece, for example, not only can you stare at it, get lost in it, a therapeutic quality that has value all its own, but I get messages every day from young singles who rant about how much they relate to the "Singles Table" title. They feel seen, understood.

And I get to paint that feeling for them. I have to paint. I have to succeed at this. I am an artist. I. Just. Have. To.

And I am.

Slowly and surely, I'm doing it. Can't they see that? Why do they keep bugging me to be something I don't want to be? To do work I don't want to do?

Sadie, of all my sisters, should get it the most. She used to. She was the one to leave Oklahoma and come to New York in search of greatness. She was the one who made me fall in love with the city.

But somewhere she changed, we changed. Probably about the second time her heart was shoved through the proverbial meat grinder. But my heart had been broken too—shoot, everyone's has. That doesn't explain how she went from wanting to be the world's best novelist to signing autographs in front of giant photos of herself, flanked by packed shelves of her own books, each pastel spine cheesier than the last, while she's lit under an *actual* selfie spotlight, at the Canton Cards trade show booth. How?

After running eight miles, I feel no better. But I know who could cheer me up.

5:55 P.M.

Me: Day One:

[Animated GIF Tiger falling off a rock]

Matthew doesn't write back, and I'm tempted to distract myself with a night out with Sam and Sally, especially since Sadie is busy catching up with her old New York friends. But I can feel the tension building in me. Between the new relationship with Matthew and the tension in my family, plus the looming stress of convention, I need to be alone. Not working alone, not alone next to someone else, just alone.

So I dive deep into one of my happiest happy places: my couch. Finally back in the world of Loya and my favorite ice cream. It's almost enough to make me forget about my unanswered message to Matthew. Finally, as I take my novel to bed, I hear the buzz that makes my heart somersault.

11:33 P.M.

Matthew: Same. Just now eating dinner.

Me: Wow, you win worst day one, then.

Lucky me. Let's try to talk tomorrow, okay?

Like . . . on the phone? What is this, 2010?

Worse. FaceTime, so I can see you.

Check for new bruises.

I hate you.

No, you don't. Night, Tiger.

Good night, Brownie Britches.

Nope, guess again.

It's the "Tiger" that gets me dreaming, envisioning Matthew and I together for the long haul. I think about his hands on my hips, his kisses that paralyze my brain, and the sound of his laugh when I tease him or share yet another embarrassing story.

I think about him with me at the next show, and I imagine him in the studio with me while I work. I know it's dangerous ground as I walk it in my mind, but I can't help myself. I fall asleep smiling.

CHAPTER 15

Susan has her game face on as we sit gathered in the conference room again. We're tense around the long, lacquered table, looking at the latest Twitter battle on the mounted TV on one end. Taking in all facial expressions, you'd think our family was about to go to war.

"Let's review what we know," she starts slowly. "They're a new stationery brand, probably print on demand, based on their hints at their website and the comments from beta users. That means cheap product, no storefronts, no big-box presence. They are unveiling their name and their app on Friday to kick off the whole conference."

"They love to troll us on Twitter," Sam grumbles.

"Yeah, but they're trolling us because we're the big dogs. They're the fleas. Do we even need to spend time and energy talking about them?" I ask, painfully aware I said "we."

"Yes, I want to get ahead of it, whatever *it* is they're launching. While they may be the fleas—an analogy I love, by the way—we are the ones with Great Dane–size overhead. We can't get behind," Dad says.

I know what he's not saying. As much as I want to be anti-consumerism and rant "stick it to the man" while giving Sadie the bird, he means layoffs. We employ about two thousand people, people with families, mortgages, hospital bills. We had to downsize a couple departments last year, and it almost killed Dad. And Susan too. As much as they are Big Corporate America, they actually know their people really well. Both of them came out of those layoffs looking at least five years older, despite the Botox.

"Well, Skye's vision for the hands-on experience was genius," Jenn pipes in with a tight smile.

Jenn is our chief marketing officer, and she blows smoke up my skirt because she can't stand me. At least not professionally. I'm sure if I wasn't so blunt with her and her team, we could be friends.

As much as I've tried to relax and not care, Canton is still my last name. I still see my dad's face, and Grandpa's, behind each product. I still feel like I can't let them down, even as I want to get the heck out of the business. It's weird. *It's just so freaking fun being me.*

Sam continues Jenn's thought. "Instead of putting out the new lines and the best sellers, we've focused across all lines of our offerings with textured paper, layered designs, pop-outs, die cuts, scents, paint, glitter, and so on. Then we've got the twelve artists, two each morning, two each afternoon, doing the live demonstrations."

"I saw all of that, and it's good. Great job, all of you. But . . ." Dad stares, finding the words. "What here convinces people that snail mail isn't dead? That physical books are better? That shopping for a gift in a store is still fun and exciting—better than shopping online?"

"Well, we've got the exhibition space set up as a gift shop for the most part," Jenn starts, "allowing them to browse cards next to journals next to vases next to candles and so on."

"We had those custom book smell scents made. We're going to have those at my signing area," Sadie adds. "It really is crazy, the nostalgia of that smell. You don't get that on a Kindle."

"And Sadie can't sign someone's Kindle." Susan gestures toward our resident superstar. "We've made sure that she and our twelve artists are available all three days to sign physical product."

"Plus, every single attendee is getting one of our hand-painted tabletop calendars and stand, gift wrapped. The paint on the cards and the wood stand is so adorable, I can't even. And they are even lightly scented. Everybody will be talking about them. Every. Body." Sam taps the table as she emphasizes each syllable.

We all nod. The calendars really are gorgeous.

"It's the quality, Dad," I finally say. Everyone jerks their heads to me in a way that makes my chest start to heat. "They go to Canton Cards for cards and gifts that are so far beyond what they can find at Wally World. They browse because every shelf has a surprise lurking there, from an embroidered pillow that says something hilarious, to a set of those hand-painted peony thank-you cards everyone loves."

"Like an Easter egg in a video game." Sally drawls the words as she brainstorms out loud.

"A what?" Dad asks.

"Sally. You're a genius."

We get to work on our last addition to our trade show experience. The day flies by, most of it not even that tense. We're all too excited about the new idea. At one point, Jenn and I have to hop on Twitter to take the newbies to school.

@CantonCards: What do you buy for the gal who's got everything? Something hilarious, handmade, or hard to describe. That's what you'll find inside a Canton Cards giftshop. Come by one of our many locations today! [Images of store interior]

Reply @NewCardsOnTheBlock: Like this comment if you'd rather shop online in your PJs—or do almost anything really—than go to an actual retail store.

Reply @CantonCards: Good news! You can live your best introvert life and shop on our website. But if you waited until the last minute (you did), actual stores are open right now, no need to wait for 2-day shipping. Also #extrovertsstillexist #extrovertsarepeopletoo

After a long, fulfilling day with no verbal sniping, the family and some of the team went to dinner. As much as I wanted to go, I chose the smart option and went for a run. This week will be so far out of my routine, with so much peopling, I need to use the tools in my anxiety tool belt. I almost texted Matthew after my run to see if he wanted to grab dinner but realized I hadn't heard from him all day. Not even his usual good morning text.

I eat a sandwich at home and dive back into my novel. I know Sam and Sally will be crashing in the door soon, so I muster up my dwindling courage.

9:23 P.M.

Me: My FaceTime availability window is closing fast

> **[Animated GIF of Cat FaceTiming]**
> Matthew: Crap I'm sorry, still at the office.
> **That's okay**
> How was your day?
> **Much better than yesterday, you?**
> No better. Looks like I'm 2 for 2.
> **Bummer. Hope tomorrow is better.**
> Me too. Let's try again tomorrow?
> Sure
> Good night
> Night

I stare at the screen, wondering what exactly is happening. Is he genuinely swamped, or is he pulling away from me? On Sunday, I did show most of my crazy to him. Scars, Band-Aids, tears, dead mother. It was a lot. And since then, he's been "busy." Yeah. Doesn't take a genius to figure this riddle out. Plus, I even told him, *You want a cute, likable artsy girl, and that ain't me, bucko! I'm a mess!* What did I expect?

He hadn't seemed fazed at the time. But like Sam says, I am intense. Paul, vanilla as he was, seemed not to mind. Maybe I, an unstable firecracker, could only ever work out with a wet blanket of a man? And that's not Matthew. Matthew is on fire too. Just like I'd feared, I'm getting burned. I don't let myself cry, but there is no smile as I fall asleep.

CHAPTER 16

Wednesday and Thursday were a blur of preparations. I had zero studio time, but I did get afternoon runs in. Sally followed me around, which I loved, and Jenn and I went back and forth about all the final details. All of it helped to distract me from Matthew's radio silence. Well, almost silence.

He sent a few texts here and there, including a link to an article titled "Why Tigers Are the Best of the Big Cats." But he made no effort for meals, coffee, a run together, no attempts at Face-Timing. Nada. Even Sam thought things were looking bleak.

Thursday night, we head to the convention center to give our exhibition booth its last once-over. Other exhibitors are milling under big signs reading INTERNATIONAL STATIONERY CONVENTION, but we don't make eye contact. Instead, we head straight to our spot. Even Dad and Sadie joined us, with event security. Not because they'd get shot or something, but because crowds may form, asking questions and wanting selfies.

As expected, our space looks amazing. Walls have been constructed to create an actual retail shop filled with cards, journals, planners, stickers, gift wrap, art, frames, gifts, candles, ornaments, pillows, and more. Everything is unique and beautiful.

The store walls open up on one side and come apart, leading into the artist exhibition areas and the bookstore section, where Sadie and other Canton authors will do signings throughout the convention.

Once we've seen everything and congratulated Jenn and her team, everyone begins debating where to go for dinner. I think about going home, even as Sally begs me to join the party. But I get a text.

> Matthew: Quick dinner?
>
> [Dropped pin location]
>
> **Me: Sure, I'm close by.**

The quick-serve restaurant greets me with cold air and the heavenly scent of fresh bread. I spot Matthew, of course with someone, Jimmy this time, in the corner. I wave before ordering a panini and then head to greet them.

Matthew stands and smiles at me, but he looks exhausted and disheveled. But also sexy. His zip hoodie sleeves are pushed up to show his veined forearms, over perfectly fitted tan pants and white sneakers. His hair looks as if he's been pulling on it, and his shadow has gone well beyond five o'clock. He wraps me in his arms and plants a quick peck on my lips.

"Hey, Tiger," he says, smiling down at me.

"Hey." I don't let him let go at the end of his hug. "Are you okay?"

He laughs. "I look that bad, huh?"

"Told you," Jimmy says from his seat at the table, with his mouth full of chips.

"What's going on?"

"Software update," Matthew says as I sit next to him.

"Like when my iPhone has an update?" I ask.

"Yes, except when we do it, something inevitably breaks," Matthew says, smiling tightly. Jimmy chuckles. "With a launch or an update, as much as we prepare, there are bugs, clients get mad, it's all hands on deck." I nod slowly. "And we have two this week."

"Wow, so you really do win for worst week," I say as I thank my server for my sandwich and chips.

"Here, Skye, I'm going to take my chips and head back to the office," Jimmy says.

"Okay." I shift to take his seat across from Matthew. He tucks my legs inside his with a squeeze.

"See you in a few," Matthew says to Jimmy as he leaves.

I smirk across the table. "Are you *ever* alone?"

He raises his eyebrows. "Are you trying to get me alone? I mean, I only have a few minutes but—"

"Oh, shut up," I say, laughing with him.

He shrugs. "I like people." He takes a sip of water.

"Ugh! People are the worst."

"What, people are the best!"

"Today I saw a guy on the subway run to steal the last available seat while a little old lady could barely stand right in front of him, and guess what he did?"

"Just sat there?"

"Worse. He started livestreaming."

"No."

"Yep." I imitate the idiot, "'Bruh! Don't forget to like and share.'" That gets me a wide smile, so I pile on. "And Tuesday, Janie sent me a pic of an actual sign at a carnival in Brooklyn, a metal printed sign."

"Uh-oh."

"It said, 'Please do not force children to ride if they are afraid.' A permanent. Metal. Sign. What's going on with parents out in these streets, Matthew?"

We both start laughing. "That cannot be real."

"Oh, it's real. You know what else is real? The last time Sam dragged us to a movie theater, right as the movie started, I see something in the corner of my eye. It's the chick next to me, a hipster on a date, and guess what she was doing?" Matthew winces with a grin. "She was knitting! Like a huge grandma bag filled with yarn, and she was just watching the screen, knitting away."

"What?"

"Yes! Like why, Matthew, why? And yesterday, on Facebook someone commented, 'I have to run some errands.' You want to know how they spelled 'errands'?"

"No."

"They spelled it 'Aarons,' like the name! A-a-r-o-n-s!"

"Stop!" he says through loud laughs.

"But I have so many more."

"Please, no!" He takes a drink while I take another big bite. We snicker back and forth until he says, "So how's your family been? The worst?"

"Intense," I say.

"When do they leave?"

"Monday. When is all your craziness over?" I ask him casually, trying to be fine with a weekend without him.

"Hopefully by Sunday."

"You gonna make it, Mr. President?"

He sighs. "I better. We just signed two huge firms in Jersey, and the team was already stretched thin before the update. And this launch is Carter's baby—he's never pushed so hard before. Everyone is . . ."

"Intense?"

"Stressed the hell out." He doesn't smile. I look at his sexy square jaw, clenching, and think of what to say. It's strange to see him anything other than confident, unflappable, assuring. He's so warm and encouraging, so easygoing, while also crazy intelligent and driven, that it's hard to think of anything he couldn't handle.

"Hey," I say, and he looks up at me. "If anyone can lead a team of nerds through multi-update-armageddon, it's you."

"Thank you?" He finally smiles.

"I mean it. I've never met anyone like you. So equally brained, left brain and right brain. You'll be okay. And they'll be okay, thanks to you."

His smile turns serious as he stares at me. "Thanks," he says softly. I get back to my panini, and we sit in silence for a minute. I look up at him, and it's as if he's trying to get back to his playful self, but he's too weighed down to do so. So I try to help.

"So, Monday night, then. What should we do to recover from this week?" I ask.

"First, we should make out." He taps the list on his fingers. "Then we should make out, and lastly, we should make out."

"Solid list, Matthew, solid list."

"I thought so." He packs up and stands to toss his trash. He crosses over to sit beside me, wrapping one arm around me and placing his other hand on my thigh. He squeezes and kisses the side of my forehead. "Sorry I can't stay," he says. It takes me a second to understand.

"Oh, uh, that's all right, I'm almost done," I say.

"What is that, turkey club?"

"Uh-huh," I say.

"Good, I had turkey too." Then he takes my face in his hands and kisses me like we're alone. Open and hard and slow. Like we're not in a crowded sandwich shop. Like we don't taste like turkey and bacon. Like he needs me. Like he wants me. My whole body responds to the way he kisses from my detaching head to my scrunching feet. I feel my legs open and my torso push into his. Then he pulls away.

"See you Monday?"

I nod.

He gets up and hustles out into the street. And I feel . . . weird. It's not a big deal to eat alone, of course. I'm happy to eat at restaurants by myself. It's just that I wasn't alone, and I was laughing and filled with feelings and then—*poof*—alone. *I don't love the metaphor I'm seeing here.* Still, I was wanting him to reach out, and he did. So I'm happy. Tentatively happy.

I get out my phone to scroll and see another Twitter notification.

@CantonCards: Tomorrow is the big day! Mr. Canton and the whole family look forward to seeing all our suppliers, buyers, collaborators, friends, fans, and fellow paper lovers at the International Stationery Convention! [Video time-lapse of trade show setup]

Reply @NewCardsOnTheBlock: Says "whole family" but means "the one semi-famous daughter"

It's a good thing no Cantons are sitting next to me as I read it because I let all the expletives fly. Now they're getting personal? I'm about to start typing when Susan calls.

"Don't respond without getting approval first!" she blurts as soon as I say hello.

"I know, I wouldn't," I say, although I maybe would. "Suze, do we know these people? Why are they getting personal? Could this be someone Dad fired or something?"

"We don't know." She lets out a heavy sigh. "Dad didn't want to go crazy trying to find out, which I agreed with at the time, but now I'm thinking maybe we should've hired a PI."

And Susan says I'm dramatic? "An investigator? Really?"

"Well, what if it's someone who signed a non-compete? We have legal recourse." She sounds resolute but tired.

I try to be helpful, feeling a bit bad that Susan bears such a big burden out of all of us. "You know, they never post anything of substance about their own brand or product, only memes and teasers."

"Trust me, I noticed."

"I mean, at least we won't have to wonder much longer, right? We'll find out first thing tomorrow? Their presentation is the opening?"

"Yep." It doesn't sound like I've helped much at all.

"I'll send over some reply ideas before I swing by my apartment to get my bags. I'll see you guys at the hotel in a little bit."

"Skye?"

"Yeah, Suze?"

"It's good to have you on the team. Really." I roll my eyes, and it's like she can hear the motion. "Seriously, think how lame our replies would be if it weren't for you."

"True." I chuckle, and she does too. "Thanks, Suze. See you in a few."

Reply @CantonCards: Says "has a Twitter account" but means "runs a Canton Cards fan account"

I also add instructions to the team to schedule tweets about our "big family" of employees, distributors, artists, and everyone else who is impacted by our business with featured personal stories. And to throw in stories of Grandpa, Dad, and Susan working together.

By the time I'm done with the email, I am fuming. They want to get personal? They want to get mean? Just wait until I see who they are and what I'm dealing with. I can handle mean and personal. Just ask my sisters.

CHAPTER 17

It's 8:55 Friday morning, and we are downright twitchy. At nine, the emcee for the convention will come out and make introductions and announcements, and then these toolbag loser dweebs are going to debut their new brand.

We are gathered to the side of the large greenroom for speakers and sponsors. I normally lay low at events, but in the greenroom, we're surrounded by industry friends who already know who I am and that I keep my art separate from the Canton brand.

And I must admit, I'm happy to be with my family in this moment. Whoever these former employees or investors are, when they exit the stage and come in to face us, well, we are a formidable group. We know how to rock our suits and dresses—even me, in a fitted but structured long-sleeve purple dress that sits just above the knee. I'm wearing a leather jacket and killer sneakers, of course, but they are wedges with a heel in them, which Susan did not find to be any consolation whatsoever. Even ally is dressed like an executive, except for the Keds she chose, which I love and Susan hates. Dad is so proud and so uptight, we would all be wearing red Ronald McDonald shoes for all he cared.

Next to myself and Sally is Sam, looking perky and impeccable, then Susan, who always looks sharp and smart in her glasses, and Sadie, whose boobs are probably a bit too much for the event, but still, she's stunning. In addition to the six of us is Jenn, who is tall and striking with her bright red hair and tailored skirt and blouse, and Nicole, whose dark skin looks incredible in the lilac dress she chose. Beyond her is Emerson Clark, our chief financial officer. He earned the nickname Icy Emerson because he rarely talks and can freeze you with just his stare, but he's British and gorgeous and extremely intimidating. Next to him is Dad, and next to Dad is Grandpa.

"Skye, my clever girl! You know artists are the smartest of all of us," he said when I saw him last night. He says that every time he sees me, and I can never fight the smile. He was a powerhouse like Dad in his day, but now he has a twinkle in his eye and a relaxed air brought on by age and the shifting of priorities.

The two men look so much alike in their flawless black suits, purple ties, and shiny black shoes, they could be brothers, even though one is in his sixties and the other his eighties. Each year we think it's the last year Grandpa will be able to come, but every year the man just keeps on ticking. Other than his board seat and being seen at events like these from time to time, he doesn't do much in the business anymore. He'll go home before the event is over, but as always, he says, "There can't be an ISC without I."

"All right, it's time for the moment we've all been waiting for!" the emcee says, pulling our eyes to the large TV monitor on the greenroom wall. "They've just secured their first round of funding and promise to change the entire stationery game. Wow, bold claim! Big promise! Let's see if we believe them, huh?" The crowd is cheering way too much for this. *It's a new card brand, everyone, not Magic Mike.* "All right, let's find out . . . who are . . . the New Cards on the Blooooock!"

The lights go out and a video begins. Instrumental hip-hop music plays over images of paper, cards, stamps. I decide to go to Twitter to see if anyone is saying anything yet. The female voice in the video talks about revolutionizing sending not just greetings, but personalized greetings.

Twitter's got nothing. Their account hasn't posted anything since last night. I'm searching through replies, looking for cues as the music gets louder and the crowd cheers. I switch to search the #ISCon hashtag.

"Uh, Skye?" Sam whispers.

"Huh?" I don't look up, as I'm lost in hundreds of replies to the Canton brand within the event hashtag. So far, the feedback is amazing. Early bird attendees love the displays.

"Skye!" Sam is almost yelling now.

"What?" I still don't look up.

Sam grabs my arm in exasperation. "Skye! Why the hell is your boyfriend on stage right now?"

"What?" my two older sisters and I say at the same time.

Everyone erupts in loud whispers.

"*That's* Matt?"

"Which one is Matt?"

"Did you know about this?"

"He's a founder of, what did they say the name was? Post something?"

"Postify?"

"Does he know who we are? He didn't say anything?"

"Well, he is hot, I'll give you that."

"Very hot."

"Was he trying to get to us through you?"

"How did you not know this? He lied?"

"Quiet!" I say, filling with so many emotions, I can't think. They pick up from my terror-stricken face and shallow breathing that I clearly don't know who Matthew is. But does he know who I am?

I'm known in New York as Skye Morgan, so that's all Matt should know me as. Articles about my work, my usernames online—I thought I'd covered my tracks.

I guess I was wrong.

We focus on the TV.

"That's right, you just hop on the app, choose a birthday card, add your own message, input the address, and hit send." Matthew is talking now, apparently. I missed some words when I was experiencing rage-induced deafness.

"For the price of a fancy gift shop card, you can find a high-quality print, add your own message, pay postage, and send it, without ever leaving your couch," Carter says. Oh, Carter is here. *Fancy gift shop card.* That means us. *"This launch is Carter's baby."* Holy crap. Was Matthew trying to hint to me? Or throwing an inside joke around right in front of my face?

"Go ahead and point your cameras at the QR code to get the Postify app and test it for yourself," Matthew says. "It's not just greeting cards. You can customize a box set of thank-you cards for graduations and weddings, then upload all your addresses and run a mass mail project." He flips through the slides of examples behind him. "You can customize, wrap, and ship gifts as well, all while in your PJs."

"We've already started to assemble an amazing team of designers and artists, and we're excited to announce that, as of today, we are the exclusive distributor of BackBeat Cards."

"What!" Dad finally says something, and we all jump. Back-Beat is a hip line of cards that we had exclusive distributor rights to, until three months ago when they chose not to renew. They were a favorite of ours, and their cards were always at the top of the spreadsheets, among our best sellers.

"Mother f—"

"Skye!" Susan stops me.

Matthew and Carter finish their presentation, which is, unfortunately, amazing. Even though we're watching on screens in the greenroom, it's clear Matthew is brilliant up there. He's at ease and making jokes, but somehow not at all performing. His white teeth gleam in the lights, his khaki suit fits to perfection. He shaved and got a haircut since I saw him last night. I hate hate hate how good he looks.

They take questions, and it becomes clear: they are here to poach artists, writers, and designers. They want the best of the best to join their app. They can't possibly offer the payment structure we can, but they can offer stock options. And they are pretty smooth with their talk of how apps are the future and physical stores are the past. With each word from their mouths, I become more angry and anxious.

The hives are out.

The splotches are in place.

But I don't care.

I am going to rip this man a new one.

I know underneath there is sadness too, but I can't think about that right now. Because they are exiting the stage and heading for the greenroom, where we are waiting like a cat about to pounce. A tiger. Not a cute tiger—a huge, hungry beast about to rip a young buck to shreds. *Shreds!*

Dad interrupts my violent thoughts.

"Skye. I'm going to shake their hands, Susan is going to shake their hands, and we are going to be civil, do you understand? Skye? We are Cantons. Do not make a scene."

Matthew and Carter explode into the room, excited and relieved. I clench my jaw. Dad and Susan make their way over.

"Finally, we meet the new kids," Dad says. "Jon Canton." He extends his hand, and Matthew takes it.

"Of course, Mr. Canton, it's an honor to meet you. Matt James," Matthew says.

Honor! Yeah, right!

"And Ms. Canton, you as well," he says to Susan, who uses her maiden name professionally. Carter follows.

"Impressive presentation," she says, somehow calm and smiling.

The next person Matthew sees is Sadie, then behind her, he sees Nicole, and that's where the first flash of confusion crosses his face. Carter says "Wait, what?" at the same time Matthew's eyes find Sam, and then they lock on mine. My jaw is clenched, my lips in a straight line, my breathing deliberate. *Do not make a scene, do not make a scene.*

"S-Skye?"

"Yes, uh, it appears you've already met some of the family," Dad says. The tension is palpable. Even Iceman Emerson looks uncomfortable.

"C-Congratulations on your launch," is all I can say through gritted teeth while I turn to the nearest door. *Must exit! Meltdown imminent!*

I push hard into the handlebars of the left door closest to me. It's the double doors that lead to the back service halls of the convention center where I can go nuclear without being seen. But of course, it's locked. I slam on it again, feeling all eyes on me.

"Other one," Sam whispers. Grunting, I push on the right door, and it finally swings free.

"Wait, Skye!" I hear Matthew calling after me. Down at the end of the wide concrete hall behind the greenroom, I spot one of those little event golf carts. *Salvation!* I head toward it, but Matthew is gaining on me.

"Skye! Wait! You're a Canton?"

"As if you didn't know that," I huff, almost running to the golf cart.

"I thought your last name was Morgan!"

"That's my middle name, as you, I'm sure, already know."

"I didn't! I had no idea! Skye, stop! I didn't know, I swear!"

I finally stop to face him. "I sure as hell didn't know either. You lied about your company, about your stupid software update this week?"

"I didn't! I didn't lie. Carter had worked for months on this big reveal today. We didn't tell anyone outside of the company."

"I don't even know you, Matthew. Who knows what else you're hiding? I'm definitely not going to find out."

"Are you serious?" He scoffs, as if he's getting angry. *What could he possibly be angry about?*

"Dead serious."

"You've got to be kidding me. You are the most closed-off woman I've ever met! You give short answers, if you even tell me about yourself at all. Skye, you said 'family business' like your dad worked out of his garage or something. You didn't even tell me your real name!"

"Well, I sure wish I had—could've saved us a lot of time and energy. Have a nice life," I say, climbing into the golf cart.

He walks around to the front of the cart so I can't move.

"So that's it? We're not going to talk about this?"

"There is no 'we.' And no, I'm not talking about it."

"Shocker," he spits.

We lock eyes in an epic staredown that would be hot if I weren't so upset.

"Move, you hoodie-wearing, soul-sucking, heartless, AI robot asshole, before I run you down!" I snipe.

His glare softens. "Fine, Skye. Fine." He raises his arms as if in surrender as he moves out of my way.

I smash the pedal down on the golf cart, but the wheels are turned, so the vehicle is launched straight into the tall stand that holds temporary event signage. With a loud thud. Of course.

I stop for a second on impact, but then—

FWAP!

The sign falls all the way over. I'm too mortified to stay there with Matthew watching, so I just floor it again.

FOP!

The loud smack of the metal frame hitting the ground fills the hallway.

CRHHCH!

THUNK!

The sign cries out under the wheels, and I'm free but—

SSSSSKKKKKK!

Oh no, I'm dragging it.

I'm dragging the metal event sign behind the damn golf cart.

So much for not making a scene. *Sorry, Dad!*

My face burns even more, but I keep driving. I drive all the way to the other side of the complex, sign dragging, where I see doors to enter the exhibition space. I park the car, duck out, and immediately find the exit. I burst outside, gasping, and head toward the hotel.

Sally: Are you okay? Where are you?

Sam: Carter says they really had no idea.

Sam: I've got to work the floor, but will you tell us you're okay?

Me: I'm fine. Back in the room.

Sally: Are you still going to help me with the Easter eggs?

Yes, but I'm going to run first. And change.

Sally: Okay

Sam: Everyone here says sorry and we love you.

What did Dad say?

Sam: Nothing really, he and Suze are on that panel of experts soon, they're getting ready for that.

Sadie: For what it's worth, he seemed like a nice guy.

He did. PAST TENSE.

Sam: Also, can we just talk about your epic getaway?

Sam: There were sparks flying on the concrete where the sign was dragging!

Sam: [Animated GIF of golf cart crashing]

[Middle finger emoji]

Sally: lololol

Sadie: It was amazing. Way to go out in a BLAZE of glory!

[Middle finger emoji]

CHAPTER 18

"Love the Witness Protection vibe you've got going on," Sam teases as we sit down for a late dinner. I roll my eyes and pull my hat down farther on my head, making it smash my sunglasses.

"Sweetheart, you're sitting with all of us at the table, I think you can lose the sunglasses now," Dad says. Everyone is smirking.

I take off the glasses and sit up a little straighter, realizing he's right. I glance around the restaurant again. It's a small tapas place, and it's well past the dinner hour, but since this is one of the few options close by the convention center, the enemy could walk in at any moment.

I am a bundle of anxiety, even after a five-mile run and darting all over the convention center with Sally to hide some of our best sellers. Writing clues and hiding the little gifts was exhausting, but Instagram and Twitter are already blowing up over it. Take that, stupid Postify Press—hands-on, in-person activities with a physical payoff.

We are dominating the convention conversation so far. I keep checking compulsively, but Stupid Face and his stupid company has yet to tweet to us after changing their username and beginning to function as a real brand rather than a teaser account. *Even better, let's never talk again!*

"He's not here, and even if he was, he wouldn't come over to our table. Relax." Susan's voice takes on that motherly tone.

"He really seemed shocked and apologetic," Sadie offers with half a shrug.

"He seemed nice enough." Dad leans in. "But they are a disaster for us. We have four retail locations on the brink of closing. We're going to have to crush them."

"Yes, Dad!" I lean in too. "Love that energy. More of that, everyone! Let's discuss *how* we'll crush them, shall we?"

"Wow, Skye wants to talk business, someone call a doctor," Sam mutters under her breath. Sally laughs, and Sadie and Susan stifle their smiles.

"Well, first we need to tighten up our relationships, make sure no more of our lines or artists get stolen away." Dad looks around like we're surrounded by spies, though there is no one near us.

"I can't believe they're offering stock options for creators." Susan stares into her glass, looking defeated. I don't like it.

"But stock options are not tangible, not cash in your pocket to pay for a new easel or laptop or whatever." I point my thumb at my chest. "And if they're all like me, they hear 'stock schmock' and their eyes glaze over."

"Good point, Skye." Dad smiles at me.

"Can we offer higher margins for them? Better royalties?" Sadie asks.

Susan is still huffy. "No, as they not-so subtly pointed out, we are already dangerously close to luxury gift prices!"

"So, we focus on what we do have." Sam grins, optimistic as ever. "Big-box stores, huge social media numbers, a whole publishing wing . . ."

We brainstorm around the table, and it is actually fun. For a moment, our differences highlight what a great team we can make when we're not at each other's throats. I get what creators want, Sadie understands the commercial side for artists, Susan knows the numbers, Sam knows how the buyers and distributors think, and Sally knows what's trendy and cool. Dad knows the vision, and Grandpa serves as our cheerleader, telling us all how genius we are. It was a dinner we desperately needed after the day we had.

Beyond my humiliation and disappointment, the app idea is crushing. It feels like Postify Press is forward, out in the future on the cusp of technology and consumer habits. And we're the dinosaur trying to keep up. We already lost BackBeat—we cannot lose anymore, or the industry will start to talk. And talk disrupts the board, our stock, and the two thousand families counting on us for their livelihood. Which explains why, even after a fun, productive dinner, the Cantons are tense. Very tense.

"So," Susan wraps up as Dad pays the bill, "Sadie, you have two signings tomorrow. Sam, you'll do the rounds again with some of these new ideas we just discussed, and you two"—she gestures to Sally and myself—"can lay low until the gala."

"Uhhhh, no, I am not going to that." I almost choke on the last of my wine.

"Not up for debate." Susan switches from sister to COO in a link.

"C'mon, Skye, you really going to avoid him forever?" Sam whines, clearly still on Team Matthew.

"Yep, I am." I nod as we all stand to leave.

Sally smirks. "Wouldn't it be better to show up looking smoking hot?"

"Yes. It would!" Sadie smirks too, loving the drama of it all.

I glare at them.

"Which dress did you bring? The gold? Oh, maybe the black one from a few years back?" Susan asks.

"Psh, I know what you two are doing tomorrow," Sam sing-songs to us. "You're going shopiiiiiiing."

Sally nods, and I grin despite myself. She's absolutely right.

———————

"I think this is the one," I say to the mirror. We're at the fifth shop we've tried, so it could be worse, but it's already lunchtime.

"Oh, it definitely is," Sally agrees.

"I'm going to have to have it taken up, though. I wonder if Dad's tailor can fit me in."

"With heels, it'll be fine."

"No, I'm not wearing heels. I know the perfect gold-jeweled platform Prada sneakers for this—look." I show Sally the link on my phone.

Her eyes light up. "You have those?"

I wince, knowing there's at least one person in the city who can get me what I need. The fact that he happens to be best friends with The Enemy is irrelevant. I mutter to Sally, "Nope, but I know a guy."

> **Me: I need these asap. I'll pay, but I need your shoe guy to find them for tonight.**
>
> Jimmy: I'll try
>
> **There is no try.**
>
> Okay, Yoda. And sorry about everything. Matt and Carter feel really shitty about it.
>
> **Let me know when and where to get the shoes.**

"So, Jimmy says they feel bad," Sally says as we head to the front register of the small but swanky boutique.

"Psh, not bad enough to text me, or try to find me at the convention," I huff as I hold up the heavy dress as we weave through the racks.

"Can I ask you something and you not get mad?"

"Sal." I smirk. "I'm already mad. I'm always mad."

"Mad *at me*, then?"

I give her a glare. "Proceed with caution."

"Well, didn't you hide things from him just as much as he hid things from you?" I don't say anything, focusing on paying for the dress. She boldly continues. "I mean, he didn't talk about his work because his partner told him not to. You didn't even tell him your real name because . . . I'm not even sure why."

"C'mon, you know how it is, being a Canton is a whole thing. Then there are a million expectations and questions. Maybe you haven't experienced it much yet, but—"

"Yeah, maybe with strangers, but with someone you're dating? Are you . . . are you embarrassed of us? Ashamed of us?" Sally asks, genuinely.

"No! Damn, Sally. Of course I'm not ashamed," I say, taken aback.

"Okay. Well. I'm just saying—didn't you both hide stuff?"

"Yeah, we did. Not a great way to start a relationship. It's better it's over now before things got even harder."

"Harder?" she asks as we wait for our Lyft. I don't respond, unsure of what she means. "It's just . . . you said your breakup with Paul wasn't hard at all, and you guys were together for two years."

I shake my head, exhausted. "I don't want to talk about this anymore, please."

She nods.

For the rest of the afternoon, as we finish our errands, we focus on the Easter egg excitement. It's been fun to do something with Sally. Since she's seven years younger, we don't get the opportunity very often. We send Jenn and her team responses to comments and clues. Still no tweets from the Hoodie Brigade, and neither of us say a word about it. Jimmy came through with my sneakers, which Sally went to get while I stayed with the tailor.

At the end of the night, my ensemble was going to be worth a small fortune and I did feel badly about it. *But this is Matthew and his stupid app's fault. If he hadn't been so charming on the plane, so sweet the last month, and so secretive—can't forget secretive!—then I wouldn't need to look so amazing at this gala!* But he did, and I do, and oh, I will.

CHAPTER 19

The Annual ISC Charity Gala is a who's who of the stationery world, including buyers from the big-box stores and even bigwigs from London and Paris. It's our only black-tie affair all year, and the glamour doesn't disappoint. The unbelievable ticket prices raise money for school supplies for underprivileged children across the US, a cause we all rally around. No one loves school supplies as much as paper people love school supplies, and all the people in this room are paper people. Well, except for Matthew—Matt—and Carter.

The realization makes me wonder how they've been received over the past two days. For a second, I feel a stab of concern for Matthew. What if they've been given the cold shoulder? What if the app isn't doing well? I shake away the thoughts. He's a big boy with other companies. He'll be fine. I, on the other hand, am so nervous and of course sweaty that I may not make it through this gala.

"Holy Toledo Batman and Robin and the Joker *and* Catwoman too!" Sam says when Sally and I join everyone in the lobby.

"Catwoman, huh?"

"Definitely." Sam's smile is so wide, I can't help but smile myself. The dress Sally and I picked is a shiny black satin, with long sleeves and a high neckline, as per usual. Along the chest and shoulders are little gold stones that sparkle in the light, twinkling down the sleeves as well. The dress hugs what little curves I do have. But what sold me on it was the very high slit, allowing my toned leg in a killer Prada to pop out when I walk.

My hair, which is piled to the front left side in big curls, shows off that the dress also has a very low back. It's a risk, because I'm pretty sure my splotches will spread there, but without it, the high neck and long sleeves would be a little nun-esque.

And that's definitely not the vibe I'm going for.

We pile into the limos serving as shuttles for the evening, all of us looking dapper and feeling chipper. Sam had great conversations with our artists today, we are selling out of all the stock in the booth, our social media team is crushing it, and no one has said anything about the Soulless Wonders and their app.

I brace myself as we make our way into the ballroom, which is already crowded and loud. The tables are donned in huge floral bouquets made of incredible paper flowers. Little number statues sit on each table, also crafted from paper. A big band is playing Sinatra, waiters are passing champagne, and the whole room somehow smells of roses even though there are no real flowers present. It's beautiful, and it's a lot. So, after grabbing a glass of champagne, I find a dark corner perfect for wallflowering. Sally follows.

"Four o'clock, his back is to us," she says softly, the absolute perfect wingwoman.

I look up and see him.

I thought I was ready.

I was mistaken.

Because he turns and there he is, wide smile and perfect face, tanned skin, piercing dark eyes, all wrapped up in a tuxedo. *Google later: Who invented tuxedos and how can I send them hate mail?*

Matthew—*Matt! Skye, Matt!*—laughs as he shakes some guy's hand, and my breath catches. It's such a great laugh. And I'm reminded of everything Sally said today. That I hid things, hid myself from him. I hear him telling me how closed off I am. I relive the moment Matthew surrendered, after asking to talk to me. After I called him names and said we weren't a "we" anymore.

I lift up off the wall I'm leaning on to go to him, to see if he at least wants to talk.

And then I see his date.

Allison, the blonde from the diner, grabs his arm.

"Oh, well, maybe they're not—" Sally starts to think aloud but is cut off by Allison, whose left hand is already clutching Matthew's bicep like she's trying to force her nails through the fabric. She takes her right hand and runs it down Matthew's arm to hold his right hand in hers. I look away before I have to endure any more. "Okay. Definitely his date," Sally says.

"A date he had to know was happening tonight," I say, before downing the rest of my champagne.

"Yeah, but you guys aren't exclusive, right?"

"Weren't. Right. We weren't exclusive. He can do whatever he wants."

"Where are you going?" Sally asks me as I leave my corner.

"To get myself a date."

I head to our tables, where I know the only male available to me will be sitting in silence.

"Emerson," I say as I sit next to him. He is a stunning man, tall and chiseled, but he's definitely earned his "Icy" nickname. He sits so straight he could be a statue, and when his crisp, light blue eyes land on me, I wonder if they might turn me to stone too. "You are my date for tonight, okay? I'm going to put my arm on you, and you have to dance with me one time, all right?"

"I don't—"

"I'll owe you one," I plead.

"I—"

"Don't make me pull rank on you, dude. We don't have to chat, no making the rounds, no shaking hands. We sit here in silence, dance—also in silence—and you're my hero. It's a win-win."

"All right," he says in his gravelly quiet voice. The man is frigid, that's for sure. I know he hates these events even more than I do, though, so I've got him right where I want him.

"Put your arm around my chair, okay?"

He sighs. "All right."

I glare at him, and he concedes.

We are not friends, but he's been around a long time. He was a good college friend to Adam, Susan's husband, so he's like family. Except he is painfully formal at all times, and never talks, so none of us girls really know him all that well. I wince at the pang of recognition. *"You give short answers, if you even tell me about yourself at all."* Still, Emerson looks divine in his tux, he's older than Matthew, and known in the city. The perfect fake date if you ask me.

The family joins us at the table when it's time for the meal. Everyone eyes us.

"Emerson is my fake date, everybody get on board," I whisper to them. Everyone chuckles and squirms in their seats, eyeing Emerson like he might melt or combust or something.

"Guess you'll be reminding me of this when bonuses come around," Dad says to him.

"Most definitely, sir," Emerson says, as if being my date for a couple hours is absolute torture. We all laugh and relax a bit. Fortunately, I can't see the Postify Press table from where I'm sitting. Unfortunately, Sam has taken the seat on my other side.

"She's a skank. And her dress is so boring. Red strapless. Yaaaaawn," she says once everyone else is having their own conversations.

"Thanks, Sam, but you don't have to—"

"And she's all over him, but he is not all over her. He seems uncomfortable."

"I don't care."

"'I don't care,'" she mocks me. "That was the most unconvincing lie in the history of all lies since the beginning of time, Skye." I sigh, and she continues. "It's okay to care. It's okay to be pissed. We're all pissed with you," she says. I squeeze her hand.

"Thanks."

"Of course."

We eat and chat and listen to the presenters as they discuss the charity and the money raised. Dad has donated the most, of course, earning our table attention and a round of applause. I make sure to lean into Emerson, who is as stiff as the banquet chair he's sitting in. Finally, the host says something about how we shouldn't let New York's finest big band go to waste, and Dad takes that as his cue. He stands with Susan, Grandpa takes Sadie's hand, and I shove Emerson so hard in the arm, he stands up, I think, partially as a reaction to the pain. He offers a hand to me, and I smile up at him like he's Prince Charming in the flesh.

I look down until we get to the dance floor, and then I look up at Emerson as he turns to dance with me. "I'm going to stare at you the whole time we dance, and it's going to be super awkward, but just deal with it, okay?"

"All right," he says again.

"What are you, Matthew McConaughey?" I say, feeling my skin burn like lava, knowing people are looking at us. Emerson does not offer even a chuckle. I look at his shirt, his hair, his nose, his eyes occasionally, which are doing the same awkward dance as my own. I realize halfway through the slow rendition of "Mack the Knife"—who knew this song was so long?—that we are basically out-awkwarding each other.

"Shouldn't we be chatting and laughing like we're super into each other?" I ask him.

"You tell me," he deadpans.

"Sorry, thank you for doing this."

"It's all r— it's fine, Miss Canton," he says, catching himself.

"What if we just dance closer, that way we don't have to talk, is that okay?"

"I—"

I don't let him object. I move my hand from his shoulder to around his neck, allowing me to hug him closely and put my head against his jaw. I close my eyes and breathe through how unbelievably uncomfortable it is. I have had worse ideas, but I can't think of them at the moment.

Emerson is as stiff as a statue, and as cold, and I'm sure my back resembles giraffe hide at this point. Mercifully, the song ends, and I open my eyes for a split second to see Matthew across the room. He's not looking in my direction, probably cringing with secondhand embarrassment.

I turn to thank Emerson, but he says "I believe I have fulfilled my obligation" and walks—no, darts, maybe even jogs—away. I am frozen for a moment. *Ass! Must check with Nicole that he is not such a jerk at the office!* I take the long way, down the wall farthest from Matthew's table, to the back bar. I let myself get a third champagne, because I ate a whole plate of sub-par ravioli.

"You run the Twitter account, don't you?" Matthew's voice comes up from behind me. I turn and brace myself.

"I don't."

"I don't believe you." He smiles at me and motions to the bartender for another scotch.

"I advise the social media team sometimes," I say, catching his scent. I force myself to take a step backward.

"I knew it. So quick. Such a smartass." I scoff and start to turn away, not sure if he's complimenting me or not. "Wait, I'm sorry about that last tweet, Skye. We ripped into our social media team. We never should've gotten personal," he says.

"It's fine." I shrug. "Business is always personal for us. We can handle it."

"Skye." He steps toward me and reaches out his hand. He looks sincere, remorseful. It almost gets to me.

"I should get back to my date," I say quickly with a tight smile.

"Emerson Clark, really?" he says, angry. I freeze my face, hoping my childish delight doesn't show up in my features.

"Really," I say sweetly. "I'm sure your date is waiting for you as well. Good luck, Matt." I turn and leave before he can say anything. I almost slipped and called her by her name, which would've really given me away as the sad, jealous stalker that I am.

I don't want to hear about her, how they met, why he's here with her tonight. Why he didn't ask me to be his date for what must be a big night for him and Carter and their brand. Instead, I beeline to Sally at our spot on the wall.

"Please tell me you have one of Dad's shotguns in your dress and you can take me out of my misery?" I say when I reach her.

Sally moans. "Hey, at least you're old enough to drink through this."

"Here." I offer her my glass, but she shakes her head, ever the good girl.

She raises her eyebrows at me. "He looked pretty pissed when you were dancing with Emerson, which, by the way, was the most hilarious thing any of us have ever seen."

"It was like dancing with a frozen robot!" We both get the giggles. "Could you tell we were faking it?"

"Well, all of *us* could, of course, since we know you both, but I don't think anyone else could tell." Sally turns to face me. "Skye, even Matt's date looked irritated at how upset he was, and Carter looked like he was talking him down."

I refuse to get my hopes up with her, but I still enjoy her little report. "He knows who Emerson is, then. The night is not a total loss, I guess."

"He also looked you up and down about a hundred times. Go us on that dress!" Her smile is infectious. I nod, and she gets carried away. "Sooooo he still likes you and you still like him! Why don't you just go make up?"

I shake my head. "We were doomed from the start. Even if we did want each other, he's frickin' enemy number one, Sal. I can't be with him now."

"Dad would get over it if you really like him. Suze too." She nudges me.

"Not worth the drama. We barely know each other." I snort. "Clearly."

For another hour, we take turns dancing with Grandpa and sampling desserts. Susan makes sure the official Canton family photo is taken at the amazing origami photo backdrop. As always, the official shot, for the event photographer and a couple industry publications, includes Grandpa, Dad, Susan, and Sadie.

Later in the lobby, we have Jenn take a few of all of us on Sam's phone. Grandpa steps down and says, "Now Jon and his girls!" And all our hearts break a little bit.

For eight years we've done this, and every time it still hurts, knowing Dad's best girl, our favorite woman in the world, is missing from the shot.

Not only did we love my brilliant mother as our mom, but we have my parents' incredible love story, etched in our minds, like it was in their letters to each other.

It's no wonder the loss inspired Sadie to start writing romance. I don't know how Dad carries on some days.

I do know my eyes aren't the only ones stinging. We quickly hop down from the steps and head to the shuttles, ready for our beds.

CHAPTER 20

I finally head to my studio Monday morning after days away.
The rest of the conference went fine, though I stayed in the
back halls with Sally, hat and sunglasses on, just in case. It
would've been pretty easy to avoid Matthew out on the floor,
however, because their booth was bright, huge, impressive, and
packed. Packed with chicks. I mean, Carter is good-looking too,
but Matthew in a suit? I get it. Still, we didn't see each other at all
on Sunday. There were no texts either.

It's a new week, though, and I'm ready to get back to work. I
head to my studio door and see an envelope, too big for the wall
mail holder, shoved in the doorjamb. It's got my name and studio address on it but no return sender. I open it, wondering why
Maud would send paperwork to the studio, since the envelope
must hold flat letter-size papers, like a contract.

Oh.

It's not paperwork.

Breathe, Skye, breathe.

It's a brilliant, technicolor, pointillist depiction of a growl-
ing Tiger on thick cardstock. My hands start to shake because
I know the artist the second I look at it. "TamPoints," just Tam

to me, is a genius street artist who sets up his wares all over the city. He usually creates cityscapes or park scenes as he sees in front of him, dot by tiny dot. I mentioned him to Matthew when I was teasing them about their apartment, saying the street vendors of New York had much better art to offer.

Heart pounding, I head to the front desk of the shared workspace.

"Hey, Leanne, when did this arrive for me, do you know?"

"That came Friday, I think, afternoon."

"Thanks." I walk back to my space and shut the door.

Friday afternoon. Sunday I'd told him about my scars. So sometime during the week, he went to Tam? During his launch? He obviously did it before the big reveal. He couldn't have had Tam create this in that amount of time, so he must've had it commissioned—*he had something commissioned for me?*—earlier in the week.

MONDAY 9:44 A.M.

Me: Look what the jerk commissioned for me.

[Photo of the tiger print]

Janie: OMG! That's one of Tam's, got to be. And it is gorgeous! Wow.

What are you going to do?

I don't know, does this change anything?

It's pretty sweet.

Yeah, but it was before. It was delivered Friday. I don't think it changes anything.

You could just tell him thank you, see what he says.

Yeah, good call.

And then GET BACK TO WORK!
Also good call.

I decide to work on my thumbnail studies and sketch and, well, stew, for a few hours before sending the thank-you text. I don't want to appear too eager, texting him first thing Monday morning.

I don't tell my sisters. It doesn't help matters for our new enemy to maybe be a total sweetheart. I already know Sam will say to marry him the second she sees the print. Definitely not telling her. My patience runs out after lunch.

2:02 P.M.
Me: I just got the Tiger print. It's beautiful, thank you.
Matthew: You're welcome.

My hand hovers over the keyboard. I want to ask how his launch went. I want to say I'm sorry for calling him those things. I want to see if he wants to talk. The three dots pop up, and I wait to see what he's going to say. But he doesn't press SEND, and the dots disappear. Since he didn't press SEND, I take my thumb off the keyboard. I stare for a couple minutes. But he's not typing.

We're really done, I guess. I think if I'm being honest with myself, I was expecting more of a fight from him. After pursuing me the way he did, I'm surprised he just let us end without talking it out. He hasn't called or texted other than those two words just now.

Suddenly I am deeply sad. Illogically sad. I only knew him for weeks. He was hardly a presence in my life—how can he now be an absence? I don't know. But he is. A giant, gaping absence.

I put my phone away. I write out a few more ideas at the studio, I run, I eat with Sam—who asks me how I'm *really* doing—I try to read. But my mind keeps spinning. I open Instagram.

To my surprise, Matthew has actually posted to his profile. It's a series of photos from the convention and the gala. He is with women in every. Single. Photo. Sure, Carter is in some, and they're different groups of women, but still. The last two are him and Allison, a selfie first, but then a candid of them dancing.

And it guts me.

He looks like a dream, so free and fun, his muscles bulging under his sleeves, his smile wide. I bet he was in the middle of making a joke. He looks happy. Of course, Allison is happy just to be within his orbit, as anyone would be. I find eyes starting to mist when I'm saved by my COO.

9:50 P.M.

Susan: The soulless Hoodie Brigade stole Whimsy and Howdy Doody too. Not renewing.

Sam: NOOOOOO!!!!!!!!!!!!!!

Sam: [Angry emojis]

Sam: [Crying emojis]

Me: [Angry expletive emoji]

Sally: What! Whimsy was my favorite!

Sadie: Two more of our best sellers? This seems like a surgical attack.

Susan: It does.

Sam: This is WAR.

Sam: [Gun emoji] [Bomb emoji] [Fencing emoji] [Ninja emoji]

Sally: [Animated GIF Prepare for battle]

I agree. It's on.

On Tuesday, I spend some good ole quality time with our tech team. I learn some interesting tidbits. One of which is that there's a site online called Down Detectives. It lets you know if a whole website or app is down, like Instagram, for example. If Instagram wasn't working for you, but you went to Down Detectives and their site said the gram was doing just fine, you'd know the problem is your Wi-Fi or your phone. I wait for my moment to use this helpful tool, and it arrives in record time.

@PostifyPress: Finally remembered to get your mom a card, but stores are closed? Our gift shop is always open! [App link]

Reply: @CantonCards Doh! postifypress.com has crashed fifteen times in the last week, according to @downdetectives. Plus, doesn't Mom deserve a card you hand-picked? Grab her some hilarious tea towels or delicious handspun toffee too. #gooffline #doitformom

I also learned from our team that the app doesn't even exist for Android users yet. That is a huge group of Samsungers that just don't have the app option at all. Sure, they can shop on the website, but it's still the opportunity I need.

@PostifyPress: Once you load your favorite addresses into the app, it's easier than ever to shop, personalize, and send cards to family and friends over and over again. New designs added every day! [App link]

Reply: @CantonCards (cough) Easier than ever as long as you're not one of the 133 million Americans who use a Google, Samsung, or Microsoft phone. (cough)

It has been no surprise to anyone that I am exceptional at trolling.

Over the next two weeks, I hit The Hoodies, as we now call them, every time there was a glitch on their site, an app update, site downtime, trouble with images loading, whatever technical issues I could find. And I, along with the team, found plenty of issues. Matthew—*Matt!*—wasn't lying when he said launches were buggy. Our guys found bugs everywhere.

The second part of our strategy was to divert marketing dollars away from traditional ads and focus on influencers. As much as I hate that term, I do fall into that category on Instagram and TikTok. Sadie, with her four million followers on Instagram, and even more on Facebook, is an actual celebrity. Between the two of us, we gathered a stellar group of women to send gift boxes to. We found excuses as to why to send them, like an influencer's birthday, or they hit one million followers, and so on. But all of them, with a little prompting, went on and on in their social media feeds about the textures and smells of the products, the uniqueness and quality—all the things our brand stands for.

On TikTok, we paid hipsters to go on shopping sprees in our stores. That was a huge hit. Suddenly Gen Z kids who'd never heard of Canton Cards wanted to go get emoji coasters at the local retail store. All our artists, writers, designers, and line vendors took note of the momentum, eager to learn and grow on TikTok as well. And the Twitter feud raged on, much to the d light of both tech writers, Manhattan business writers, and the few journalists who cover stationery or the odd bit of Canton personal news.

@PostifyPress Mom-and-pop gift shops started in the 1700s—over 300 years ago! It's 2022. Skip the shop and go straight for the gift. [Link]

Reply @CantonCards: Oh, yes, if there's anything America needs more of, it's apps launched by Hoodie-Wearing Technigarchs, not family-owned mom-and pop-businesses. [100% emoji]

I expected at least some retort about hoodies. I could tell their social media team still kept an eye on us, but I got the feeling Matt told them to hold back. Silly boy. This is war. Worse, this is business. I reveled in their weak efforts.

@CantonCards: Happy 66th birthday to us! Three generations of Cantons have taken pride in offering you the absolute best cards and gifts for your loved ones. Thank you to all of our customers across the globe [Employee group photo with Mr. Canton at Canton HQ in Tulsa]

Reply: @PostifyPress: Wow, the white tube sock game is strong, Mr. Canton. You're even older than our dads (who've already retired). Mad props.

@CantonCards: Ageism is something we take very seriously at Canton Cards. We have many employees and collaborators who are still working in their sixties and even seventies, like Don, who is the artist behind everyone's favorite dogs from our DogGoneIt collection! [Image of Don drawing dog cartoon]

I found myself getting more aggressive on Twitter as more time passed without hearing a word from Matt. At the same time, he started posting a lot more to Instagram. Every single post was a group shot, I assume from work. In each one, some chick is grabbing Matt's arm like she's staking her claim. Which is hilarious since I've yet to see the same woman hanging on him in two consecutive posts. Matt looks gorgeous in all of them. And happy.

I, on the other hand, have been less than happy. Maud is thrilled, however, because breakups and corporate battles are apparently great for art. I am painting faster and better than I have maybe ever. I didn't expect inspiration to come from the family business, but here I am, staring at the latest in what we've decided is my Texture series. All the talk of hands-on experience got my mind working in overdrive about different surfaces and what their titles could be.

So, Maud is giddy, Janie has stopped hounding me, Susan and Dad are elated, everything is wonderful. Except for me. My stupid heart, somehow, despite my many, many warnings, had begun to hope for a future with the sexier half of The Hoodies. A future that is clearly history, since I've yet to hear a word from him. I turn off the studio light with a sigh, glaring at the Tiger print I should've hidden away. Instead, it stares at me as I work, reminding me of all that could have been.

I pull out my phone on the way to the subway and turn it back on.

My heart stops.

Matthew: Ageism?!

And Don and his dog doodles, are you kidding me?

Well played is an understatement. We're not worthy.

Me: [Animated GIF woman bowing]

[Animated GIF tiger attacking]

Your boys ready for this weekend's game?

Always.

We'll see.

[Animated GIF of the Sooner Schooner tipping over]

Please do not send me football memes.

[Texas football meme]

[Texas football meme]

[Texas football meme]

Unsubscribe.

I don't know what to say after that. I don't care about football, of course, but it was something fun and neutral to say. My whole stomach is clenched. I want to keep the conversation going so badly. But anything else I ask or say would be either something personal or something about work, and both options seem bleak. So I say nothing. No more text bubbles pop up from him.

As I hop on the subway, I feel that weird mixture of disappointment and hope, like bitter lemonade with a barely sweet aftertaste. You know if you go back for more it'll be sour and drying, but you can't help yourself. He texted me. With a tiger GIF, no less. It takes considerable effort not to smile as the train nears my stop.

CHAPTER 21

"**Y**ou're going!" Sam yells at me from the bathroom.

"Ughhhhh," I say to my mirror.

"We always go. We've never seen him there before. We're not bailing because he *might* be there," she says as she stomps into my room. "Didn't you say he has a killer bachelor pad with a giant TV? I'm sure all three of them would rather watch there than at the bar."

I consider. She makes a good point.

"Plus, you look *hot*. And so do I, and so will sexy Ben the bartender if he still works there. Let's roll!" Another fine argument. She's wearing a football jersey as a very short dress, with boots and a jean jacket. I went with long-sleeve Spanx arm tights (thank you, Sara Blakely!) under a jersey tied to be a crop top, with very high-waisted jeans. And my red and white Vans, of course. Only a couple inches of my midriff are actually showing, but it still feels sexy and fun. Exactly how I need to feel.

We're both rocking high ponies and the dangling red earrings we always wear for this game. Football people, of which I am just a close observer, are super into weird traditions and even weirder superstitions. If we don't wear these earrings, the sporty women in my family insist that the Sooners will lose to the Longhorns.

Sam repeats her arguments all the way to Sideline, a huge sports bar (by New York standards) that is hosting the Red River Rivalry game. Which means beer specials, cheap nachos, and the game showing on all their TVs. There's an online New York alumni group for both OU and Texas, and they co-host the event. And Sam is right, we've never seen Matt at this event in the last three years we've attended.

We make our way inside, and within steps, Sam is squealing. She makes new friends at this thing every year, which is fine with me, because it provides a group within which I can hide. Waving and smiling, I follow closely behind Sam. Of course, the place is loud and packed. I scan the room and don't see any sign of Matthew. Not sure if I'm relieved or bummed? Both.

I see Emerson and two of his equally tall, handsome, positively icy friends. We barely wave at him, and he barely nods at us. can't believe I danced with that pompous ass. Sam gets us each a beer, delighted to find Ben the bartender still works here.

While she chats, I keep scanning, taking in the camaraderie and side-eye action between the two sets of fans. It's amazing really, how small the world can feel when you're actively looking for connection. It's as if it's always there—we just don't take the time to find it. Here tonight is just one small percentage of all the heartlander transplants, and it feels like a lot. It's a happy feeling, even if drowned out by lightweight girls, mansplaining bros, and too many TVs.

Just before kickoff, I decide to head to the bathroom before it gets gross. I check myself in the mirror, feeling confident. An definitely bummed. I'm bummed he's not here—I can admit it to myself. Maybe I should've texted back earlier this week with a quick *Ha, yeah, Texas sucks. Oh, and sorry for calling you a heartless robot!* But I didn't. I head out of the bathroom hallway in a hurry to get back to the group before kickoff. And I run right into a wall of tall, sculpted muscle in a tight shirt and jeans. I die a little bit when I look up.

At Ryan.

"Hey, Stormy girl," he says. I experience a visceral reaction to the nickname. Funny how something that once made you swoon can later make you swear. And sweat. Simmer. Seethe. *Okay, time to actually say some words now, mouth!*

"Ryan!" I give a tight, nervous smile as I sense blotches starting on my neck. The smile prompts him to pick me up and spin me around. I give a small laugh involuntarily. Ryan is a big guy, a hot surfer type. Not gorgeous, not stunning—hot. Hot in a way that makes you think he scored poorly on his SATs. He didn't. He's actually a genius—cunning bastard. But he doesn't look it.

"Let me get you a drink, the game's about to start." He leads me to the bar with his hand on my lower back as if it never left. I catch Sam's attention, and her eyes grow wide, then tiny. She mouths *What the hell?* And I give her my own white-eyed glare with a shrug. He gets me a Corona, my favorite beer, not like that's hard to remember. I move to get closer to Sam, but she's dead center in a circle of people, naturally.

"Wh-What are you doing here?" I ask when Ryan turns to me with my drink.

"We were going to watch the game anyway so we figured we might join the party. I still had this OU shirt from you, so, why not?" He smiles down at me.

"Oh," I say. He gives a nod to his friends at a table but then turns back to me. The bar erupts for the singing of both fight songs, and then again for kickoff. I take a long sip of beer when things quiet back down, and Ryan is smiling my way again.

"So, how have you been?" he asks.

"Uh, good. Yeah, great. How about you?"

"Yeah, doing good. Made VP of East Coast finally," he says in a way that makes me think he really did have to struggle awhile to get it. The man knows how to sell. He'd been a killer salesman for my dad when we'd met.

He has a way about him. He isn't naturally magnetic like Sam. It's more like he knows he can charm anyone, be with anyone, celebrities, politicians, royalty. So when he is choosing to be with you, talk to you, you feel special. He has an edge too, a mean streak, but you feel like that streak is only toward outsiders, while you're on the inside of his protective bubble.

"Wow, that's amazing! Congratulations," I say, smiling more as the beer kicks in.

"Congrats to you, Stormy. I saw an article on you in some magazine at the office!"

"Oh, yeah?"

"Yeah, and the art was incredible and"—he leans down closer—"and you looked really damn good . . . just like tonight."

I blush in a way that makes me mad at myself. I don't want him to have this effect on me anymore.

"And you're blowing up on TikTok too, I couldn't believe it." Something flashes across his face. "I mean, I can believe it, totally, I just couldn't believe I hadn't heard, hadn't seen you or your shows around town."

"Well, thanks," I say, hesitant.

"Will you come sit with us? Please?" He puts his hand lightly on my shoulder. It's possibly the most sincere I've ever heard him. So I nod. Sam eventually sees me walking and shakes her head as she mouths *No!* with some other choice words in and around it.

We sit and have nachos and watch the game, chatting during the slower parts and commercial breaks. He has his arm around me in a protective way, a possessive way. I don't hate it. And I hate myself for not hating it.

At the start of halftime, Ryan launches into a story about us. It's a favorite of his to tell, where he claims we were on a romantic stroll through Central Park, when I demanded we try to sneak into the Museum of the City of New York. He always paints himself as the voice of reason, and me as this daredevil, just desperate to get in to see the exhibits because I loved New York so much.

"That is *not* how it happened!" As I say it, I cross my hands wide for emphasis. Of course, one of my hands hits Ryan's full pint of some fancy IPA, which explodes all over both of us. And—because that's not enough—I manage to wipe out a couple plastic souvenir cups that bounce on the floor, making the world's loudest *bong-bong-bong* noises while throwing ice everywhere.

"Shit! That's cold!" Ryan jerks to wipe his now freezing, wet crotch.

"Sorry!" I say, embarrassed.

"Damn it, Stormy! Still as klutzy as ever!" His face grows red like it's about to pop, as if I meant to make this mess. As I mop up with napkins, he launches into a monologue to his friends about how often I fall down. Or break things. Or behave in some way that is unbearably awkward. And they laugh because it's hilarious, and I half smile, because the stories are true.

"Hey, Skye," a familiar voice says next to me. I look up at Matthew, mortified. Now he's here too? I really should just never leave the house. "Can I help you get another drink?" he asks.

"Who the hell are you?" Ryan says.

"This is Matt, a f-friend from Texas," I say as I start to stand, eager to disappear. "I'll go get you another one of those," I say, and Matt leads me away from the table, his hand on my back. After a few steps, he takes me by the hand and detours, leading me outside the front door.

"I'm sorry, I spilled his—"

"What? Skye." He scoffs. "You don't need to apologize to me. Who was that guy?"

"That was Ryan," I croak out, so softly maybe the whole situation will disappear on the breeze.

Matthew takes a small step back. "Oh, so you guys are, uh—"

"No! No. He showed up here tonight and just asked to get me a drink. I haven't seen him in years."

"Phew! Because what a winner. Wow." He shifts back toward me, his body tense.

"Yeah, well, thanks for rescuing me!" I smile with fake enthusiasm. My voice quivers, as do my hands and really all of my nerves.

"Hey." He puts his hands on my shoulders, then hesitates. "I don't know what happened with him, but it was like I saw you shrinking at the table. Like you were a smaller you. A less you, you? I don't know if that makes sense." He drops his hands and pops his knuckles as if he's nervous.

"It does." I nod, my eyes starting to sting. "Matt, I—"

"Matthew," he corrects me softly. Now the waterworks are really building in my eyes.

"I-I'm sorry." I sniff. "For what I said to you. You're not heartless. Or a soul-sucker."

He smirks. "I do rock a good hoodie, though."

"A *zip* hoodie. So much worse," I joke, grateful for the slight release of the tension between us.

"Oh, they're worse?"

"Definitely."

He grabs my hand, interlocking our fingers. "I'm sorry too. I wish we could start over," he whispers.

"Even if we did, what about work?" I squeeze his hand, hoping he won't change his mind.

"You think two people from competitor companies have never dated before? We could figure it out." His eyes look at me with all the hope I've been trying not to feel. I shiver as I look up at him, my wet shirt and jeans feeling colder out in the breeze.

He sees the goosebumps break out on my skin. "Let's get out of here. Want to go watch the game at my place?"

I smile and nod.

"Let me text Jimmy to close our tab in there."

CHAPTER 22

The game was a nice distraction, keeping things easy and fun in light of the looming necessary conversation. As we watched the Longhorns crush the Sooners, it was as if we were right back to being us, weeks ago. He gave me a shirt and basketball shorts to wear, which felt like such a boyfriend move. We sat so close, my left leg was almost on top of his right, and during an Oklahoma fumble, he gave me his deepest condolences and kissed me on the side of the head as if he'd never stopped.

Now, though, we're sitting with our backs to his headboard, legs stretched out straight, each with a bowl of cookies-and-cream ice cream, quiet and hesitant. I feel as though I should start, being the *closed-off* person that I am. But I'm not sure where to begin.

"I—"

"Why—"

We laugh at how awkward we are.

He nudges me. "Go ahead."

"No, no." I can't look up at him. "Please, save me."

He puts a hand on my thigh and gives me a squeeze. "Why don't you start with douche bucket back there."

I almost choke on my ice cream, laughing at the name he chose. "Douche bucket?"

"What do you want me to say, fucking asshole?"

"Language, Mr. President. You can't talk like that around a Canton."

He deadpans a glare at me. "Let me know if you see one."

"Oooookay." I take a deep breath. "So. He worked in sales in our New York office, that's how I met him, right when I first moved here. Sadie was still here then, but she was pretty busy, and Ryan offered to show me the sites. He can be so charming. And he was.

"He liked all my quirks and teased me, said he supported my ambitions in the art world. But then over time, it was like he was on this trajectory and wanted me to come with him, support him. He wanted me to give up studio time to wine and dine clients, wanted me to throw my name around more. It's funny actually that you said I shrank next to him. I felt like I stayed the same, and he just got bigger. I mean, I don't have a big personality like Sam."

"Hmm, I think you do." He puts his spoon in his bowl and pauses, cocking his head. "Not like Sam, but you're so . . . feisty. Even if you're not talking, your face gives you away. How smart you are, how you see everything around you. That you have some hilarious, spot-on smartass comment to say about every single person in the room."

I give a small laugh. But on the inside, I'm not chuckling. I can't believe how three sentences can make me feel so seen, so understood. I feel my eyes start to water, so I take a deep breath, blinking through it.

He nudges me. "So, then? He cheated on you?"

"For months. And I had no idea. For someone who sees every-thing, I was blind. Granted, I was painting, working, and working hard. Which annoyed him. I wasn't with him at the office much, but other women obviously were. And as a sales rep, he was out in the city all day long, 'taking meetings.'" I say this with air quotes. "I caught him in the office. It sucked so bad. Not just for me, but because he was like a rockstar in the company, killer at his job, so fun and engaging, and everyone loved him. Then my dad had to fire him because of me."

"Uh, no." Matthew's voice gets loud and gravelly. "*Not* because of you. Because *he* was an idiot."

I sigh. "Right. The hard part was that it had been going on so long. I felt like I couldn't trust anyone after that, or myself, my own intuition."

"Wow." He slouches back into the headboard. "So, then I hid something so huge from you."

"Right," I mumble, getting back to my half-melted ice cream.

"I would've told you Sunday. Actually, I probably would've called you Friday, that morning, right after, to tell you how the launch went. Carter just begged all of us to wait until the announcement."

"And then you—" I stop myself.

"What?" He nudges me again.

"And then you would've gone to the gala with Allison? I mean, we weren't exclusive, so you had every right. It's just—"

"Hey." He grabs my thigh again and waits for me to look up at him. "We had had that planned for weeks, before you and I were really dating. And that was the only date, she and I weren't *dating* dating. Plus, explaining the gala would've been hard to do without the app and the reveal, which I couldn't tell you about."

"Oh."

Silence settles between us for a minute.

Matthew swallows. "What about Emerson?"

I start to laugh. "He wasn't actually my date."

"What?"

"He's a family friend, he's worked for Dad forever, and I forced him to dance with me, which was terrible. Ter. Ri. Ble!"

He points his spoon at me. "Serves you right! I was going to get up and cut in on the guy, but Carter stopped me. He got to touch you in that dress and—" After a long sigh, he shakes his head and squints at me. "You owe me, Tiger."

"What! What about you? Allison was holding your hand like you two were engaged."

He grins. "Yeah, about that. You think I was just going to let it slide that you somehow know her name? How, Skye?"

"Because I am a petty psycho stalker, obviously. Don't change the subject! She was all over you. It was freaking torture watching it."

"Okay." He relaxes beside me. "I guess we're even then."

I am not relaxed. I push myself to say what I need to say, but the words won't come all the way out. "Matthew, I can't . . ." He takes my bowl and sets both bowls on the side table. Then he shifts me so I'm perpendicular to him, my legs bent over his. He pulls me closer with his left hand on my hip and leaves it there. His right hand is draped over my legs, and he just looks into my eyes, waiting. "I just can't date around. I am not built for it. I get too all up in my head, anxious about the other dates, other women. I understand if that's not what you want. You're a very social person—"

"Social person?" he interrupts, smirking.

"Every day you post a new group photo with at least three girls trying to climb in your pants, and I'm sure you are out with people all the time, and that's great. Fine, let them in your pants. I just can't . . ."

"Share my pants?"

"Ughhh, you are the worst." I look to the ceiling and feel my face turn crimson.

"Sorry." He stops smirking and squeezes my hip. "Seriously, Skye. I don't want to date other people."

"You don't?" I let my eyes land back on his.

"I don't."

The relief makes me ramble. "But I'm closed off and uptight and I have to take things really slow and honestly any one of those pant-climbers would probably be more fun."

"Those pant-climbers"—he pulls me to his lap, so I move my legs to straddle him—"would all be boring. You are the most interesting woman I've ever met. And the way you see people, your critical eye, it makes me . . ." He considers his words. "It makes me feel like a badass that you'd choose me."

I wince. "Critical is not exactly a good quality."

"That's BS. If there were no one to ask the hard questions, and problems that need solving, humans would never achieve greatness. And when you told me that night, before the presentation, which you didn't even know how much was on the line, but you encouraged me, it meant a lot, Skye. Because it came from *you*."

I don't know what to say, but I know words won't be adequate anyway. Our faces are so close, I can see the start of laugh lines around his big brown eyes. His stubble is the perfect length, his hair mussy from the stress of the game.

I am panting, because of how his words make me feel, because of how hard his chest is under my hands. Because of how fiercely he looks at me. I fist his shirt, about to give in, but then pull myself off him. He looks confused but patient as I sit facing him with my legs crossed.

"I meant what I said, Matthew. You are so great at what you do, and at leading. And . . . on that stage? I mean, forget it! Game over! So, I mean." My voice cracks. "How? How can we be together when your company is freaking enemy number one of my entire family legacy?"

"We're not the enemy, though. Now, we shouldn't have started the Twitter war—which we're losing badly, thanks to you—but really we're a different model. I mean, are all the big online stores the enemy?" His warm eyes plead with me, but I can't stop myself from pointing out the obvious.

"Oh, most definitely. The big sites with next-day shipping are killing all in-person retail, everywhere. You know that."

He gives me a squeeze, begging me to give in to him, to us with his hands. "Your campaign right now is brilliant, though focusing on the experience, the textures and surprises. You guys are killing it."

I squeak, torn by the conflicting emotions. "You poached three of our best-selling lines from us. You guys are thieves!"

"I think by 'thieves' you mean 'skilled negotiators.'" He's smiling as if this isn't a huge issue. "Can't we just not talk about the specifics of work? Keep it separate?"

"Sure, until we're home for Thanksgiving. 'Hey Dad, you remember Matthew, the guy you're trying to crush into oblivion.'"

"Honestly, it's pretty cool to even be on the great Jon Canton's radar," he says.

I squint up at him. "Not radar. Crosshairs, Matthew, crosshairs. And Cantons don't lose."

Finally, he grows as serious as I am. "So then why do you hide your name? You have to admit it's weird that publicly only Sadie and Susan exist."

I hesitate, and he pulls me closer to him, leaving his hands on my legs.

"I guess it is kinda weird. We each have our own reasons. Sam is so trusting, she's been burned by fake friends and ambitious boyfriends a million times. When she moved here, she decided to keep a low profile. Especially since there are actual sites and magazines based here that would hunt her down for photos. She's so gorgeous and her personality . . . like I said, she's been burned before. Sally is still so young, just starting her junior year at OU this year, and it's overwhelming enough that everyone in Oklahoma knows all about us, so we just shield her from the national stuff."

He studies me for a second. "Isn't that exhausting? All the hiding?"

"Not really, it's just how we do things. Until each of us is ready to 'come out' as a Canton, so to speak."

"And the reason for best, coolest, sexiest Canton?" he asks, tracing small circles on my thigh with his thumb.

"I want to make it on my own as an artist. No strings pulled by Dad, no comments that I only sell paintings because of my last name."

"Skye, your work speaks for itself," he starts.

"Doesn't matter. I need it. For me. I have a lot I want to prove. I want to make enough to quit my part-time work with the company, make a name for myself in the art world, a big one. Like Sadie. But without her or Dad. All on my own." I don't say more than that, because it already feels like I've said so much. I can feel the exhaustion of the conversation in my bones. But I want to keep sharing, keep getting closer to the amazing man in front of me.

"Okay, I can understand that. But, like, I was going to find out at some point, right?" he asks slowly.

"Of course, I had even thought about inviting you to come meet my family sometime during convention . . . you know, before."

"So, Ms. Morgan, can we try this? Just try keeping things separate and see how it goes?" I nod, but I'm not looking at him. I'm mad at myself that I can't just be relaxed and fun and move on to the make out portion of our evening. He seems to sense all of that in me. "What is it?"

I sigh. "I'm sorry, it's just . . . you know about Ryan now, but I don't really know anything about you and Lauren. It would help me to know more about that."

"Okay, what do you want to know?" He's not at all bothered, thank goodness.

"Well, I mean, you guys moved out here together, so you must have been really serious?"

"Engaged, actually." My eyes go wide, and I suck in a breath. He adds quickly, "Sorry, I probably should've said that the first time we talked about this, but that was like our second date?

Anyway, yes, we were serious. And moving here together, we clung to each other at first because of the culture shock. And after a while, the excitement of New York wore off, and she didn't have a real need to be here for work, wanted to settle down back home. I wasn't ready for that. She basically said it was her or New York, and I chose to stay."

"Ouch," I say.

"The ultimatum or the fact that I said no?"

I hitch a shoulder. "Both, I guess."

"It was a good breakup. I think that really for a lot of the time we were just comfortable, safe. More in a routine than we were in love. We stayed friends," he says. I'm not sure if the friends bit makes it better or worse. But I'm not about to ask him *not* to be friends with her. She's back in Texas—how much of a threat could she really be?

"Thanks for telling me," I say.

"Of course. Now we just have to talk about one more thing. It's really important." His face falls, serious.

"Okay?" A flash of sweat forms on my palms. I can't think of anything else left for us to dig into.

"Did you know sparks were flying behind you when you made your great golf cart getaway?" He bursts out laughing.

"Ahhhhh! Shut up!"

He jumps up and barrels me over, pushing me back and pinning me down to the bed. "I mean, the noises of that sign when you just laid it out—it was like a monster truck rally."

"Oh my gosh, stop, so embarrassing." He pins my hands up above my head.

"It was amazing. And you look so hot when you're mad. I exhibited a lot of self-control not jumping into that golf cart, Tiger."

I pull my body up to challenge him, but he has me pinned. "Yeah, well, I'm mad right now."

"I know," he says in an altogether different deep voice. Then his mouth is on mine, finally, with a moan from both of us. He's not soft, he doesn't hesitate, and neither do I. He still tastes sweet and cold from the ice cream, and the feel of his weight on me is otherworldly. "I . . . missed you . . . a lot," he says to my mouth.

"I missed you too." After a lifetime on my mouth, his moves his lips to my earlobe, my neck, the start of my collar, where the big shirt he loaned me hangs loose. Without thought, out of pure need, in one quick motion, I pull my shirt off. I need his hands on my skin, more of my skin.

He pauses for a second and runs a finger along the small amount of cleavage created by my hot-pink push-up bra. "Have I told you you're the sexiest woman in New York?" he whispers. I smile wide and nod and pull his head down, but he doesn't come down to kiss me. Instead, he kisses the spot where his finger was, then runs his tongue along the edge of the cup of my bra. I shake at the sensation. The move should be called the bra remover, because it was. And lying there, exposed from the waist up, scars and all, he cherishes me with his eyes and his hands and his mouth. He touches, kisses, licks, and nibbles all over every inch of skin that's available to him. I moan his name, gasp it, sigh it.

I push him up and pull off his shirt as I sit up on my knees to put us chest to chest. I was not prepared for it, for him. He is more defined than I had imagined, which is saying something

Not huge and bulking, but rather hard and chiseled, everywhere. The man has no fat on him. But he also has defined pecs and . . . an eight-pack. I counted. I swallow.

"Okay. You are doing a lot more than running," I say, staring.

"Little bit." He chuckles. Then his arms are around me and his mouth is claiming mine again. My chest tingles at the feel of his sparse, dark chest hair. His hands spread wide, feeling all up and down my naked back. When he begins kissing my neck again, I feel myself losing my grip. And it scares me.

"Matthew," I manage to say.

"Mhm."

"It's late." He groans, but I tense up. "I'm not quite ready."

"Mhm," he says as if in a stupor. His mind finally catches up to what I've said, and he stops kissing me. "Oookay, of course, okay."

I get back into my bra and his shirt and call an Uber since it's so late. He gets his shirt on too and hands me a sweatshirt from his closet. It's breezy out, and the thoughtfulness of that—just the small gesture of him thinking about my comfort—nearly gets me out of my clothes again. He walks me out, past his door and elevator, all the way down to the curb.

As my car is pulling up, he says, "So, just to make everything completely clear, you now have a boyfriend."

"I do?" I smile up at him.

"Uh-huh." He leans in and gives me one of his excruciating almost-open kisses.

"Night, Tiger. Text me when you get home."

"Okay."

CHAPTER 23

I brace myself before I walk out into the kitchen. I know Sam was already home when I got in and is already up now, just waiting to pounce. I check last night's messages again.

SATURDAY 11:03 P.M.

Susan: Okay, which one of you hussies didn't wear their lucky earrings!

Sadie: Yeah, we want names.

Sally: I did.

Sam: Earrings are on. We just suck this year.

Sam: BUT!

Sam: Guess who dared to show up to the bar last night?

Sally: Please say Matt.

Sadie: ???

Sam: EFFING RYAN!

Sadie: No

Sally: NO!

Susan: WTH

Sam: Yep and he was being his asshole self.

Sam: And then guess who swooped in and saved the day?

Sadie: You?

Sally: Best sister everrrrrr!

Sam: MATTHEW

Sadie: OMG

Sally: YESSSSSS!!!

Susan: I repeat: WTH

Sam: Ryan was SO PISSED!

Sam: It was glorious

Sam: Highlight of my life when he realized she just up and left the bar.

Sadie: She left with Matt?

Sally: Wish I could've seen that

Susan: Me too!

Sadie: Did she leave with Matt?!

Sam: She did!

Sam: Hope this wasn't a secret, Skye LOL

Susan: OMG

Sadie: Where did they go?

Sally: #TeamMatt

Sam: I don't know

Sam: She hasn't texted.

Sam: Will keep you abreast of the situation.

Sam: lol breasts

Sam: [Animated GIF of various cartoon breasts]

Susan: Oh boy. Let us know when YOU get home okay, Sam.

Sam: K!

SUNDAY 1:20 A.M.

Sam: I just got home and guess who is NOT HOME?!

Sally: Bow chicka wow wowwww

Sadie: What!

Susan: She better not stay the night with him!

Sam: She won't.

Sadie: I agree, she won't.

Sally: I don't know, he's pretty dreamy.

Susan: He's the enemy, Sally. Take a cold shower.

Sam: Aw Matt's not the enemy!

Sam: He's the one for her. I'm telling you.

Sam: I mean, they met on a plane.

Sadie: LOL. Maybe you do read too many of my books.

Sam: I must hasten to bed now, fair ladies!

Sally: lol It's not books, it's Bridgerton.

Sadie: Bridgerton started as books!

Sam: Not Bridgerton. Skye's got me hooked on the Loya series.

Sally: You too?!

Sadie: Oh, so she'll read romance, just not written by me.

Sam: [Awkward face emoji]

Sally: [Awkward face emoji]

Susan: EVERYBODY GO TO BED!

2:03 A.M.

Me: Home. And for the record, I also wore my earrings.

The second I make a sound on the hardwood floors, I hear Sam's happy Ricky Ricardo impression from the kitchen, "Lucyyyyy, you have some 'splaining to doooooooo."

"Ugh. Coffee, Ricky," I mumble.

I step into the hall and see her beaming at me from our little dining table. "More like tea, which you need to start spilling."

"Clever," I mumble as I pad into the kitchen, stepping around Gus. "Well, you saw Matthew show up. I guess?"

"Ooooooo back to *Matthew* now! I love it! Eeeeeee!" She drums her hands on the table in a fit of glee.

"Too much, Sam. Too much."

"Okay," she whispers.

I pour coffee into the mug she left out for me. "Did you see him at the bar?"

"No, I had my back to him. It wasn't until I heard your big spill that I looked over, and he was walking toward you. He looked so pissed." Her voice gets dreamy. "Like he was going to punch Ryan out for scolding you over his stupid beer."

I sigh. "He wanted to. It was so great, honestly. We talked about everything. And now . . . I officially have a boyfriend."

Sam's face lights up like Times Square. "What! Permission to squeal?"

"Granted."

She screeches in a way that makes me want to both smile and flee.

"So, what about the whole corporate enemies thing?" she says after a sip from her giant mug.

I pull my lip through my teeth. "Ehh, for right now, we're keeping work separate."

"Totally. You can do it. I mean, until the Twitter feud, you dreaded anything Canton Cards anyway, right?" She clinks her mug with mine. "Easy peasy."

"Yeah. Right." I hesitate. I had actually enjoyed working in the business over the last few weeks. This realization makes me feel things. Weird things. I shift our focus.

"And who did *you* end up with last night? Bartending Ben?"

"I did find my bosom heaving in the arms of Lord Benjamin, yes." She bats her eyelashes. "But 'twas only because Lord Jimmy had departed."

"No. Whatever that is, no."

"It's your fault," she cries, back to her normal accent. "I can't put that Loya book down. Jaylyn is totally me. Funny, strong, brave."

"Really? I saw you more as Jaylyn's lovable little sidekick who never shuts up." I smirk. She flips me the bird and leaves the room. "Have a good day!" I call after her.

I hear the buzz of my phone as I sit by the window with my coffee. My sisters have been incessant this morning, but I'm not dealing with that right now. Especially not Susan and her questions about how exactly this separation of life and business is going to work. Because I have no clue. And I don't want to let my mind run away with all those questions just yet.

I want to relive last night and how protective Matthew was, how sweet. I can't get over how well he seems to know me, see me, after such a short time. And I definitely want to go back to the moment his mouth breathed how he missed me onto my skin while his hands explored all over my torso. But my phone interrupts my reverie. *Just let me have this, Susan!* But it's Matthew, with a "good morning" and a GIF of a Tiger either just waking or just falling asleep. I send him a good morning reply, smile, put my phone on Do Not Disturb, and head to get dressed.

———

Janie and I sit at our favorite café across from the Flat Iron Building. It's a bit rowdy for us, but less crowded on Sundays. She and I agree this somehow makes their shoestring fries even tastier.

A lock of dark hair falls into her gorgeous face as she leans into the small black-and-white checkered table so she doesn't have to raise her voice. "I'm happy for you, I am. I am just . . ."

I smile. "A crusty old cynic like me?"

"Hesitant," she finishes. I nod and take a bite of the burger—a beef burger—we're splitting. Ever supportive, she doesn't eat meat whenever her boyfriend is around, which is often, because, like Matthew, he is a people person. "Mmm. Don't tell Theo, but this is the best thing I've put in my mouth in months." We laugh and she continues, after a few quiet bites. "So, when you told him about Ryan, did you mention the scars?"

I throw her a look. "The scars started when Mom died, Janie, not from Ryan, you know that."

"And you know that you spiraled after that breakup. All your bad habits went into overdrive. You didn't paint for months."

"I didn't have the coping tools I have now. Plus . . ." I pause as a server rushes by. "That was about losing myself, not the breakup."

"Exactly. Lost yourself in his big personality. Matt has some serious personality, Skye. Promise me you won't lose yourself again." Her voice is loving but serious.

"I promise. I was pretty miserable without him the past three weeks, and I've been painting more than ever. Look, I'm here with you now, we're headed to the studio, instead of meeting him for brunch like he wanted. It's not the same, believe me, Janie."

"Okay. I believe you. Let's finish up, I want to see these goose bumps."

We get back to eating and chatting all things Loya, her obsession matching my own. But in the back of my mind, her warning has freaked me out a little bit. Matthew does have a big, wonderful personality. But she seems to believe me, for now. But . . . do I believe me?

_____

In my studio, Janie says she officially concedes, hands up in surrender, when she sees my work. So far in the Texture series, I have a large close-up of a woman's skin with goose bumps, a square of moss that looks so real, someone is guaranteed to try to touch the canvas during the exhibition, a big piece that shows a bedsheet-size roll of actual-size small bubble wrap, and one close-up of a woman's hair that I'm still working on.

Janie works at my desk while I work on the hair. I put on one of Sadie's playlists for us. When my sister writes, she needs different moods of music, but without any words. Beyond just classical or theatrical, she gathers the best mix of instrumental covers from all different genres. Janie appreciates the playlists too, since her genius brain is crunching numbers, forecasting projections, and doing other mathematical things I don't understand.

After a few hours, we decide we have done enough Sunday hustling. We have said zero words between us, our phones have been in airplane mode, and we are as happy as can be. I needed this, and so did she. After a quick run, my internal tank will be fully recharged, meaning I'll be more than ready to pour a little of myself into my boyfriend. *He is my boyfriend! Huzzah!*

Never think "huzzah" again, you giant dweeb.

6:02 P.M.

Matthew: Brunch was so lame without you. Dinner?

Me: Sure

We're here for happy hour!

[Dropped pin location]

Okay, see you in a few.

When I walk up to the table, it's clear the guys were talking about Postify. Matthew doesn't seem to care though, quickly wrapping his arms around me and kissing me in the way that makes it seem like fifteen hours apart, for him, was fifteen too many.

"Uh, just a reminder you're in a public place," Jimmy announces at us loudly. Carter clears his throat as Matthew ends our kiss, seemingly coming back to his senses. *Stupid senses!*

"Yeah, yeah." Matthew pulls out the seat next to him for me.

"Hey, Skye." Carter chokes on the greeting. *Okay, so it's gonna be awkward for a while.*

"Hi." I smile around the table. "Uh, how's it going?"

"Better now that you're not ripping us apart on Twitter anymore," he snaps.

"You guys started it, I was happy to finish," I snipe quickly Matthew gives him a glare that could cut glass, which softens only slightly when he looks back at me.

"Oh, shit, sorry. No work talk. I'm doing fine, thanks," Carter mumbles into his beer.

"Where's Sam?" Jimmy asks.

"We're not staying long," Matthew says, thankfully.

And we don't. After Matthew finishes his beer, we head to a cozy little Thai place. Our conversation is easy and fun. I learn all his favorite things and file them away in my brain: Snickers, a specific color of blue (not royal, not baby, but a bright medium blue like the sky, pun not intended), Michael Scott memes, street tacos, Muse, Tetris, pancakes over waffles (*blasphemy!*).

We talk more about our families than ever before, and I force myself to open up. I love the way his face glows sharing about his family, the same way he does about his work. They have a close, healthy bond, and it shows. I know I'm not lighting up the same way he is, but I remind myself that doesn't mean I love my family any less. We've been through unthinkable heartbreak together. Tragedy changes the dynamic, and I try to extend myself and them some grace. Matthew doesn't press the issue, happy to listen to whatever I'm willing to share.

As we talk, he squeezes my leg under the table, he holds my hand, he plays footsie like we're a couple of tweens, and he barely looks away when a guy and a too-interested girl stop by and say hello to him. I am annoyed at the intrusion until he introduces me as his girlfriend, and then I experience some sort of happiness seizure where my thoughts stall and my smile involuntarily spreads so wide, it's got to count as a workout. Then it just kind of freezes. *Earth to face! Come in, face, you're embarrassing us! Please respond!*

We decide to grab an assortment of desserts from a bakery and take them back to my place. Sam is thrilled to see us, of course. But I glance up and realize she's deep into a rewatching of *Dawson's Creek. Warning! Sister meltdown imminent!*

"I'm, uh, in the mood to watch something funny. Think we can pause your thousandth visit to Capeside, Sam?" I ask her.

"Okay, but only because of this chocolate peanut butter bar you brought me," she says. The speed at which she is consuming desserts confirms my suspicions. Something's up with her.

"Matthew, what's the funniest show you've ever watched?" I turn to him, eager to help Sam abort her trip to Sad Town.

"I feel like this is a test," he drawls, hesitant.

"It absolutely is a test." I nod, left hand on my hip as I grab the remote with my right.

"Godspeed," Sam whispers with wide eyes.

He straightens with confidence in his guess. "The obvious answer is either *The Office* or *Parks and Recreation.*"

"Oooooooo, so close," Sam says.

His eyebrows shoot off his face. "What!"

I can see Sam's mood lifting already as she explains. "Those are second and third, respectively, but our particular favorite is *New Girl.*"

"No way." Matthew shakes his head. "Absolutely no way that show is funnier."

"That show? You've never watched *New Girl?*" I say, a little too passionate about television.

"Ahhhhh! Yasssssss! Now we get to see you experience it for the first time!" Sam squeaks. Then she switches to one of her impressions. "You're like one of the youthsss."

"Yes," I join her. "Youthsss who eat chut-a-ney and smoke crack cuh-caine." This sends my sister and myself into a fit of laughs.

"What . . . is happening?" Matthew looks a bit scared.

I give him a pat on the shoulder. "Schmidt mispronounces things, you'll see."

After a couple hours of the show, which he concedes is hilarious, I stand and grab Matthew's hand.

"No more *Dawson's Creek*," I say to Sam as I hand her the remote.

"You can't keep Pacey and I apart, Skye, it's true love," she calls after us.

I sigh, giving up, much more interested in showing my boyfriend my room for the first time. I don't know why it makes me nervous, but I suppose it's a reflection of me. And I like it, so I guess I hope he does too.

My bedroom furniture is a mix of styles, like the rest of the apartment. I have a really nice upholstered bed that I splurged on, with a small Ikea desk, plus a shabby chic chest of drawers with my jewelry displayed on top. Everything is white and light gray, which makes the art on the walls pop.

"Hey." He points at one of the cityscapes on the wall, a pointillist piece by Tam. I smile and nod. "Where's your tiger?"

"At the studio."

"The studio no one sees?"

I smile and bite my lip. Obviously, he's going to get to see the studio. I want him to see it. But I'm not above making him work for it. *What? Where did this confidence come from?* As Matthew crosses over to me and puts his hands on my hips, I know the answer. "I've got to be honest, it's a lot . . . tidier in here than I thought."

"Um, I'm sorry, are you implying I am a mess?" I say.

"I believe the term *you* used was 'hot mess.'"

"I tend to get twitchy if my space is all cluttered. But it's not perfect, my closet is overstuffed, my drawers are embarrassing, and ugh, inside my desk . . . but I can just close those things away."

"I like it," he says, drawing closer.

"Yeah?"

His mouth moves to my neck. "Probably good you keep it so tidy—don't want any tripping hazards, sharp edges."

I feign being offended. "Ugh, you know what, I'm feeling kind of tired, so maybe you should just—"

But his mouth is on mine before I can finish. After the scene with Ryan yesterday, I realize the difference. Matthew is somehow always laughing *with* me, but not *at* me. Something in how he looks at me, the tone he uses, it's never made me feel small or stupid. Instead, he makes me feel adorable? *No. Adored. Damn He makes me feel adored.*

I am filled with so much feeling for him, it takes over my hands. I pull him onto the bed, and again we make out like we were born to kiss each other. And my hands do a lot more exploring this time, but I have to shush his moan. And stifle my own. We shudder, whisper, laugh, mouth things to each other. But as we get lost in each other, and as our bodies eventually start to move in a rhythm, he pulls at my shirt. I grab his hand.

"We should stop," I say. He says okay as he kisses me. He seems disappointed but not upset. "Sam can hear everything."

"I kind of hate your sister right now," he says, panting with his eyes closed.

"I kind of do too." I squeeze my hand that's on the back of his neck. "I'm sorry."

He opens his eyes to meet mine, shaking his head. "Don't apologize. We have plenty of time," he says, and I believe he means it. And again, I'm filled with emotion—*emotion, not the L-word*—toward him. I really, really care about him. I'm not sure how much longer I can wait to show him just how much.

CHAPTER 24

The next few days are a blur of painting, running, and meeting Matthew at random locations he sends me. I realized quickly that he has less flexibility than I do and appreciate that he basically wants me to meet him everywhere, every day.

It's a bit annoying that he's always with coworkers or Carter, but we usually don't stay with the group, thankfully. We grab coffee, we run, we have dinner or dessert. We haven't had a chance to finish our makeout sesh where we left off, unfortunately. And maybe fortunately. Because I want to jump his bones.

Who thinks "jump his bones"?

We don't try to meet up in the middle of the workday, and that's all right with me. Because I am a painting fool. Maud is thrilled and thinks this might be the series that gets me a spot at Culture in Midtown. It's one of the bigger galleries, and its shows always gain media attention. Media attention like *The New Yorker* and other publications well beyond ArtTok and small online columns. It will be huge if it happens, even if they just let me have five or six spots. The pressure is gnawing at me, but long runs and productive days are keeping it at bay.

Professionally, the Twitter feud is behind us, but it's still good Matthew and I aren't discussing the business. Because we lost another favorite line to his company, a gift line this time, with gorgeous acrylic coasters and trays and other tchotchkes. Needless to say, Dad is livid. I don't know what Susan has told him about my new official boyfriend, but I hope nothing. Not that he can say anything—I mean, I am twenty-seven years old. But it would take tense feelings between us to the next level. *Like, is a tightwire over molten lava a level? Because that's where we'd be.*

When I heard the news, I was conflicted, both irritated with Matthew and excited for him. He works long hours, and I know he cares deeply about the work, even if we don't discuss it. So I want him to succeed, of course. But it feels like his success comes at the cost of ours—of Dad's, I guess. I don't know if I should congratulate him or even mention it. Probably not mention it. It would just put a damper on his parade, to think about his gain as my loss.

I hear a knock on my studio door as I shake my head, trying to get focused on the canvas drying quickly in front of me.

"Delivery for you—very cool-looking," Leanne says, handing me a large potted plant. It looks like some sort of aloe or succulent, bright green with almost white stripes across the leaves. It's in a modern white pot filled with pebbles on top of the soil. I am already smiling as I check the card.

Tiger Aloe
If you paint this, the title needs to be
"Shameless Bribe for Entrance to Studio."
—Matthew

FRIDAY 2:00 P.M.

Me: Bribe accepted.

[Dropped pin location]

Matthew: Yes! Can I pick you up there for happy hour?

Actually, I still need to run and then change.

Can I show you tomorrow?

Can't wait!

"Well, well, well, is tonight the night?" Samantha is beaming at me from my doorway.

"What?"

"That dress is smokin' hot. Like *Dear Matthew, I'm Ready, Please Deflower Me* Hot!" She laughs.

"No! Not ready for any deflowering. Which, does that even apply here? I don't think so. Anyway. It's just that I only saw him in running stuff this whole week, so I wanted to look cute."

"Well, you failed. You do not look cute. You look sextastic, and tonight is the night! I'm telling you!" It's a skin-tight, plain olive-green dress with buttons down the front, but I've thrown on white platform Guess sneakers and a chunky jean jacket. Sam is just excitable.

———————

So, tonight's the night?" Janie says under her breath when we greet her and Theo just inside the bar.

Really?

"See? I told you!" Sam breaks into a fit of loud laughter, which doesn't even matter because the music in the bar is blasting.

"Shut up! Can't a girl just wear a dress if she wants?" I ask, sounding squeaker than I'd like.

"No," they both say back to me in unison, smiling.

Ignoring them, I wave to Matthew off to one side of the bar with his gaggle of people, which I notice includes Allison this time. He meets us halfway, with a huge smile that still catches me off guard.

It's beyond that he's drop-dead gorgeous—it's that his smile is so happy and full, it pushes your face to smile too. Which mine does. He pulls me into his arms tightly and pulls away just enough for a firm, happy peck before greeting my friends.

"Hey, I'm Matt!" He has to yell to Theo over the noise. Then he turns to Janie. "Good to see you again, Janie." She smiles with a tight nod. It was sweet of Matthew to invite my friends to join him and his friends for their celebratory drinks, but now I'm wondering if this was a bad idea.

I try to tell her to be nice via ESP, but I know she'd just reply that this bar is too terrible for niceness. It is. It's trendy, cold, loud, and should have a sign posted warning about seizures. They have a martini special, so Matthew, while keeping his hand in mine, gets me something that tastes like an orange creamsicle.

"So, you're at Drive Capital?" Matthew yells to Janie. She just nods. "Very cool. Didn't they base that Netflix show off your boss?" She nods again. I give her my widest, angriest eyes, but she looks around to say, *As if we can actually talk in here, anyway?* Luckily, Theo jumps in and carries on a normal human conversation, albeit at a crazy volume.

Janie and I go into Watch Mode.

Sam has decided to make Allison her new best friend, a spy mission I'll be happy to hear detailed reports from later tonight. She's also still making eyes at Jimmy, who is focused on Breasty, the brunette from the office I've yet to meet. Allison keeps eyeing Matthew and appears to be chatting up Carter to make him jealous. That's my guess based on the laughing and touching. But Carter doesn't seem to be picking up the vibes she's putting down.

As Matthew talks to Theo, he wraps an arm around my waist under my oversize jean jacket. He splays his hand out, discovering how tight the thin fabric is, stroking down my side. I look up at him, but his face shows nothing as he talks to Theo. While Matt is still focused in on their conversation, his hand slowly moves to the small of my back and then down, grabbing my butt by the handful. He does it again and again, slowly, casually, without once looking at me. My heart pounds louder than the club music in my head, and I cross my legs and squeeze automatically.

Eventually, Theo turns to say something to Janie, and Matthew whispers "I like this dress" into my ear. He tortures me with the same slow stroking, sometimes running a finger under the edge of my skirt on the back of my thigh, for what feels like an hour, until a few plates of appetizers arrive at the group's pub tables.

We all gather around to eat, with everyone but Janie and I yelling in conversation to each other. After enough nachos and french fries to settle my growing martini buzz, I take off my jacket. Within seconds, Matthew is standing behind me, arm around my waist, his *substantial* arousal obvious behind me in his jeans. I feel myself start to go weak in the knees, trying to remember we are in a public place surrounded by his coworkers. Every time I try to pull away enough to stand and think, he tucks me right back into him.

Janie has reached her max, so she and Theo make a polite exit as the rest of the group gets another round of drinks. Matthew eventually moves from behind my back to my side as he pays the tab. I wonder if it's just the food or everyone's drinks he's covering. He doesn't even look at the total on the bill as he hands his card. I feel a bloom of pride at his success, his companies he launched from nothing. I marvel at him, this Texas boy taking over the tech scene in Manhattan, and then feel a stab of sadness that I can't ask him how Postify is doing, can't celebrate with him.

"We're headed to Nova now!" Carter yells to Matthew. Matthew gives him a nod and helps me shrug my coat on. I squeeze his hand as we walk out, because I cannot handle another loud bar. Outside, I take a deep breath in the break from the thump of the club speakers.

"Matthew, I'm sorry, but I am not up for Nova," I say, and he puts his hands on my neck.

"I know," he says with a small smile.

"I'm sorry, you should totally go, and I can just see you tomorrow."

He scratches the back of his neck. "Well, we *are* celebrating, so I should probably be there." His voice is tight as he says it. I hate that I can't ask him for more information—celebrating the new line they signed? Celebrating more funding? "Let me get you home first."

"I can take the subway, it's fine."

He pulls me into him and slides his hand down my back as he kisses just under my ear. He whispers, "You're not taking the subway in that dress, Tiger."

"O-Ok-kay." Unsurprisingly, I am having trouble speaking.

———————

He gets out of the Uber at my apartment, and my palms start to sweat when I realize he's coming up. If he so much as whispers in my ear, I'm getting naked. It's science at this point. I can't fight it anymore. I'll probably rip my flimsy dress in half myself. He takes my hand and leads me up to my apartment. At my door, I turn to put in the key, but he stops me and turns me back to him before I twist it in the lock.

He slams his mouth onto mine and opens me up with his tongue. A moan escapes from both of us. He puts his left hand on the door just above my head and his right on my waist, grabbing so hard it almost hurts.

"If I come in," he says in between kisses, "I will want to stay." I moan an okay. He kisses along my jaw to my neck. "And I promised them."

"Uh-huh."

"But this dress." His hand moves from my waist down my thigh to the edge of my skirt. He kisses back up my neck as he lazily runs his fingers along my leg where the fabric ends on my skin. He kisses me slowly, with long, full sweeps of his tongue as I feel his knuckles move lightly along the inside of my thigh under my skirt. His hand moves upward, and I let out a whimper.

Is he going to do what I think he is right now in the hallway?

His warm calloused knuckles continue north, so slowly I may combust. He pulls away to look into my eyes as his knuckles finally find my underwear. "Is this okay?" he whispers. I nod but look around, worried about neighbors. We're at the end of the hall, and there are only two other doors, but someone could come in or out at any moment.

"Skye," he says, and my eyes meet his. "If someone comes, I'll stop, okay?" I nod again, and without really thinking, I arch my back, pushing myself into his hand. He smiles, a confident smile that's like an inside joke between him and my body. What even! This is the hottest thing to ever happen to me!

I close my eyes and breathe, as he's still just barely touching me with his knuckles, driving my pulse to the edge of full-on cardiac arrest. He stops moving his hand. *No, don't stop!*

"Skye, look at me," he says softly. I open my eyes and see his hunger staring back at me beneath his dark lashes and heavy lids. "Say something," he whispers.

"Y-Yes, please," I manage to get out, and his fingers do what I want, in one firm thrust, without hesitation. He keeps his eyes on me as he takes me with his hand, chuckling and shushing and telling me how sexy I am in between light kisses. I can't believe what is happening, how gorgeous he is, how kind his eyes are, how intense everything feels. It doesn't take long for me to explode around him, right there on my doorstep.

He kisses me through it, holding me up around my waist with his left hand and then pulls back to stare. "So beautiful," he whispers.

"Holy crap," is all I manage to say.

"Oh, yeah?" He chuckles as he pulls away and fixes my dress back into position, wiping his fingers on the fabric.

"Yeah." *And I love you and that was the best thing I've ever felt in my life!* I take another deep breath.

"Good." He leans in to kiss me, and I kiss him back, wrapping my arms around him to hold him as tight as I can, tight enough to show him how I feel. How *much* I feel. How big my feelings are and how much they scare me. He pulls away, resting the end of his nose on mine and says, "I'm sorry I can't stay."

"Pretty sure you just made it up to me," I say. He chuckles.

"I'll see you tomorrow?" He starts to pull away.

"Uh-huh." He stands back with his hands on my waist.

"At your studio, right?"

"Yep." I smile, then squeeze my hands on his forearms, happy that he's so excited to see another piece of me.

"K. Now please go inside so I can stop touching you," he says.

"But I don't want you to stop touching me." I bat my eyelashes at him. I squeeze his arms again. He's going to have to force me out of his arms at this point. He takes a deep breath.

"Inside, Tiger, you're killing me." He turns me around and unlocks the door. He pushes me gently at the small of my back. I turn around to say goodbye. He rests his hands on either side of the door. "Freeze, woman."

"Okay." I let out a little laugh.

"Don't move."

"Okay."

"I'm serious, no touching, no sounds, nothing."

"Okay, jeez, bossy."

He leans down and gives me his signature goodbye barely open kiss, and just as I am about to devour him, he pulls away. He starts backing up. "Good night." Then he turns and leaves, and I watch him go. "Close the door, Tiger!" he calls back as he heads down the stairs. I laugh and I obey, still reeling from the best—*what, twenty minutes? Who am I kidding, five minutes!*—of my life.

CHAPTER 25

I am a bundle of nerves and excitement when Matthew knocks on the heavy door. I slide it open to see him there, looking as gorgeous as ever with slightly mussy "Saturday hair," as I call it, two coffees, and a bag of donut holes. I quickly lift up on my toes and kiss him hello, my hands on his firm chest. I give his own teasing kiss back to him, my lips parted just the slightest bit.

"Mmm," he lets out as I pull away. "Good morning." He flashes his full wide smile down at me, and my breath hitches. He's tanned and tall and gorgeous and standing in the doorway of my sacred place.

"Good morning." I almost giggle as I say it, I'm so happy. I step back and let him take in the space. His eyes go to the easel in the center first, then the canvases drying along the edges of the room, on the floor propped up against the walls. I pull the door shut and watch him.

His eyes slowly take in everything, as if he's trying to memorize it all. He rotates as he surveys: the shelves, the tiger print, his aloe plant by the window, the floor pillows. He glances back at me with a grin when he looks at my desk and sees a small ceramic bowl filled with fun-size Snickers.

"For me?" I nod. He walks over to get a closer look at the canvases. I left my smock from yesterday on the stool next to him, and drop cloths, cardboard, rags, and pallets are all over the floor, some still wet.

"Watch your step," I say, realizing. "I probably should've told you not to wear good shoes."

"I don't care about my shoes," he says softly. He turns back to me at the door where I'm a bit frozen. He smiles again. "This is . . ." He pauses. "I was going to say it's really cool, but that's not enough to describe it, Skye." I make some sort of happy-squeal sound involuntarily.

"Isn't it awesome? I still can't believe I have my own studio space."

"Awesome isn't a good enough word for it, either." He rotates back around to the canvases. "Will you talk me through them?" he asks, and my heart combusts at the question.

"Of course." I grab the big floor pillows from the corner and put them out in the center of the room, making sure they're dry. "But here, let's eat."

We sit closely, facing each other, as I talk him through some of my ideas for the series, pieces, and titles. He nods and laughs as he chews.

"'Nature's Serta Mattress,' huh?" he asks about the working title I have for the moss piece. "Do you know this from experience?"

I laugh. "No, it's from the first Loya book. I think I'll add a hashtag to go with it so all the fans know."

"I know you like epics, but what is it with you and that series?"

I think about it, swallowing a bit of donut. "The main character, she struggles with her emotions—like, her thoughts and feelings get away from her." I take a sip of coffee, and he waits. "It's not quite the same, but it reminds me of my anxiety."

Understanding washes across his face. "So, she learns how to master them."

"Yeah, and becomes this amazing badass hero."

His face turns mischievous. "And then gets freaky on some moss?"

I laugh. "She does not get freaky! It's a romance. They're . . . enraptured. He t*akes* her."

He nods, still smirking. "Uh-huh."

"Ugh, shut up!" He chuckles at me, his eyes sparkling.

"And the hair?" he asks into his coffee. I blush. Then sigh. Then look away, hoping he will let it go. He nudges my knee with his.

"Do you know whose hair it is?" I ask him. *You better not!*

"Sam's, maybe?" He winces. It's a similar color, so, not a bad guess. Mortified that I'm going to have to tell him, I look up and sigh again. "What? Who is it?"

I stare at him. "You really don't have a guess?"

"No, should I?" He looks genuinely confused. Then the light bulb sparks on. "You're embarrassed . . ." His smile bursts across his features like a firework. "Allison!" I nod. He laughs. "Oh, I cannot wait to hear the title for it." He puts down his coffee. I shake my head. "Is there such a thing as rage painting, Skye? Were you *that* jealous?" He moves forward to me and puts his left hand on the outside of my legs, leaning over me. "What's the title?" He's beside himself.

I shake my head. "You know, this isn't fair!"

"What's not fair?" He nuzzles his nose into my neck.

"You got jealous too. Of Emerson, of Ryan."

"I did." He kisses me softly along my jaw.

"Yeah, but you didn't *show* it. Not fair."

He pulls back to look at me. "The day after the gala, I was so pissed I ran twelve miles."

"Really?" I try not to show how happy his admission makes me, but my smile erupts. *Traitor!*

"Thinking of you in that dress the whole damn time." He puts his right hand firmly on my neck. "And the only reason I didn't hit douche bucket in the face that night was because you were more important. Getting you out of there was more important."

"But you wanted to?"

"He had his arm around you like you were his! I hated it so much, I think I may have blacked out. Luckily, you spilled his drink to snap me out of it."

I scoff. "You can always count on Klutzo here to come through."

He pulls back again, looking angry as he drops his hand from my face and flexes it. "Don't call yourself that. And"—a muscle in his jaw twitches—"why did he call you Stormy?"

I sigh and shake my head, hoping to diffuse the tension in his face. "It was just a stupid nickname. Stormy Skye, you know? He tried to play it off, but really it was his way of saying I was grumpy or too moody or whatever."

"He's an idiot."

"No arguments here." I shrug. I lean into him and whisper, "I like Tiger much better."

"Hey." He stops me softly as I lean in to kiss him. I pull back my brow pinched. "I know I tease you, but tell me if I take it too far, okay? If I make you feel like that." I shake my head in protest as he puts his hand back on my cheek. His voice matches the caress. "You're not a klutz, you're distracted. Your mind is always busy, thinking, working on something, and I love that about you, okay?"

Love! He said love!

"Okay," I whisper, and before I finish the word, he's kissing me like he's got something to prove. We kiss and kiss and kiss, and I can't get enough. The way he commands my mouth—hot, hard, soft, tender, long, slow, fast. He moans and says my name and whispers Tiger, and everything he does heats me from the inside out.

Finally, he breaks away, resting his forehead on mine. "I should go. I know you want to work today." I nod, and he stands, sighing, and pulls me up with him.

"What will you do today?" I ask him, looking up and wrapping my arms around his middle.

"Watch football with the guys. Work a little bit." He leans down and kisses me, then adds, "Think about you." I kiss him back, and this time I have something to say with my mouth on his, my tongue against his, my hands scraping down his chest.

"Stay a little longer?" I say as I fist his shirt in my hands and move my kisses to his neck.

"Okay," he breathes. I pull back to look at him and move my hands to his belt. He freezes, and I look straight into his eyes.

"There's something I've been wanting to give you," I whisper. He sucks in a jagged breath. I get down on my knees.

"Skye, you don't have to—"

"I know."

But I want to.

And I do.

And it's the most sexy and powerful I've ever felt in my life. To see this gorgeous, confident, unaffected man lose himself, standing on my speckled drop cloth. He's frozen in place in his gray shirt, surrounded by my bright canvases, pieces of my brain, my soul, splattered on all sides. I love that he can barely get out the words about how amazing I am, how good this feels. He doesn't last long at all, and he cries out my name. He struggles to stay standing as I smile up at him. I put his boxers back in place and pull up his jeans as I stand.

"Well," he says softly as he watches me, "I really, *really* love your studio." I let out a small laugh. "Basically my new favorite place. In fact, I don't know how I can leave now. I may never leave." He takes over working his belt.

"Oh, yeah? What about, you know, the company you're running?"

"I quit." As soon as he finishes his belt, his hands cradle my face. "That was incredible. You're incredible." Then he kisses me slowly, lovingly, with gratitude I can feel in my cheeks where his fingers hold me. He pulls away and stares at me, his eyes searching. *Oh, Good Lord in heaven, he's going to drop the L-bomb for the first time . . . after a blow job?!* My heart ratchets up to a terrifying speed again. He takes a deep breath and pulls me into a hug instead. "I guess I probably shouldn't quit."

"No, you shouldn't. You're killing it lately." I exhale. He kisses me on the top of my head.

"All right. I'll go." He reaches a step behind me and grabs a handful of Snickers off my desk. "Wait. I have to know the title," he says, gesturing to Allison's hair.

"Well, see how the strands are so shiny?"

"Yeah?"

"And I'm going to add tiny bits of neon yellow so it'll be obnoxiously bright." I pause. "Then I'm thinking I'll call it 'Dull,'" I say with a sheepish smile.

He bursts out laughing. "Holy crap, that's perfect."

"Really?"

"Could not be more spot on." I contain a squeal. He leans in, kisses me again, slowly, lovingly, until I'm weak in the knees, then he pulls away and bolts out the door with a smirk.

It takes me awhile before I can think straight enough to start painting. When I can form thoughts again, my eyes zero in on my Tiger Aloe and my body misses the warmth of Matthew in my small space.

I think I love him.

Crap.

CHAPTER 26

SUNDAY 9:05 A.M.

Me: How are you feeling this morning?

Matthew: [I'm Dying Meme]

Good time last night?

How good could it have been without you?

Fantastic point.

Brunch?

Can't, something is up with Sam.

Really? She seemed great Friday?

She had bread AND potatoes yesterday. She's borderline suicidal.

Lol what?

Carbs = Spiraling

You're a good sister.

I'm not.

You are. I'll see you later?

Probably.

Probably?

You can't make it without me for a day?

[Friends Meme: Ross Saying "I'm Fine"]

I'll make it up to you . . .

His response takes a few minutes.

Matthew: I am no longer fine.
[Loved "I am no longer fine."]

I put my phone down and shake off my smile. Sam needs me, but also, I need a day. Or two. I am feeling so much, so strongly, so fast . . . yeah. I need a day.

"Who are we watching this morning?" I ask Sam as she pads out from her room.

"We?" She starts to smile as she pours her coffee. "You're going to watch with me today? What about Janie?"

"Janie isn't spiraling into her fake relationship with a *Dawson's Creek* character," I say dryly.

"What? I'm fine." She avoids my eyes.

"You had fries and a chicken sandwich yesterday *with* the bun. I know a cry for help when I see one."

"You noticed my lunch order?"

"I notice everything. What is it, too much alone time? I know I've been busy." Sweet Sam is my opposite in so many ways, especially when it comes to recharging our batteries. If I people for too long, I am exhausted, needing hours or days alone to recuperate. I don't think Sam can people for too long. Too much time alone, though, and she withers like an unwatered plant.

"No, well, maybe, but I don't think so."

"C'mon, Bob." That gets me a grin. "What's going on?"

She sighs and looks out of our gorgeous windows. Gus finds his way around her ankles, showing just how much of an emotional support cat he really is.

"Or should I ask *who* is going on?" I add.

"That's the thing, isn't it. There's never a who," she says, her eyes glassing over.

"What? There's always a who. You could be on a date every night of the week if you want. And some weeks you do!"

"But . . ." Her voice cracks as she plops into one of our small dining nook chairs, still gazing out the window. "No one ever lasts."

I get up and stand behind her chair with a hand on her back. I hate seeing her downright forlorn like this.

"Hey, that's not true," I say, unsure. The truth is, I can't remember the last time Sam was in a real relationship. It has been a year at least. And it hadn't lasted that long—a couple months? But I am not about to concede any of that. I try my best to find the small, empathetic, comforting section of my heart and think with it.

"It is and you know it. You're just being nice, which honestly shows just how bad things are!" She laugh-cries. "Two months, Skye. That's the longest a guy has lasted, and that was last year!"

Wow, I really do notice everything.

"You just haven't met the right guy, right? And think of all the people you meet, the places you go, the experiences you get to try—you are having so much fun, aren't you?"

She sniffs and eventually nods. "I guess, yes, I do have fun. I love my life. I just . . ." She takes a sip of coffee to steel herself. "I see you and Matthew, and I want that. I want my person. But you know how I am. I'm just . . . too much."

"No, you're not. You're—"

She cuts me off. "I am, and I know it. Too excited, too open, too eager, too emotional, too everything. The longer a guy is with me, the more he sees of my too muchness and—*poof!* He bails."

I rub her back without trying to protest.

"Did Jimmy bail? Or Bartender Ben?"

"Pff, Ben won't even ask me out on a real date. And yes, Jimmy lasted for two 'hangs,'" she says in air quotes, "before ghosting me."

"He ghosted you? We just saw him on Friday," I say.

"Yeah, he stopped responding to my texts weeks ago. Friday was awkward, but I just ignored it."

"You're amazing, Sam. And he's a moron."

Her eyes start to mist up again. "Thanks for saying that, bu I mean, is every single man in New York City a moron? You sai it: I've dated like a million guys, are all one million of then morons?"

"Yes. When it comes to you, yes. They can't see you."

"Ugh, they can, they just don't like what they see."

"I would've agreed to that idea, too, about myself, before Ma thew. He gets me. Like really, really gets me."

Her head jerks up.

Then her face lights up, and she gasps, causing me to take step back.

"You love him! You're in love with him." She jumps out of t chair, almost knocking it over. "You *love* him! Ahhhhh!"

"All right, I take back everything I said about you."

"No no no no no! You feel *seen*! I knew he was the one for you, I *knew* it!" She starts jumping up and down.

"Hey! We're talking about you here."

"And I heard you loud and clear. I just need to find my Matthew, right?" I sigh and pinch the bridge of my nose. She giggles. "Right?"

"Right." I let her combust before bringing the conversation back to her. "Someone will see you for all that you are, Sam, which is so much, and this time I mean that in a good way." She scoffs. "I'm serious. Some man will see you and get you and he'll need all of you, and your emotions and loyalty and love and enthusiasm and hope—and it won't be too much for him. It'll be exactly the right amount." She barrels into me so hard, some of my coffee spills out onto the floor.

"I'll clean that," she says into my hair. I laugh. "Thanks, Skye."

"You're welcome. Now, which skinny-jean-clad, suspiciously hot preacher are you subjecting me to today?"

She squeals as she grabs the remote.

SUNDAY 6:22 P.M.

Matthew: So? How is Operation Sam going?

Me: Well. Too well. It's turned into a full-on girls' day and night.

[New Girl Meme: Nick yelling "Help me"]

Tell me where you are, and I'll come save you.

No can do. No boys allowed.

You'll have to survive without me until tomorrow.

[Broken heart emoji]

"Just let him come meet us!" Sam yells over my shoulder. I barely hear her over the rousing rendition of "Sweet Home Alabama" that's happening on the small stage in front of us.

"Absolutely not, Nosey McSlutterson." I tuck my phone away and give her a death glare for reading my messages.

"You said this looked fine!" She tugs at her tight, obscenely low-cut dress. It's dim in this small bar, with black walls and black tables and a few neon beer logo signs. Still, I think every man in here has squinted through the haze to sneak a peek at her.

"It does. The girls look great," I say, as Janie nods in agreement.

"They really do! That's why we should have Matt join us 'cause he'll bring Carter and Jimmy," Nicole says.

Sam's face falls.

"Jimmy is a dickwad," I say.

Nicole looks between Sam and me. "Wait, you and Jimmy?"

"No, not really," Sam says softly. I'm surprised she didn't share the details with Nicole, since they are so close. But maybe Sam had picked up on the same vibes Janie and I had: that Nicole was interested in him. Or maybe my sweet little elephant-hearted sister was tired of sharing about the city's many ant-brained little boys.

"Aw, Sam, I'm sorry. What happened?" Nicole squeezes Sam's hand on the table.

"The usual: two dates and then radio silence."

"Did you sleep with him?" Sam shakes her head no, but her cheeks say no wasn't the complete answer to the question. And her eyes beg us not to pry.

"Good! Not worth it. Now c'mon, Sam, it's showtime." I pray none of my online followers or offline acquaintances are in the small bar with us as I lead a very excited Samantha to the small stage.

"I can't believe I got you to agree to this," she squeaks.

"Never question my undying love and devotion ever again," I deadpan as we take out the microphones.

"What song did you pick?"

"Your theme song," I say with a too-sweet smile as "Wrecking Ball" starts. She laughs and flips me the bird as I belt out the first verse. If there's one thing all Cantons love, it's karaoke. I prefer it at home under lock and key and security-guarded door, but Sam needs cheering. As we sing, I'm happy to see her eyes brighten and her shoulders lift. Her smile explodes the more I make a fool of myself, so for the last chorus, I decide to go all out.

As I sing the last line, drawing out the words "wrecking ball" in all their angsty glory, I decide to lunge into a squat with my microphone on its stand, tipped, rockstar style.

But I forget that I'm me.

A klutzy doofus who is most definitely not rockstar material.

My foot just barely, barely misses the edge of the tiny stage. My left foot descends to the floor below but catches the metal edge of the platform, leaving behind what feels like a large chunk of my calf on a sharp corner. I manage not to fall completely onto my face, which has turned a deep shade of crimson. I manage to stand upright in front of the stage and the handful of fellow karaoke goers cheers. *Someone, anyone, please just kill me.* I take a small bow, since everyone is staring, and limp back to our table.

"Why do you insist on moving your limbs?" Janie shrieks as I get to my chair.

"To walk? To live?" I gesture around with both of my hands.

Nicole looks pale. "You're bleeding pretty bad."

Ugh, of course I am. "What's new?"

"I'll go ask what first aid stuff they have," Janie calls over her shoulder, already on her way to the bar.

"Oh, Skye." Sam sighs as she reaches us.

"I'm sorry. I should know better than to let loose and have fun, huh." I wince. The pain has begun.

Wise, calm Janie returns. "You gotta go home and clean this, c'mon."

"Yeah, it looks really bad." Sam's eyes look concerned, but I also catch her shoulders sag in disappointment.

"Hey, Janie can take me. You guys stay here, sing a few more." I try to sound cheery and not like I'm in serious pain.

Sam's shoulders hitch back up a tiny bit. "Are you sure?"

"Of course." I put the wad of napkins Janie found onto the scrape.

"These napkins were all they had," Janie says.

"Of course they were, look at this place." I make a show of looking around the bar, and all four of us start to laugh. Janie carefully wraps bar napkins around my leg with duct tape. *Perfect.* I curse at myself for letting Sam convince me to wear a dress instead of jeans, which would've helped considerably.

SUNDAY 7:14 P.M.
Janie: You're going to need a new running partner for a while...

She starts a new group message and sends a photo of me in the back of the Uber with my left leg crossed over my right. I'm giving her a thumbs-up, a shrug, and a wince-smile.

Matthew: What the hell????

Me: Karaoke!

Matthew: Where are you????

Janie: Ubering her home now.

When our Uber arrives at my building, Matthew is pacing out front. When I see him, disheveled and worried in his sweats and T-shirt, I know.

I know that I am gone.

Done.

Annihilated.

Totally and completely lost in love with this man. He opens the door and grins down at me.

"Tiger." He says it as a greeting, but not a completely happy greeting.

"I was trying to cheer Sam up," I say, which sounds more like an apology than an explanation. Before I can say more, he leans down and scoops me up, cradling me in his arms like a bride. *Not like a bride. Like a superklutz who should never leave the house! Keep it together!*

"Uh-huh. Did she ask you to do a tap dance?"

"I think I'm going to head home, Skye," Janie says behind us.

"Okay, thanks, Jane, love you!"

"Love you too. Text me later." She gets back in the Uber.

"You didn't need to come White Knight me again. Janie has fixed me up a million times," I say, staring up at him.

"I don't doubt that." He chuckles down at me. I feel the familiar pink arrive on my cheeks and a burning sensation seeping across my chest. He stares down at me. "But that's not her job anymore." Then he kisses me softly in the middle of the staircase. He pulls away to kiss my forehead, and I feel my face start to cool.

"Matthew, I—" *No! It's too soon! Abort!*

He slows his pace. "Yeah?"

"Thank you," I manage to say.

"Well, you're not getting off scot-free," he says.

"I'm not?"

"No. I'm going to need a complete second-by-second play-by play of what happened."

"Ughhh."

"Were there sparks? Were you facing forward or backward Did you hit your chest again? Should I inspect you?"

"Ahhhhh! Shut uuuup!"

"What song was it?" I freeze, and he knows he's found a gen *Oh, look, the burning is back in my cheeks.* "C'mon, I'll put yo down, and you're in no position to climb stairs, Tiger." I shak my head. "Okay, putting you down."

"Okay! It was . . . 'Wrecking Ball.'"

"By Miley Cyrus?" he almost shouts. "That's the most amazir thing I've ever heard. Damn, I l-love this story."

Did he almost just say it?

"I'm going to need to hear your rendition, please."

I motion over my shoulder. "I'd rather you throw me down these stairs, seriously."

"And you were just so caught up in the passion of the song that you flung yourself from the stage, huh?"

"I hate you." I laugh.

He starts to whisper-sing the lyrics on the last flight of steps, barely panting at the work of carrying my weight up six flights. We are both laughing by the time he gets us into my apartment and deposits me on the couch. He finds the first aid kit in the bathroom and makes quick, soft, quiet, sexy work of bandaging me. Again. He grabs me a water and two Tylenol and sits next to me on the couch.

"How bad is the throbbing?"

"Pretty freaking bad," I say, closing my eyes. He puts his hand on my thigh and gives me a squeeze. "Um, about that inspection—"

"I was just kidding, Tiger. You need to sit there and drink water. Have you eaten?"

"No, we hadn't ordered yet."

He orders us some dinner, and we watch a few *New Girl* episodes. He clears our trash, gets me more water, and sits back beside me again. He takes my face in his hands and kisses me softly. I lean into him, but he pulls back.

"Hey. You need to Uber to your studio the next couple days."

I shake my head. "I'll be fine!"

"Um, excuse me, this is about me."

"Oh, really?"

"Yes, I want my running partner back. So you need to take it easy so you heal really fast. In fact, if it's still throbbing tomorrow, you may need to go to urgent care. Okay?"

My eyes go wide. "I do not need to go to urgent care!"

"We'll see." He kisses me slowly, but not softly. I let out a moan, wishing I wasn't an idiot with her leg wrapped in Band-Aids right now. "I want to stay, but I have a very early morning." He kisses me again. "And I don't think my staying would allow you to get the rest you need." More kisses. "Because you are so sexy." He kisses me a little harder, and I whimper. "Even with a gimpy leg." He kisses me one last time and then rests his forehead on mine, smiling wide.

"Okay," I whisper.

"So I'll see you tomorrow. Promise me you will Uber."

"Fine, I promise." He kisses my forehead and lets himself out. I recline my head back and breathe in the air that still smells of him, then fall asleep there on the couch, with a smile on my face.

CHAPTER 27

MONDAY 1:43 P.M.

Me: I GOT CULTURE!

Sam: YASSSSSSS!!!! I knew you would! Congratulations!

Sally: What?

Sam: The big art gallery in Midtown!

Sam: Skye finally scored a spot at one of their exhibitions!

Sadie: Culture!?! Wow! Skye, way to go!

Susan: Amazing, Skye! I'm so proud of you!

Sally: Does this mean you've made it?

Sam: Yes! She has! They'll do a write-up in the New Yorker.

Sam: AND she will raise the prices of her pieces by A LOT!

Sam: [Animated Schitt's Creek GIF David saying "I think this is it!"]

Me: I did it!!!! I got a spot at Culture!

Matthew: Of course you did. Way to go, Tiger.

Can I take you out for dinner to celebrate?

Well . . . they gave me TWELVE pieces! The second largest spot!

[Animated GIF: Pretending to be Shocked]

I just heard from Maud, so we need to make our game plan.

Then I need to paint my face off.

You gotta eat, though, right?

I need to meet Maud first. Not sure how the evening will go.

Okay.

TAKE AN UBER.

[Eye roll emoji] I will, Susan.

Susan?

Basically calling you my mother.

I take that as the highest compliment then.

[Heart emoji]

Me: I did it!

Janie: Hell yeah you did!

How many?

TWELVE!!!! AHHHHH!!!!

You got this. Get to werk, queen.

TUESDAY 9:00 A.M.

Sam: I'm showing them the flowers, Skye!

Sam: I am dead! Terminated! Deceased!

Sally: What?

Sam: Look at what Matthew sent her yesterday!

Sam: [Photo of bouquet]

Sadie: OMG It's as big as Skye!

Sally: That is the weirdest, brightest bouquet I've ever seen

Susan: What kind of flowers?

Me: Twelve different kinds, twelve stems of each.

Sam: Get it? For her 12 pieces for the Culture show!

Sam: Most definitely NOT from CVS!!!

Sam: I'm telling you, he's *the one*

I'll let him know you're thinking of proposing.

Sadie: Hell, with those flowers, I'm thinking of proposing too!

THURSDAY 9:35 A.M.

Matthew: How's my running partner today?

Me: Ready!

You sure?

Yep, more than ready. I am vibrating after three days off.

Vibrating . . . I'm done at 11, can I come work there until go time?

If by work, you mean work silently and hideously at my desk, then yes.

I'll be mute and utterly disgusting.

Impossible.

You can't NOT talk.

[Animated GIF "That's hurtful"]

See you at 11. Please bring sustenance. [Kiss emoji]

B y the time Matthew arrives at the studio, I'm floating on a cloud while also twisted tight, as if my whole body is closed like a fist. But just seeing him calms me the slightest bit. And the street tacos from his favorite food truck don't hurt. We kiss and eat and laugh and kiss some more.

"Okay, thank you, now please go be completely uninteresting over there at my desk," I say, dragging myself back to my stool.

"Yes ma'am."

"No stretching, no sighing, no sexy typing."

"Sexy typing?"

"If someone can sexy type and keep me from painting, it's you."

"I cannot make any promises about my typing."

I get a playlist started and opt for one of my cute lightweight aprons rather than a full smock.

We work for four hours, with only a couple staring sessions, him at me and later me at him, and a few bathroom breaks each. Matthew stepped out for a couple of calls, and I feel a twinge in my gut.

I know he went into the hall to give me quiet, but I also know I can't ask what the calls were about. Were they good or bad? What is he working on today? His business is his baby, and I can't ask him how it's doing. But he returned happy and content, so everything must be fine.

We manage not to talk or touch, which has me feeling as tight as the canvas stretched across its frame in front of me. Somehow not talking or touching has turned me on as much—okay, probably not as much—as the opposite would have. Still, I'm making progress on the current piece, a close angle of a fuzzy fur pillow on a velvet chair. I don't notice right away that he's closed his laptop and come up behind me. He puts his hands on my shoulders and begins to massage my tension away.

"Didn't I say no touching?" I ask, taking my brush down off the canvas.

"You didn't, actually." He whispers in my ear, "Keep painting." He kneads with his thumbs and then says, "Plus, you didn't want me."

"Hmm?" I ask, but it's a moan. His fingers feel like heaven.

"You didn't tell me how hot you are when you're painting." He says it into my ear and then kisses my neck. My arm starts to slack as I tilt my head to give him access to my neck. "Don't stop."

raises my arm. I manage to touch the brush to a spot on the canvas that is untouched and will be covered later, because there's no way I can produce any worthwhile strokes.

His left hand continues to pinch at the worries in my left shoulder while his right moves forward . . . and . . . down . . . and under my shirt . . . and his fingers play along the edge of my entirely too tight sports bra and . . . *oh.* He pulls his hand back up and out with a chuckle.

"Ah, ah, not quitting time yet." He moves my arm up again. I pretend to paint, acutely aware of his right hand and waiting for its return. A string quartet version of "Somewhere Only We Know" is playing through my speaker—it's nearing the end, the strings pushing, growing, adding to the tension in my core.

His hand finally returns, flat and firm, just below my bra. His mouth moves to the other side of my neck, and his fingers move down under the waist of my leggings. My legs open without my permission. But his hand is moving so slowly, I have to groan and let my head fall all the way back. He lets out a soft laugh and kisses up my jaw. His hand keeps moving. *Please oh please oh please.* When his fingers find my center, he curses under his breath at the blatant evidence of the effect he has on me. But I am not even embarrassed. *This is the steamiest thing that has ever happened in the history of steamy things. And it's happening to me!*

His long fingers go to work, but it's not enough. And then the song changes to a cover of "Madness" by Muse, his favorite, and I can't wait anymore. I drop my brush to the ground and stand and pull him up. I collide into him, sealing my mouth to his and pulling up his shirt at the same time. I kiss him desperately, begging, pleading.

"Clothes," I manage to say as I pull off my apron. He helps me with my shirt, and I pull off my tight sports bra awkwardly, and I think of my scars for a fleeting second but shake the thoughts out of my mind. He's down to his boxers when I pull off my leggings, and then I look back up at him, from his chocolate eyes to his built chest and defined abs. I swallow. I'm in just my light blue thong, wishing I'd put on sexier underwear, black or lace or something. Until he says "Wow" while studying me. This is the first time I've stood exposed in front of him like this, and I'm surprisingly unashamed. He says it again, a whisper, and it strikes like an arrow to my heart, exploding with warmth and making my eyes sting.

"Wow yourself," I say, then move down to the floor pillows that are still in the middle of the room from lunch and pull him down with me. He is tense and panting, but his kiss is slow and long as he hovers over me. I whisper his name and pull my underwear off. When I grab at the elastic on his boxers, he pulls out of our kiss and moves to my ear.

"Can I taste you?"

Is this my life? I am close to bursting just from his voice asking those words. I nod. I tense a bit, my mind wondering about how thorough my shower was earlier. I also think through our previous conversations about this, about our pasts and that I'm on birth control. I'm grateful we already talked it through and hopeful he knows I'm finally ready.

But the way he kisses down my neck, my chest, the invisible center line down my stomach . . . I forget the details. I am so near the edge already that by the time he looks up at me with a smile I have to clench my hands into fists. When he kisses me, there, realize I didn't know what I'd been missing out on all this time. Everything is so perfect, synced in my brain, and I'm so close, I don't want anything to change.

"Is it okay if I put this song on repeat?"

"What song?" he says, smiling at me. I grab my phone as fast as I can, shaking because of what he's doing with his fingers, and put the song on repeat and turn it up. I reach up to put my phone on the edge of my easel, out of our way, and of course, *of course* I knock the palette off its perch. To keep it from falling directly onto us, I smash my hands around it. My fingers are covered in thick paint. I let out a shaky sigh, knowing I've ruined our moment. *The* moment.

But Matthew chuckles and pulls the palette from my hands, sets it aside, and then links our hands together as he kisses my neck. He lets go so he can position his mouth right back where it was, placing hand prints on my thighs. My hands go to his shoulders, leaving prints on him too.

"That is hot," he mumbles, looking at his hand prints on me before resuming his kisses at my center. I focus back on him and the music and my smudgy hand marks on his body. In minutes, I am overcome. "Matthew!" I'm not quiet, and he smiles as he kisses his name from my mouth.

"So gorgeous, Tiger," he says as he rubs his nose along mine.

"Matthew," I say, a command this time, pulling at his shoulders. But he doesn't budge, and kisses along my collarbone leisurely. But I can feel him, just as ready as I am against my thigh.

"Are you sure? I can wait, Skye," he says into my skin.

"Yes! Quit torturing me!"

"But it's your turn to be tortured," he says as he pulls off his boxers and kisses quick, light brushes all over my torso.

"What?"

"You've terrorized me. I've thought about this for so long."

I squeeze his shoulders so tight, my fingernails dig into him. "What?"

He looks into my eyes. "Since you pulled your hoodie down and took those headphones off."

He positions himself over me, grinning, glistening with a thin sheen of sweat, and blinking slowly. I realize what he's saying. Since the plane. *Wait, since the plane?*

"Really?" I barely say, all of my emotion getting caught in my vocal cords.

"Really." And as he says it, he crushes into me, putting his forehead on mine as I take a breath. He freezes for a moment, both of us adjusting, savoring. He looks in my eyes and starts to find a rhythm that I feel in every cell. We make love together, slow but hard, wanting more, wanting to be closer, fuller.

He whispers yeses and calls me Tiger. He says wow again and again and tells me that I'm beautiful. He says that I'm his and looks in my eyes, puts his forehead on mine, and runs his hands everywhere. He says my name as we both explode together, in a rush that annihilates my senses like nothing I've ever felt before

I thought I knew what good sex was before. I thought I knew what pleasure was, what intimacy was. But here in my tiny studio, on shabby paint-covered floor pillows, surrounded by canvases and drop cloths, with sloppy hand prints on my skin, I realize the truth.

I hadn't known actual love before.

But now I do.

CHAPTER 28

"Just tell him. He's seen the inner workings of your mind for weeks now—it's not like he'll be surprised." Janie salts our plate of Sunday shoestring fries and shared (beef) burger at our favorite spot. We grabbed a spot by the window, and Janie's burnt-orange scarf matches the trees lining Madison Square Park across the street.

"I don't know." I take a fry. "I just don't want to be the lame downer girlfriend. He wants to be going and doing and wants me with him. What If I'm, like, holding him back?"

"It's not holding him back at all. He can do what he wants—you're not stopping him."

"That's true, I guess." I sigh as Janie studies me. "I knew eventually we'd have a rough patch. I just figured it'd be about business."

"I did too. And I don't even think this qualifies as a rough patch. You haven't even talked to him."

"Feels like one."

"That's your baggage talking. He's not Ryan. You guys are so solid. It's been a month of nothing but puppy eyes and hot sex and swapped keys and gifts. You even had your amazing Post-

291

man and Stamp couples Halloween costume. It was so cute, I almost threw up in my mouth."

"I still can't believe I found a hot dress with a stamp pattern on Amazon. Score another one for the Hoodie Brigades," I say, and we both laugh.

"How's his hoodie life going?"

I grimace. "I have no freaking idea!"

"Whoa. Simmer."

"Well, it drives me nuts! There have been days lately when he comes over and he's disheveled and his mind is elsewhere and I can't ask about it." She makes an "eek" face, understanding. It kills me not to know things, and she knows that about me. "Something is up recently for sure. Not to mention the many times we're out with his team happy hour-ing or celebrating, and it's like they can't speak freely around me. Stupid Allison gives me the side-eye across the room."

"Stupid Allison," she spits in solidarity.

"So, maybe that's part of it too."

Janie nods. "And *your* other life? How's the Canton empire holding up?"

"Good, actually. Stabilized. We haven't lost any other vendors sales are fine, not fantastic or anything, but on track for what we'd projected. If we have the holiday season we're hoping for we won't have to close any more locations next quarter."

Her thick brown brows shoot up. "That's a lot of 'we' you jus said."

I shake my head. "I know, but after the Culture show, I'm ou I'll make enough if they all sell, and Maud has some social medi partnerships she thinks we can land after the *New Yorker* piece

"Love it. How are you feeling about the show? Just a couple more weeks!"

"Pretty good, actually. I mean, obviously a nervous wreck and hardly sleeping or eating, but good."

"Good. And you finished the *big surprise*?" She emphasizes the last two words, letting me know exactly how she feels about the gift.

"I did." She shakes her head at me, but I hold my ground. "I know, I know, I didn't really have the time, but I wanted to. I can't wait."

"I guess that's love."

"I guess so." I smile. I haven't said it yet, and neither has Matthew, but it's so obvious at this point, I'm not sure what I'm waiting for. Maybe just not to be first. *Coward.*

"So, are you meeting him now?"

"Yeah."

"Just tell him how it bothers you, tell him what you need, so it's off your chest and you can go back to being disgusting together."

"K."

"Hello," he says in his low, sexy voice that kills me. He's leaning against the door of my studio, two coffees in hand.

"Hey." I reach up and give him a kiss and take the coffee marked DECAF.

"How long today?"

"Seven or eight."

He wraps his big, firm arms around me. "That bad, huh?"

"It's more like ten or twelve miles bad, but I don't have the time."

"We can go later, even in the dark. I'll be with you." I wince, and he catches it. "What?"

I take a deep breath. *This is not that big of a deal—just say it!*

"Um, well, I need to tell you something," I say.

"Okay?" He squeezes his hands on my hips.

"I am . . . struggling." His face twists up with concern. "No, no, I mean, I'm fine. Anxious, obviously with the show and every-thing. But I just need . . ." I don't want to finish my sentence.

"What, Tiger? Need what?"

"Well, I don't know if you notice this, but you are literally al-ways with people." His face scrunches even more. "And that's fine, I know that's how you like it. And that's great! But I just need . . . less. Less people."

"What?"

"People, Matthew. We are always with your roommates, your coworkers, or Sam." He tilts his head at me, still confused. "I want to keep up with you, I do. But I just can't." The rest of the words rush out. "I can't do all the happy hours, hanging with the guys, watching shows with Sam. I feel like I'm never alone. I feel like I'm about to snap."

He responds slowly. "You want to be alone?"

"No! I mean, yes, sometimes. Here, mostly. But I know, Mat-thew, I know you want to be with people and I'm trying, I am." My eyes start to well.

"Hey." He grabs my right hand, where I'd absently started picking at my thumb cuticle. "Slow down for a second." He mas-sages my hand in his. "What do you want, Skye?"

"To paint by myself."

He stops massaging my hand and starts to laugh. I look up at him.

"That's it? You're all worked up because you want to be alone in your studio?"

I squeeze where I'm holding his forearms. "Why are you laughing!"

"Damn, woman, I thought we were about to break up! You scared me!"

"But it's not just the studio time."

"Okay, then what else, Skye? Just tell me, it'll be fine." He kisses my forehead and then gazes down at me, smiling and waiting.

"I just can't keep up. Like I said, I can't be with people all the time, with your friends all the time."

"Do you want space? From me?" he asks, his smile fading.

I rub my hands along his skin. "No! Not you. Just everyone else."

"That's fine, totally fine. I don't need to go to all that stuff."

"You do—you need people."

"Hey." He tilts my chin up to look at him. "You're people. I just need you." He kisses me softly, and a tear makes its escape down my cheek. He pulls away and wipes my tear and says softly as he searches my eyes, "Is that all? What else?"

Rip the Band-Aid off already!

"I need to stay here for Thanksgiving. I know I was going to meet your parents and we already booked the tickets, but—"

"Fine, Skye. That's totally fine." He holds my face in his hands, but it's his eyes that grip me with their intensity.

"It is?"

"Of course. You have your show the very next weekend—I should've thought of that."

I jut out my chin, sure this can't be so simple. "Your parents, though."

"We can do it over Christmas. They'll understand." His voice is firm, as if it's all settled. I finally let out a sigh of relief and wrap my arms around his middle. I squeeze, and he groans. "Man. I think I just lost a year of my life."

I smile up at him. "I'm sorry."

"Did my hair turn gray as we were standing here? Am I bald?"

I laugh and wipe my eyes, loving how he always eases the tension, loving how he comforts me, loving him.

"I can make it up to you," I say, tightening my grip around him.

"Oh, you most definitely can." He unwraps me from him. "Tonight. After you've painted and run and maybe had a hot bath and read your book."

"I don't need—"

"You do. I'll take the guys out so you can have my apartment to yourself. My tub is better." I start to cry again, and he takes my face in his hand. "Did you think I would be mad?"

"I guess? We had a plan. We already bought those tickets."

"I'll transfer yours to Christmastime. It'll be like a fifty-dollar transfer fee. Done. No big deal at all." He kisses my forehead and then cheeks and then nose. "Now, I'm out of here. And I'll see you late, late, *late* tonight." He kisses me quickly on the lips. "When you will comfort me about this near-death experience today."

"Okay." I laugh quietly. I almost say it. "I—" *Just do it!* "Um, I, . . . thank you. Thank you for understanding."

"Thank you for telling me." He kisses me one last time. "I'll see you later." He ducks out the door, closing it behind himself.

CHAPTER 29

I smile at myself as I put the finishing touches on Matthew's present. Tonight is his big birthday bash, which I assured him I most definitely did want to go to. I'm not about to let all his many female coworkers wish him a happy birthday in my absence.

I also know he needs me. The last few weeks have gotten harder and harder for him. After I told him I needed more alone time last week, he pulled away. I don't think he was hurt or angry, but he's going through something and I can't be there for him. Or maybe I could, but he doesn't want to ask or share because he knows I'm under pressure too. Either way, it really sucks.

I do know some things, and they aren't great. After first poaching product from us and a few other brands, Postify has struggled. Their initial number of beta testers was much lower than they'd hoped, according to the tech blogs. It seems there are some people out there who still want to go pick a card or gift out in person, which is great news for Canton Cards. But of course I feel badly for Matthew, which has been putting me in a sort of emotional whiplash.

I can see it in his eyes the last few days, especially at dinner or dessert after work. He and Carter left their active roles at In-put.co to put all their time and energy into Postify. They're still stockholders and advisors, for multiple companies, but Postify is it for them now. And it kills me that I can't talk to him about it.

I think it kills him too, but he's built differently than me. He doesn't hold things in and stew—he thinks out loud. And he always has a whole crew of people around to talk to and commiserate with. But shouldn't his girlfriend be one of those people? Shouldn't I be the team captain? His partner in everything, including work? I think I should. But I have no idea how we get there. Even after I leave the company, I'll still be a Canton. It feels hopeless.

I shake my head.

I don't have to solve that problem tonight.

Tonight is about surprising and celebrating Matthew.

I hear his knock on the door and hop over to open it, giddy. He looks crisp and clean in a white button-up shirt, untucked, and dark jeans. He's replaced his hoodie for a heavier dark gray jacket.

"Hel—"

I kiss him before he can finish. "Happy birthday, handsome," I say.

"Thank you. You look amazing." I shrug on a black coat over my simple but sexy black wrap dress. I pull the door shut behind me, and he reaches for my hand. "You're ready?"

"Yes, and we have to make a stop on the way."

"Okay, what about Sam?"

"She's meeting us there."

"Okay, where's the stop?"

"You'll see."

I get our Uber so he can't see where we're headed. On the way over, he's distracted, frowning down at his phone. I don't say anything, not sure how to help. He eventually looks up.

"Skye, this is not on the way."

"I know, but it won't take long."

"I probably shouldn't be late to my own party."

"It's literally the only party you can be late for! They can't start without you," I tease.

"Isn't that rude?" He huffs. He's never this short with me.

"We'll be quick," I say softly and look away. He doesn't apologize as he gets sucked back into his phone. *He's stressed. Be easy-breezy. It's his birthday.*

We pull up to his apartment.

"We're here," I say, squeezing his leg to get his attention.

"My apartment?"

"C'mon, you said we need to be quick!"

"Okay?" His foul mood starts to dissolve into curiosity as his usual smile returns.

"Close your eyes," I say when we're at his door. I get us in and lead him by the hand to stand in the living room. I am shaking with excitement. "Keep them closed!"

"I am!" He's smiling wide now. I position him to face the wall on the side of the living room. While he was at work, I sneaked in with Janie to replace the cheap, generic cityscape print that hung there. In its place I put one of my own.

It's a longhorn, brown and white like the Texas mascot, Bevo, looking downright pissed, like he could take on the world. The sky is Matthew's favorite shade of bright sky blue behind the cow, and his eyes sparkle in such a way the canvas looks wet. He looks like he could charge right off the wall and into the room. I'm over the moon about how it turned out. And I know he will love it.

Next to the canvas I put a title card directly onto the wall. I went through a thousand options but decided to settle on something snarky, something that felt like our beginning on the plane months ago. Since Sooners always say "Texas Sucks" as more of a life motto than a game time cheer, the card reads:

Series:
Things That Suck
Title:
It Killed Me to Paint This
#yourewelcome #boomer

"Okay, open."

"Skye," he whispers.

It was worth it. Adding an extra, very large, very importan painting to my plate right before my show. Right now, to see h jaw drop and his eyes mist, it was worth the lost sleep and extr thumb Band-Aids and missed meals. Worth. It.

He walks closer and sees the card and laughs as he touches with his index finger. He shakes his head in disbelief.

"Well? Do you like it?" I'm beaming.

"It's . . . I . . . I can't . . ." He turns back to look at me. "I love Skye." He takes a step toward me. "I love you." He kisses me te derly, wrapping me in his big, warm arms. My heart is pounding from happiness and the realization: he said it!

But fear grips me. Just a second ago in the car, he was so distant, not himself. We're headed into a night that will be an hours-long reminder of the huge part of his life I can't be a part of, can't discuss, can't share. He pulls away, and I whisper "Happy birthday" with a smile. He kisses me again, deepening beyond happiness to desire. I pull away. "We better go, I'm making you late."

He holds me from pulling away for a beat, studying me. He lets me go and exhales softly. "I'm sorry I was a dick earlier. This is well worth being late." He turns back to look at his gift as I start to walk toward the door, tugging at him. "Wait!" He snaps a picture of it with his phone. "My dad is going to be so jealous. Everyone is going to want one."

"Oh, no, I almost died finishing that ugly beast. Never again!"

He laughs and follows me out.

In the car on the way to the restaurant, I wonder how to recover from the fact that I didn't say those three words back to him. He's quiet but seems more tired than angry. I squeeze his hand and decide to explain how I pulled off the surprise, who knew, who helped hang it, and a million other things. He scolds me for taking time to do it with everything else I have going on, kissing me on the head and thanking me. We relax together, and I decide I'll tell him as soon as we reach our next tender moment.

He unlocks my phone and looks through more of the photos I took of the painting, AirDropping all of them to himself, going on about how much his parents will love it. By the time we pull up to the restaurant, we are downright high on affection for each other.

But it doesn't last long.

Not for me, anyway.

Because while this is a birthday party for Matthew, it's also a Postify party. Every employee is here, plus employees, investors, and partners from their other businesses. It almost feels like a who's who of the New York tech scene. After we walk into the restaurant, which is entirely reserved for us this evening, Carter pulls Matthew away to talk to suit after suit. Thankfully, I spot Sam and Allison near the drink table.

"Skye!" Sam screeches as I approach. "So! Did he love it?"

"Yep, he did."

"I bet he just died. Was he shocked?"

"Yep," I say.

"Shocked about what?" Breasty (Heather) says as she joins our little circle.

"Skye painted Matthew a huge, killer longhorn painting for his birthday. Hung it up in his apartment to surprise him."

"Aw, that's so cute," Allison says.

Cute? It took me days to finish, looks like an actual cow walking through the wall, and she's calling it—me, my relationship with Matthew—cute? I grip my champagne glass and force a smile. *You're stressed and tired. Do not make a big scene out of this.*

"I was just telling Sam how happy we all are for you. We never thought we'd see Matthew settle down," Allison purrs through a pinched smile.

Breasty laughs. "Right? He dated his way through every woman in tech it seemed like."

"Guess he needed someone *not* in tech, then," I say, fake laughing back in their fake faces.

"Carter always said it didn't matter who he dated here because Lauren was waiting back home." Allison sighs dramatically.

"Lauren?" Sam asks.

"His ex-fiancée," I say. *I know all about her, but nice try, Allison. Really subtle.*

"Yeah, they broke up, but Carter said the breakup was just temporary, that the plan was always for Matthew to move home and for them to get married, after he had mastered things here."

"Which, let's be honest, he definitely has." Breasty gestures around the room full of powerful, genius, well-dressed executives.

"Mhm," I say. My smile fades to a tight grin, as much as I tried to keep it in place.

"But hey, maybe you're right." Allison mirrors my own fake smile back at me. "He just hadn't found the right city girl to distract him from his college sweetheart waiting for him in Texas. You know how college sweethearts can be."

I did know, from my parents and my sister. You didn't get over your first love, not easily anyway. In Oklahoma—and Texas and many other flyover states, I'm sure—you married them. If they broke your heart, you thought about them, pined after them, grieved them.

At least, I guessed. Sadie never let us discuss what happened. Whatever it was, it had crushed her beyond recognition. She has yet to recover. Sam notices the color leave my face, knowing exactly where my thoughts led me.

"You know what?" Sam spits. "If this Lauren is just sitting around waiting on a man a thousand miles away, how great could she be, anyway? C'mon, Skye, Jimmy wanted to talk to you about some New Balance shipment that just came in." We wind around to a separate part of the restaurant with only a few men chatting. "Don't even waste your time thinking about it. He is crazy about you." I nod, breathing. "Right? Right, Skye?"

"Right. You're right." But I can't look her in the eyes.

"Not all college sweethearts stay in love and get married—in fact, most don't." I can only nod. "You can just ask him about it, right? Surely those bitches just made up that whole plan thing. Even if Lauren is sitting around waiting for him—which, uh, barf—that doesn't mean there's some plan or that he agreed to it or is planning on it. He's not planning on it! He has you!" My nods have slowed. "Remember, he came to your show three months after your meet-cute. When you had a boyfriend. And he stalked you on Instagram, just waiting to ask you out. He was taking you to meet his parents next week, right? He loves you, Skye. He does."

"Okay. Okay, you're right."

She is probably right. So why does everything in my head and my heart feel all wrong?

CHAPTER 30

I smile and stretch, feeling the warm late-morning sun coming through the window. After the early ambush at the start of the party, things got better. Matthew could tell something was up and kept his hand on my waist the rest of the night. He introduced me to a million people as his girlfriend, telling them all about my work and his birthday gift. He glowed at me, stole kisses, and whispered compliments in my ear. He offered to leave early, but I insisted he stay and that I stay with him. I could tell both gestures made him happy.

In fact, the night was almost perfect. Just those two witches and then a few moments where conversations about work were clipped. He was gracious about it and tried to be subtle, but it was awkward. More than one man gave Matthew a confused look when he said he didn't want to talk about Postify. How could he not?

On the way home, he'd gotten pulled into some emails and his face fell. I didn't ask, couldn't ask, but I wanted to. When we got home to his apartment, we forgot all about everyone and everything and just focused on each other. As always, it was earth-shattering and mind-blowing. Just not mind-blowing enough for me to quit thinking about Lauren and Postify and how I still needed to say I love you but couldn't bring myself to do it. Still, we fell asleep in each other's arms, happy and content. Then, as a gift to both of us, we didn't set an alarm this morning. It's Sunday, after all.

"Good morning, gorgeous," he says.

"Hey." I smile at him.

He leans over and gives me a quick kiss. "I'm going to start some coffee and get in the shower. You need anything?"

"Water?"

"Okay." He gets out of bed, and I enjoy the view. His tan sculpted back flexes as he leans over to pull on shorts. "Are you ogling me?"

"Absolutely."

He smiles me his wide breath-taker.

"Speaking of"—I stifle a yawn—"all our photos from las night are on your phone, where is it?"

"If it's not on my nightstand, it must be in my pants."

I lean over on his side of the bed and find his dark, tight jean from the night before. I smile, thinking about how I'd basical ripped them off him.

Matthew sets the water down on the nightstand and kiss my forehead before heading into his bathroom. I find our phot and flip through. It really was a great party. And damn. He rea is gorgeous. I didn't look too bad myself last night, and Janie right. We're kind of disgustingly cute together. I select my favc ites to AirDrop to myself, when a message pops up. I almost dr the phone.

Lauren: Good, can't wait to hear all about it! See you Friday!

My heart detonates. I sit up so fast, I am instantly light-headed. No, *nonononono.*

Before I even register what I'm doing, my thumb taps on the notification. I am confronted with their conversation. Their very recent conversation.

Lauren: Happy, happy birthday, Matthew. I hope it's wonderful, you deserve it. [Heart emoji]

Matthew: Thanks

Lauren: Saw the latest Tech Insider article. That guy's a moron with an education degree from a tech school. Financial Columnist my ass. Don't sweat it.

Matthew: Ha! Thanks. We're doing really well.

Lauren: Good, can't wait to hear all about it! See you Friday!

What? What Insider Article? This Friday?

I take a deep breath and glance to check that Matthew is still in the shower, which of course he is, because he just got in. The messages before that are from months ago, before me, so I don't read them. The few I read and reread a million times are the only recent set of exchanges. He doesn't invite her to see him on Friday—it's just assumed. Maybe a family thing? A party? A reunion?

Wait. I was going to be in town with him.

But I canceled. Friday was going to be the day we drove up from Dallas to Tulsa to see my family. Now, Matthew is free that whole day.

I can't help myself. I text Carter and ask him if I'm going to miss any big parties or family reunions since I bailed on the Thanksgiving trip. After a minute that feels like a year, he says none that he knows of.

No. *Please no.*

The only answer is that Matthew invited her to see him on Friday by phone call. Sick in every cell of my body, I click on his outgoing calls. He called her. Three days ago. They spoke for five minutes.

I go back to Matthew's home screen and lock his phone. I set it on the counter like it's on fire, hands trembling. I get dressed as fast as I possibly can, grab my phone and purse, and dash out of the bedroom door. Jimmy looks up in confusion at my sprinting to their front door.

"I feel really sick!" is all I can think to say before slamming their door behind me.

Once the elevator doors close, the tears start. I don't really feel them or hear myself sobbing, even though I know it's happening. I also don't feel myself get an Uber or text Janie that I'm coming to her place. I'm almost surprised when I find myself at her door, as if I didn't get myself there.

"Theo! Can you make a fresh pot of coffee?" she calls out as she pulls me in. She doesn't say anything else—she just hugs me. Hard.

She hugs all the sobs out, not asking one single question. When I finally start to settle, she pulls me to the couch and sits me down. She goes to get coffee and puts a warm mug in my hand. Then she sits and waits.

I start with what Allison and Heather had said at the party and end with running out of Matthew's apartment. My phone starts to buzz. Janie takes it and turns it off.

"Okay. Skye. We don't know anything concrete. Calling her and texting her and seeing her this week—none of those things are actually cheating on you."

"But he kept it from me. He's kept things from me from the start. We started our whole relationship on a foundation of omission!" I'm crying again.

"That's true, but just because you didn't tell him your last name, does that mean you weren't honest about everything else? That you don't love him now?"

"No, but cut the crap, Janie." I pace back and forth, spitting the words at her. "It looks bad. Admit it."

"You're right. It does." I don't know if her concession makes me feel better or worse. "Don't you want to ask him about it?"

"I don't know. I guess? Except it'll hurt too much. I felt like I couldn't breathe. I had to get out of there. It was like I was on fire. I'm still on fire." I stop my stomping long enough to put the coffee down and shake out my hands.

"All right, maybe you should go for a run?" she offers tentatively. I nod. "Okay, well, you can't run in that, so maybe go home and—"

"No. I can't see him, he'll come find me. He knows where I run, and I need time. I'll just run here. Can I borrow some clothes from you?"

"Of course. But you have to take your phone with you." I groan in protest, but she adds, "Leave it on DND, and I'll just track you with Find My Friends. If you run for a million miles, you won't check in and we'll all think that with your luck you fell into an open manhole in Queens or something."

"Okay."

———————————

I run. I run and run and run. But the pavement doesn't do its job. It doesn't take all the feelings I pound into it. The worry doesn't fade. The pain only grows. The questions compound. I feel like a fool, more and more with each step. Even if he isn't cheating.

He didn't tell me she was at home waiting for him.

He didn't tell me he'd called her.

He didn't tell me he was going to see her. To see her! In person!

When I canceled our plans, he didn't offer to stay here with me.

He didn't beg for me to join him.

He can't tell me everything.

He can't give me all of himself.

And he can give it to her.

They are going to talk in five days, about his work. About his pride and joy. And she will be there for him, his longtime love who was before me, who knows him deeper than I do, longer than I have.

She'll be the one to make jokes and encourage him. She'll be the one to squeeze his arm and look into his eyes and tell him he can do it. He can build Postify into something great, something that eclipses all the competition, which includes me, my father my family, my whole world. She can do that. And she will. In five days.

We were built on lies by omission. It's a sandy foundation that won't weather the storm. And I'm not staying around to drown when it all gets swept away. I'm not.

I will not.

"I wasn't sure you'd be able to make it up the stairs. Was that the longest you've ever run?" I nod as she hands me some water as I enter their little bohemian getaway of an apartment. "Well, way to go. There's something. New PR. How long, twelve?"

"Fifteen." I plop myself down on the square of tile surrounding the front door.

"Dang. Then what? You should've been back hours ago."

I gulp the water like it holds the answers to all my unanswered questions. I wipe my mouth with the back of my hand. "Then I walked."

"He asked me where you were." I jerk my head up at her. "I said here, not feeling well. I told Sam the same."

"Well . . ." I throw my head back against her door. "That's the freaking truth."

"You look terrible. Did you get water? Have you eaten? It's almost four."

I use all my energy to get up. "I should eat. I did get a couple waters along the way."

She nods and heads to the kitchen. Their apartment is the most Theo place I've ever seen. I follow her past their small living area of bright colors, textures, and artwork until we reach the kitchen. I lean against the kitchen wall that's painted a banana yellow. Without asking, Janie, a contrast to the space in her practical, slim-fit, all-black sweat suit, hands me some ibuprofen and water.

She rummages through the fridge as she talks. "So? Do you feel better after the run? What are you going to do?"

"No, and nothing today. Tomorrow, I will end it."

"Whoa, wait, end it?" She slams the fridge door shut. "Over one phone call? That's what the pavement told you? Maybe you ran on the wrong streets."

"Very funny." I sigh. "He's going to see his ex-fiancée in a few days, a reunion *he* initiated and didn't tell me about. I'm out." She's not convinced as I press off the wall and move into the kitchen. "Listen, I just told him I need more space. I canceled our Thanksgiving. I can't be there for him about his business that is his whole life! It all adds up."

"Adds up to what?"

"To nothing." I motion with the watter bottle before taking another big gulp. "To the end. To the perfect combination of things that have sealed our fate. It's over."

Janie stares at me, holding sandwich supplies in her hand. "I think maybe it's good you're not doing anything today. Maybe sleep on it."

"I will, but it won't change my mind. You were right about last time, I was shattered. I'm not getting busted up this time. I'm walking away in one freaking piece, Jane. Whole, and intact. On my own terms this time."

She sets everything down on the counter. "What if it's not what you think?"

"Doesn't matter what I don't know. What I do know is enough. I'm done."

She drops the conversation and starts unpacking meat, cheese, and lettuce from their packaging. I decide to face the music waiting in my phone.

Matthew: Why did you leave? I can take care of you if you're sick Tiger?

Where are you?

???

Skye, why are you at Janie's and not at home? Talk to me

Whatever is wrong, just talk to me about it?

I'm officially worried now, Tiger.

Me: Sorry, turned my phone off to rest. I'll see you tomorrow

Can I come take care of you? Soup? Ice cream?

No thanks, I'm still at Janie's. We'll talk tomorrow, okay?

Not really, no. I'll come there.

Please, Matthew. Please don't, I'm gross.

I'll run there, then I'll be gross too.

I'm gross enough for the both of us.

Call me so I can talk to you?

What is this, 2002?

Please talk to me, Skye.

I'll talk to you tomorrow, I promise.

Okay. Feel better.

One of the thousands of tight coils in my body relaxes the tiniest bit. The trauma, for today, is over. I eat enough of the terrible, sprouted-bread, vegan-turkey, fake-cashew-cheese sandwich to give me energy to get home.

Luckily, when I get home, Sam is out running errands, so I quickly shower and get in bed. I don't get any sleep. Instead, I think through all the scenarios for tomorrow, where I break up with the love of my life.

CHAPTER 31

Matthew: Good morning, beautiful, how are you feeling?

Me: Better, thanks.

I've got some donut holes with your name on them.

Thanks, but I'm hanging with Sam this morning. Can you do dinner?

Sure. Let me know if you can get away earlier.

Okay

"Okay, so, I get that we are pissed. He should've told you. Hate hate hate all of that. But. You're going to hear him out before you end it, right?" Sam is pacing in our little kitchen, absorbing the news.

"I'm sure he'll do some talking, but it won't change my mind."

She sighs heavily. "You really think this is worth throwing it all away? Everything you have with him, the happiest I've ever seen you in your life, over one call? One meetup with an old friend?"

I stroke Gus in my lap as I correct her. "Old fiancée."

"Even so, what if he was meeting with her just to tell her to quit waiting, that he found someone else?" Her eyes are so hopeful, I have to look out the window next to me.

"If that was the plan, Sam, why wouldn't he have told me about it?"

She crosses from the kitchen to the table where I sit. "Because he didn't want to worry you?"

"That's BS." I look back at her. "In what world would I *not* want a heads-up that he's calling, texting, and going to see his ex-fiancée."

"Okay, you're right." She finally concedes enough to sit down. "I think I'm swearing off love altogether."

"Don't say that to me. Say that to someone who'll tell you, *'No, don't swear off love, it's worth it!'* We both know it ain't me, sister."

Our phones buzz in unison, and it's as if Susan has entered the room.

"Speaking of sisters." Sam picks up her phone. I focus on petting Gus, knowing my sister will tell me whatever the latest news from our fearless COO is. But Sam doesn't say anything. I look up, and her face scares me.

"What? Is it Dad?"

"Just look," she says softly, scarier than ever.

I pull up my phone. Susan sent us a Twitter notification. I tap to see the latest lame attempt at shade I need to deal with.

NO. NO NO NO NO NO NO.

"No!"

@PostifyPress: Retweet: @TheTulsaWorld The Man Behind the Envelope: Jon Canton. Read our feature on the founder of Tulsa-based stationery giant Canton Cards, seen here with his son, Jonny, and his granddaughters, from left, Susan, Skye, Sadie, Sally, and Samantha. [Article Link]

I tap on the link, my breath ragged.

"Shit," Sam whispers next to me.

I scan to the part I hoped I wouldn't find. It's at the end, just a footnote in a long story about Grandpa and Dad. Just a few paragraphs to blow my entire existence into smithereens.

> *The Canton daughters are as creative as they are devoted to the family mission. Susan, 34, sits next to her father at the billion-dollar helm, while Samantha, 25, assists in East Coast sales in the brand's Manhattan offices. Of course, millions of fans, readers, and viewers know Sadie Canton, 31, romance author and screenwriter. But she's just one of the artists in the family. Skye Canton, 27, is an up-and-coming painter in New York City, followed by hundreds of thousands of fans on both TikTok and Instagram @APaintedSkye. The middle sister also serves as a brand consultant for the family empire, advising on the brand voice and marketing efforts. No wonder Jon has dubbed himself the proudest father and grandfather in the great wide world of paper.*

I let out a whimper when I scroll and see that below the image of us together from the convention lies a photo of my work, shot of "He's Just Not That into You," pulled from my Instagram and embedded in the article. And of course, my Instagram profile is linked directly from the article, as is the photo. I run to the sink and throw up.

"It's all right, Skye, it was going to come out someday, right? Guess that day is today," Sam says quietly from the hall outside the bathroom. She picks up her phone and paces as she talks to Susan. "How did they get it? Did any New York publications . . . oh okay. All right . . . yeah, she's here. She just threw up in the sink. I know . . . yeah, that's what I said. It's okay. We'll be okay. Uh-huh . . . yeah, I'll tell her. Love you too. Bye."

She comes back to the bathroom doorway. "They don't know how *Tulsa World* got that photo, or your Instagram. Grandpa obviously did not say anything about us or approve the photo. Suze wants you to call her."

I throw up again, even though there's nothing in my stomach.

"Skye?"

"Give me a minute." The room is spinning. I'm sweating. can't think.

"Skye, this could be a good thing. Think of all the exposure fo your Culture show. I mean, now it's out, maybe it'll be a blessing right?"

The Culture show. I dry-heave again. Sam is rubbing my bac I think.

"Maud," I croak out.

"What?" Sam steps back as I straighten and walk back aroun the counter to my phone. I send Maud the article link. I send it Janie too. Neither of them needs any words. I lock my phone. T Twitter notification is still showing on the alerts on my scree along with texts from Susan.

I feel a new wave. "They tweeted that, Sam. *Postify* tweet that."

"I'm sure Matthew didn't know or approve that, though, Sky

Would he have? No. Even if he was pulling away from n even if he was headed right back to Lauren's waiting arms, w would he try to ruin me on his way out the door? But what if things at work had been really bad? What if Postify needed this win over us? Was it a win for them, though? *No. Just a loss for me.* And Sam and Sally. The article mentions Sam's role in sales and that Sally is a junior at the University of Oklahoma. Sharing that photo did nothing for them, for any of us.

The photo.

"The photo . . ." My legs give out, and I sink into our couch.

"What?" Sam sits down beside me.

"Where else would they get that photo? Matthew knew my phone password, and he sent himself stuff from my phone all the time."

She puts her palm on my knee. "Why would he do that though, Skye?"

"To screw us! To mess with the mighty Cantons!"

"No, you're not making sense. Even if—which I do not believe this and I think is crazy and very far-fetched—*even if* he was about to break up with you and go back to Lauren, he wouldn't do this just to hurt you. He has no reason to hurt you. And he's a good man. He wouldn't do that."

My voice cracks. "Do we even know that? That he's a good man?"

She squeezes my knee. "Yes, we do."

"Pff, we know that he kept his business from us when he *sup-posedly* didn't know who I was. I am done talking about him. I don't care anymore. This is so over I can't even think about it, because now I have to do damage control and try to stop the bleeding. What did Susan say about the New York publications?"

I can see the hesitation cross her face. Finally, she answers: "Once Postify retweeted it, they all retweeted it too."

"Damn it!" I yell, jumping back up to my feet and scaring Gus.

"Skye, try to think about how this could be good for you. The cat's not going back in the bag."

"And you? And Sally? You didn't want this either!" *Why isn't she more upset?*

"No, but I wasn't trying to hide a separate identity. And Sally doesn't care, not really."

I cross to the window, looking out at the city that now knows all our secrets. "She should've been given the choice, Sam."

Sam stands and draws close behind me, talking softly. "None of us were given a choice, Skye. We were born Cantons. This is our life. And honestly, it's great, our life is great. This is not that big of a deal, you'll see."

I turn and glare at her, seething. She doesn't understand. And I am not going to explain things right now.

"I'm going to shower. I'll call Susan and Dad and anyone else back later. Tell them I need a minute! *I need a damn minute!*" I yell, surprising even myself.

I cry in the shower, trying not to think.

I dress in running gear, pull my hair back, and chug some water. Then I face my phone. I have missed calls from everyone which irks me because every single one of them knows I hate talking on the phone. It's as if they want to pour gasoline on me as I go down in flames.

9:32 A.M.
Maud: So, today is the day. This will be fine, Skye. Doesn't affect your show.

I will text you about any press opportunities.

Might be best to get ahead of this rather than look like you're hiding.

9:34 A.M.

Janie: You earned that Culture spot on your own, and everyone in your world knows that. This changes nothing. Who leaked it?

9:42 A.M.

Matthew: I just saw it, I had no idea

I had them delete the retweet, but it was too late.

I'm so sorry.

It wasn't us, Skye. I swear to you.

Please talk to me.

I can't talk to him. I go to the studio and paint. And I cry. I run six miles straight, and I cry. I walk back, and I cry. I go home and shower and scream under the hottest spray I can stand. Maud continues to tell me everything is fine. Janie says to take my time. My sisters say they're sorry and they're mad too.

Matthew sends me locations all day, begging me to meet him. I ignore him. I try to eat, but I cry again, and I can't stomach any food. Sam stops trying to comfort me. I don't join her to watch trash TV. I just go to sleep and, unsurprisingly, I cry.

TUESDAY 7:33 A.M.

Matthew: Please talk to me before my flight out in the morning, Skye.

Please, Tiger.

I love you.

Somehow I feel him outside the heavy door of my studio before he knocks.

"Please, Skye, let me in—just for a minute."

I sigh a deep sigh that shudders through me. *Might as well get it over with.*

I open the door but step back as he reaches for me.

"Skye, I didn't know, you have to believe me. I screamed at the team. I told them to delete it, but it was too late." I can't look at him. He talks faster. "Marcy, the intern, she honestly thought it was nice. She thought she was following our instructions to extend the olive branch. I believe her. She didn't know."

"Where'd they get that photo, though, Matt?" I emphasize the t's in Matt—not Matthew—because I am too hurt and too furious to rise above pettiness. To rise above retaliatory hurt. His face falls.

"Skye. Look at me. I would not do that to you. You know that. I love you—please don't do this. Look at me." I don't. He takes a step back in frustration, turning around in a circle, like he needs somewhere to put his energy. "I know you didn't want this I know you're upset, but this will blow over. New York has no memory, you know that. Everyone will forget your last name in a few days, and this will all be over."

"In a few days, you'll be in Texas." I throw the words like knives, but he doesn't understand why.

"Okay, so come with me. Or I'll stay here," he says, reaching for me.

I recoil. "Do not. Touch me."

"Skye, I don't understand. Can you—" His voice breaks. "Can you explain it to me? I mean, it's just one article, and c'mon, it's just the *Tulsa World*, not the *Times*."

It's the use of the word *just* that kills whatever humanity I had left in me. I feel myself become pure pain.

"Go, Matt. Go home. Go to Texas. Go to Postify. Go live your life. We're done."

"Are you serious right now? We're done? Over an article I had nothing to do with? What are you not telling me?"

"What am *I* not telling *you*?" I turn my back to him, trying to compose myself. I fail. The words come out loud and jagged. "What about what you haven't told me? You're going to see your damn fiancée on Friday, Matthew! I saw the messages!" I watch him deflate like a balloon.

He swallows. "It's not what you think."

"It doesn't matter what it is! What matters is that—surprise surprise—you didn't tell me." I squint at him. "What else are you not telling me? Like how you knew I was a Canton all along? How you waited to drop that photo to mess with us when things were going poorly for you?"

"Skye." His eyes plead with me. "You know none of that is true."

"Do I? Your investors are worried, your beta numbers are shit, your reviews are in the toilet—what better time to screw with our competition." I sneer and add, "If you can even call us that."

He shakes his head. "You're mad about Lauren. And you have every right to be. I should've told you, and we need to talk about that, but you need to believe that I had nothing to do with the article." He reaches his hands for me and raises his voice. "I would never out you, even though I don't know why it's so important to you, because you won't let me in!" He moves his hands to pull at the back of his neck in frustration. "I know there's more you're not telling me, Skye. Just fucking talk to me!" he yells. Immediately, he adds, softly, "Sorry. I'm sorry. Please just talk to me, Tiger."

"We're done talking. You are a liar and a cheat like every other dick in this city. You can go back to Lauren and live happily ever Maybe she'll keep up with your running around from group to group, noise to noise, business to business, idea to idea, distraction to distraction so you never have to sit and be with yourself."

He takes a small step back. "Be with myself?"

"Yes, just be alone, be with yourself, be with negative emotions, deal with your inner shit like a man, not a scared little boy who has to be with his little friends all the time. Dating his way through his entire company—*companies, plural*—so he doesn't have to eat a dinner by himself, God forbid! I'm sure Lauren is great with all that. I wish you two the best. We're done. Leave."

He backs up farther, panting, and stares at me. His nostrils are flared, his eyes glassy.

I know.

I know in the back of my heart that I just crossed a million lines and said the most hurtful things I could think of. I know I crushed him. I know later I'll regret some of it. But right now I can't really feel or think beyond my own blinding pain.

"I never lied to you, and I would never lie to you." His voice is low and scraping, like it hurts on its way out of his throat. "I was going to tell Lauren about us because Carter thought she was waiting for me. I didn't want her to wait for me because I was ready gone. I did not leak that photo, or plan that tweet, or know you were a Canton. I just . . . I just met a beautiful Oklahoma girl on a plane and fell in love with her. Stupid me." He doesn't hesitate as he leaves, he doesn't look back, he doesn't close the door.

My heart is screaming in my ears. For a second, I want to run after him, to grab his hand. But I just keep seeing the text on his phone, the outgoing call. I see Ryan having sex with the intern on his desk at our office.

I hear her voice: "just."

Just just just.

I don't follow him. I close the door and sit and weep.

CHAPTER 32

Two Weeks Later

"Rise and shine, porcupine." I hear my bedroom door open. "Sadie?"

"In the flesh," she says, sitting on my bed and looking like she just came from a photoshoot or something. My sparse, quiet room is now filled with so much Sadie, from her floral scent to her clanging wrist bangles to her bright aqua shirt that matches her eyes.

I groan. "What are you doing here?"

Sadie sighs. "Sam realized she was a little out of her depth with you."

"What?"

"She tried, bless her big sunny heart, but she is not equipped for whatever darkness you're marinating in. Which, judging by the smell in here, is a soup of wine, tears, sweat, and what is that other smell—garlic? Pizza sauce? Ugh."

I roll my dry, swollen eyes. "I'm fine."

Sadie leans into my personal space. "False. You look like death stretched over bone. You stayed here alone for Thanksgiving, you barely made an appearance at your opening, you're not running, you aren't answering emails, or even texts, you're drinking, your thumbs are raw, and you're not painting. C'mon, get out of bed."

She tries to tug my white duvet off me, but I pull it back. "Um. No. Goodbye."

Our tug-of-war leaves me half-covered. "I will take a photo of you right now and post it on my Insta Stories and tag you."

"No, you won't." I hear the camera sound clicking repeatedly. I sit up and try to snatch her phone.

"Sadie! Cut it out! Leave me alone!"

"Get in the shower, and I'll consider it." I glare at her. She glares back. "See, this is why Samantha called me in. You don't scare me. I don't bluff, and you know it. I'm about to hit post." I throw her the most disgusted, hateful expression I can as I get out of bed.

I scream internally in the shower, that Sadie of all people is here, to witness me like this. And that she's right. Sam was never going to win a battle of wills with me. And I did need a stupid shower. I'm mad that I feel significantly better after I've dried off and put on fresh PJs, which Sadie dug out for me.

She appears in my room just as I've finished getting dressed. "C'mon, food next. I made a spinach salad." I grunt my objection. She calls from the hallway, "Yes, vegetables. When is the last time you had any?"

I follow her out into the open living, dining, and kitchen space. "Sadie, really, why are you here?"

"Because, believe or not, I love you. Sit. Eat."

I sit at the little table. "Where's Sam?"

"Hiding somewhere you can't hurl insults at her." I wince, and she catches it. "Yeah. You owe her a million new apologies for the last two weeks." I start eating the salad, angry that it tastes amazing. Sadie sits and works on her phone while I eat, saying nothing. Once I finish, she refills my water and sets her phone down.

She puts both hands flat on the tabletop. "So, Skye, what is this really about?"

"Ummm, my reputation was destroyed and my boyfriend left me?"

She looks up as if pained. "Wrong, try again."

"If you know everything, then why don't you just tell me what my problem is?"

"I am not sure what it is, but I know what it isn't. It isn't just about Matthew, who was amazing and you're an idiot for losing."

"Wow." I choke on a bit of salad. "Thanks, sis, for the pep talk. Glad you flew across the country for this. Really, great."

"It's also not about our name or your art, which congratulations, by the way. You sold every single piece, with three pieces going to bidding wars. So, whatever is going on here, I don't think it's really about your career."

"Did you see the *New Yorker* article?"

"I did. It's their job to hate the new girl. Your name made you an easier target, but we both know that overall your show was critical *and commercial* success." She studies me, in a way that reminds me of how I study others. I don't love it. "Is that it—are you afraid to be a commercial success? Are you afraid of achieving your goals?"

"No, and I was *this* close." I pinch my fingers. "So unbelievably close to succeeding on my own."

She cocks her head. "What are you not telling me, Skye? What is it that has you so scared?"

"I'm not scared."

"Takes one to know one. Only some deep fear can wrap you up so tight about your name and your secrecy. What is it?"

I let my fork crash onto my plate. "I don't know! I don't know Sadie!"

"Bullshit. Have you been going to your therapist? What does she say?"

"I'm not going to talk about my therapy with you. Can you just go? I showered, I ate, I'll go for a run, and you can watch my location."

Sadie raises her voice. "Why do you need to succeed on your own, Skye? Just tell me! Just say it! Just say whatever it is you're so mad about."

I put my head in my hands, exasperated. She is relentless.

"You think I can't handle whatever it is? I can. For shit's sake just spit it out already so that—"

"For Mom! Because of Mom, okay?" I screech it out.

Finally, my bulldog of an older sister softens the tiniest bit. She draws out her words, trying to understand. "You want to make Mom proud by *not* sharing her last name?"

"Not make her proud." My voice cracks, and my eyes start to sting again. "Prove her . . ." The words get stuck. "Prove her wrong."

Sadie sits back, confused. "Prove Mom wrong?"

"Right before she died, one of the last conversations I ever had with her . . ." I take a breath to keep from sobbing. "I told her I was changing my major to art, even though it wasn't what they wanted, and she . . ." I fist my hands, trying to find some strength left somewhere, just to talk. "She said, 'No, Skye, surely you're not going to waste your genius *just* to be an artist? That's what you intend to do with your gifts? With your mind? *Just* paint little pictures?' She"—Sadie grabs my hands—"She was disgusted, Sadie. Not just disappointed. And then a week later, she was gone."

Sadie's shoulders sag. "Oh, Skye."

"And I was so mad, you know? Mad that she didn't understand, that we were so different, that she just left before we could talk about it, before I could explain it to her. That painting, that art . . . wasn't a waste that . . . that I-I wasn't a waste."

Sadie comes around to my chair and holds me. She lets me sob. When I can finally breathe again, she pulls us up and over to the couch.

"I'm so sorry, Skye, that you've been carrying that alone all these years." She scoffs. "She really did a number on us, didn't she."

"What do you mean?"

"I know I loved Mom. Still do. We all do. But she was an actual genius, a leading orthopedic surgeon, married to a titan of industry. We didn't exactly have normal expectations to live up to."

"She was proud of *you*, though. She loved that you were an author."

"What!" Sadie snorts in disbelief. "She thought I was going to graduate and write memoirs, Skye! Nonfiction manifestos! She would hate hate *hate* my work."

I laugh suddenly and unexpectedly. "Really?"

"Absolutely. I think she'd be proud of my success, and yours too, by the way. One hundred percent. But would she be a fan? That's a hard no."

"And that doesn't bother you?"

"Sure it does, some days." She clears her throat. "Just like having a sister who says I sold out my soul when I started a publishing business from scratch and negotiated my work onto the big screen with almost zero help from anyone because I was just 'the card guy's daughter.'"

I look away. This is already a lot. I'm not sure I can talk through our issues right now too.

She goes on. "Look, I know somewhere deep down you know this, but I'm going to say it anyway." She leans forward to catch my eyes with hers. "If I couldn't write anymore, if my creativity dried up and the words wouldn't come, and I changed to do something else professionally, would I be any less valuable then? Would I be a waste?"

"Of course not," I say, sniffing.

"If Dad made some major mistake and lost the whole business, ruined thousands of people's lives, was the embarrassment of the industry, would you love him any less? Would he be less of our dad?"

"I see what you're getting at."

"Right. He'd still be the hard-ass driver who pushes us. He'd still be a hidden goofball underneath, a loving grandpa, a secret ly super-romantic husband, and on and on and on." She squeezes my hands. "Skye. We. Are. Not. What. We. Produce. We are not our work. Our value isn't in what we do. You seem to have forgotten. It's separate, inherent. Human being equals value. The end. Fearfully and wonderfully crafted in the image of God, as Susan would remind us."

"Okay, okay, I get it."

"And, sister, I'm thirty-one. You're twenty-seven. We are too old for this parental nonsense. They're not going to love every single thing we do. We have to let their pride—in our general work ethic, brains, strategy, success, you know they're proud of all that—we . . . have to let that be enough."

"And you think she would be?"

"I have no doubt. And Dad is too." She lets go of my hands and sits back to think. "Soooo you don't want to be a part of the business because, what, that would disprove your success?"

"I guess. I wanted to stand on my own two feet, my work, my success, financial stability, all of that."

"And now that's all gone because of some balding, fat tool sweating at the features desk in the back corner of the *Tulsa World* office?" I laugh. I had forgotten why Sadie used to be my best friend. That sentence sounds like it could've come right out of my mouth. She stands and crosses to the freezer as I think about my answer.

"It feels like it's gone to me."

She fills two bowls with ice cream and comes back to the couch.

"Well, you should rethink that. That gives Baldy way too much power. You're already successful, Skye. Own it. Recreate it. Come up with a new vision, one without Mom's random, not-thought-out commentary in your head. If she'd known what would happen, how that would affect you for almost a decade, she never would've said that." We eat ice cream in silence for a couple minutes. It's nice. I feel the tiniest bit less lost.

"So. We're on a roll here. You and me, let's go there."

"Let's not. I'm exhausted," I plead.

She snaps back even though her is mouth full of ice cream. "Oh, you wannatayanap an I'll wait?" She swallows. "I cannot promise drooling-slash-snoring photos will not *not* get posted."

"Ugh," I point at her with my spoon. "You are a raging bitch, you know that?"

"Hello, Kettle." She bows her head and flourishes her own spoon. "C'mon. Why'd you stop reading my books? And don't say you don't like the genre, because you *did* like the genre at one point."

"Maybe I just stopped liking the genre then? I mean, it's just so—"

"Predictable, cheesy, riddled with tropes and clichés, I know, I know. But every genre has its built-in go-tos. You can watch a Marvel movie and predict what will happen. Even mysteries and thrillers have a formula to them, and you can read a fantasy novel and quickly guess how the magic works, even in your precious Loya series, which, admittedly, is fantastic."

"I told you!"

"The point is, it's not the genre for you." She braces herself but as always, goes boldly right to the heart of it. "So is it just my success? Did you just get jealous?"

"Jeez, Sadie, you're so—" I cut myself off and start to laugh.

"What?"

"I was going to say intense, and I realized that's exactly what Sam says to me."

"Samantha," she deadpans. "The walking, talking emotional rainbow fireworks show, says *we're* intense?"

"Right?" I say, and we both laugh. She stares at me, waiting. "I did read your books at the beginning, and I did like them, but . . ." I falter.

"But what, Skye?" She takes on a tone like she's cheering on a toddler. "C'mon, you can do it, I believe in you."

"But they were all Sam! Every damn book was Samantha. A fun, lovable, sweet, happy, big-eyed, extroverted dream girl!" The words fly out like they've been bubbling in a pressure cooker. I mean, obviously not exactly Sam, but gah, don't you get tired of writing her over and over? And I mean, yes! She's so likable. So easy to root for. I know that. I just started to feel like maybe that's how all women were supposed to be. Your readers must love it and identify with it, and most women do tend to be more bubbly and social and that's just . . . not me. None of your books were me. Maybe a quirky sidekick character from time to time, but I just started to feel . . . bad. So." I shrug, spent. "I stopped reading."

Sadie sits back and stares at me with an unreadable expression. Then she starts to laugh, not a full laugh, more of a giggle. A strange giggle. She sounds unhinged. *Uh-oh, I did it. I broke the family superstar.*

"I did. I did write a version of Sam over and over for a while. course readers love her—you know why? She's easy to read. She's easy to write! She's easy to love. E. To the Z. And that's

KELSEY HUMPHREYS

what readers want because reality is anything but. Real people are hard. Real relationships are hard. Real romance is hard. Real love . . . well, I think you're drowning in its wake right now, so you get it." She gets up and crosses to Sam's bookcase. "But Sam is real. She's not perfect, either."

"No, but it started to feel like you clearly didn't like me, my personality," I say, sniffing again.

"Be honest, Skye, and I'm not asking this to be mean, I'm asking this because I've had to ask myself: Do *you* like you?" My throat starts to close with a new set of sobs, so I say nothing. "My guess is—and I'm an expert here—the answer to that is 'No, no most of the time.' But there's a lot to like, Skye. The problem i you're so hard on yourself, you can't see it. That's why you pus people away, snap, and say the meanest thing you can think o But you've come a long way, with your therapy and runnin and work—you know you have. You and Sam have a wonderfu friendship now, and Matthew too, before you blew it up. I thin getting over this deep hurt with Mom is probably a huge missir piece."

I just nod.

"So, yes, I wrote variations of Sam over and over, but afte cut my teeth and hit of few of the best-seller lists, readers gre more patient and I grew stronger. Able to bare it." She runs h fingers along the titles.

"Bare what?" I ask, confused.

"Writing us. Writing you, writing me. Writing Mom, eve Writing funny stories on top of hard, real complex charact with baggage." She pulls three of her later books off Sam's C to Sadie Shelf across the small living room. "These three are y

A little of me, a little of all of us, probably, but in my head, I saw you, and . . ." She closes her eyes for a moment, and when she reopens, I realize they're wet. I haven't seen Sadie cry since Mom. "And I hope I did you justice."

"Sadie, I—"

"It's all right. I get it. But you should read them, at least one. *Sarah's Last Stand* is the strongest, despite the fact that her life's work is—wait for it—running a lemonade stand." We both laugh. She heads to the kitchen counter. "I've got friends to see and a few things to pick up while I'm here, but I'll be back later."

"Okay," I say, knowing she wants to leave as much as I want to get back in my bed. We each do what we want, but this time I climb under the covers with a new book.

CHAPTER 33

Monday 11:03 A.M.

Me: Aaaaand I'm weeping.

Sadie: Yeah?

It was so good, Sadie. So good!

And you said some things in there, about me.

You see me. You get me.

I do. And I love you, Skye.

I love you too. I'm so sorry I missed out on so much for so long.

Same.

"Oh no, we're back to the crying phase?" Sam walks into the living area. "I thought we were in the 'stare silently out the window so long I think you're asleep' phase."

"I finished it." I hold up *Sarah's Last Stand.*

"So good, right? I love that one."

"Yes, but . . ." I start to cry again. "I think I screwed up, Sam."

"What?"

"Some of the things she wrote in here, Matthew said those same things. He saw me, he really knew me and—" My voice breaks. "He loved me, like no one ever has before."

"Aw, Skye." She rushes over and puts her hand on my back.

"With that stupid article, I was so upset, all that stuff Sadie got out of me, with Mom and all of that that we all talked about on FaceTime, it was so deep I didn't even really know what I was reacting to, not really. And I was still blindsided by the Lauren thing—I just snapped."

"How very unlike you," she says, sitting across from me with a sarcastic smile.

"I know. And Sam, ugh. I said some awful, awful things."

"Again, I'm shocked to hear that," she deadpans.

"I know, okay? But I just flashed back to Ryan and how he had all those texts and calls, walking in on him in his office that day. It was like PTSD seeing that text pop up from Lauren on Matthew's phone. And Matthew said, 'It's just one article.'"

Sam makes a yikes face. "Uh-oh, trigger word."

"Exactly."

"Okay, so you get him back."

"I'm pretty sure I'm too late."

Sam sits up taller, as if hope is filling her spine. "It's only been two weeks."

"Yeah, but not one text, not on Thanksgiving Day. Not on opening night. Not even a lame excuse like returning our spare key. He doesn't look at my Instagram anymore. Nothing."

"Well, okay, so it's too late for you to just text him or call him but seriously, have you learned nothing?" She points toward Sadie's three books on the kitchen table next to me. "Grand gesture, Skye. Big, fat, grand gesture."

I take a deep breath. "Okay. Grand gesture. But what? I mean in the books it's always the man who screws the pooch. Women are easy—they want romance, but what would a man want?"

"I have no idea." She pauses but proceeds to have ideas. "I think just think about his favorite things. And what would wow him. And something that takes significant planning and thought and effort on your part. And groveling. You gotta grovel."

"Right."

"And you need to pull it off fast."

My voice is pinched from the pressure of what I'm thinking of attempting. "Why?"

"Christmas. He'll go home and so will you. You don't want to wait until after, do you?"

"Ugh, no." I shudder. "Thanksgiving without him was bad enough."

"All right then. Grand, thoughtful, something he'd love, with-in"—she pulls up her calendar—"two and a half weeks."

I nod. I'll think of something . . .

TUESDAY 7:20 A.M.

Me: We need to call in a favor.

Maud: WE do?

I need you to call John at Beanie's.

Beanie's?

Yep. The whole place.

When?

Two weeks from yesterday...

WHAT!

Trust me. I'll pay him, I'm loaded now, remember?

WE are loaded now. ;)

On it.

FRIDAY 10:22 P.M.

Me: [Image]

Is this going to work? Am I crazy?

Janie: Yes and yes. Are you still at it? It's past our bedtime.

Yep

Don't forget to eat!

Eh, food is for the weak.

DoorDashing you now.

MONDAY 1:02 P.M.

Maud: John is totally overcharging us!

Blast that last name of yours!

Me: Ha. I'll just forward the bill to dear ole Dad.

Wait, is that an option now?

Please tell me we're doing that.

NO, WE ARE NOT DOING THAT!

Shame.

SUNDAY 8:04 P.M.

Me: [10 images]

Sam: AHHHHHHH

Sam: It's amazing!

Sam: The grandest of grand gestures! I love it! He will love it too!

Sally: It's perfect!

Sadie: I may or may not be stealing this idea for a book

Me: No stealing!

Susan: I'm praying hard for you! C'mon, Matthew [Prayer emoji]

Sally: Me too [Prayer emoji]

Sam: [Prayer emoji] [Prayer emoji] [Prayer emoji] [Prayer emoji]

Sadie: It's beautiful, Skye.

Sadie: Also: [Prayer emoji] [Prayer emoji] [Prayer emoji]

This is it. I'm shaking, and not just from nerves.

I'm so tired I can barely stand. The only thing I've consumed in larger quantities than caffeine in the last two weeks is ibuprofen. My fingers burn, my neck aches, my back is throbbing. I haven't had time to run much, but it feels like I just did another fifteen-miler.

And, like my sisters, I've prayed. And cried. And talked to my therapist, more openly and honestly than before. I've actually talked a lot, for me, anyway.

I've talked (even if via text) to Dad and my sisters more in the last two weeks than probably the last five years combined. Janie has been there too, listening and pushing me not to give up, on any of it. Maud has thrown herself into this project like a diehard rom-com fan, though she'll deny it.

And it's all been worth it, or it will be, I hope.

I think I've done something he'll love, that's special, for just the two of us, but grand enough to at least get him to listen to me. And if he will agree to listen, I'm finally ready to talk. *Please, Lord, let him agree to meet me!*

Beanie's is a small coffee shop, but I couldn't have handled a bigger space, anyway. I managed to finish five 18x24 canvases, which is small for my usual work, but perfect for Beanie's and my two-week deadline. Then there are the two larger ones.

The last one, the big one, if nothing else, will hopefully get him to talk to me. I wrote my heart out in strokes of acrylic. I explained what happened with my mother, and Ryan, and the word *just*. I wrote how much I missed him and how scared I was and how I hoped it wasn't too late. I wrote about every time I almost said I love you, in great detail. I wrote that I'd rather quit the business and stop talking to my family about the industry, just so I could talk to him about Postify.

I spelled out how proud I was of what he'd built. That I wished I could've comforted him when things went wrong. I wrote about how my big opening that I dreamed of for years sucked, because he wasn't there.

I wrote that I hated running without him. I wrote I loved him more than anyone. That no one had ever loved me like he did. I repeated "I didn't mean what I said" over and over. And "I'm sorry" over and over. And "I miss you" over and over. I wrote it all out in thick black paint.

I take a deep, shaky breath, paste the pin into a text to Matthew, and hit send.

MONDAY 8:00 A.M.

Me: [Dropped pin location]

TUESDAY 8:00 A.M.

Me: [Dropped pin location]

WEDNESDAY 8:00 A.M.

Me: [Dropped pin location]

THURSDAY 8:00 A.M.

Me: [Dropped pin location]

THURSDAY 4:08 P.M.

Me: Should I resend it? I'm guessing his flight leaves tomorrow. What if he didn't get them? What if he changed his number? Or blocked me?

Sam: I asked Carter if he got them, and he said yes. Per your stupid and very strict instructions, I did not ask any more questions!

Susan: Don't resend.

Sally: Don't resend.

Sadie: This is your grand gesture. Resend.

What if he already left town?

Sam: I lied!

Sam: I asked Carter when his flight was. It's tomorrow.

!!! Did you say anything else? Did you ruin the surprise?

Sam: NO! I asked those two questions: did he get your message, has he already left town. Carter said "Yes" and "No, tomorrow"

[Broken heart emoji]

Sadie: Resend it, Skye.

Sam: How long do you have?

John will keep Beanie's open until 10 for me.

THURSDAY 5:00 P.M.

Me: Matthew, please just swing by. Closes at 10 p.m. [Tiger emoji]

[Dropped pin location]

With every passing minute, my heart breaks a little more. I am sitting across the street in an office lobby, with their permission, like I have all day, every day this week. I have gone to nearby restaurants and worked a bit, but mostly I have gone out of my mind. By Wednesday, I decided I had to run, or I would explode, but I stayed on a one-mile loop surrounding Beanie's.

The receptionists at the office where I sit with my phone had smiled and cheered on Monday, but tonight as they leave for their happy weekends, they look at me like I am on my way to a funeral. And right now, I feel like I am.

Only a couple hours left until it's really over.

My phone buzzes. *I said I would give you an update if there was one, Samantha!*

> THURSDAY 8:03 P.M.
>
> Matthew: [Dropped pin location]

I let out a cry that disturbs the security guard. I stand and start to leave and realize I need to gather my things. Panicking, I shove everything in my backpack without looking—my laptop, phone, sketchbook, coffee, keys, and jacket. Then I bolt across the street, legs wobbling. I send up a prayer that Matthew will be willing to listen.

CHAPTER 34

MATTHEW

'm almost running to this random coffee shop like a tool. I don't know why I waited so long. Well, that's a lie. I was hurt, it's not exactly rocket science. I was hurt and angry. I can feel that I look like hell, though Carter's told me enough times that I could take his word for it. I haven't been able to sleep, food tastes bland, coffee isn't working its usual magic.

She had told me, warned me. She said there are people who don't know what to say in an argument and later they think of all the perfect comebacks in the shower. Then there's her. She shared a few fights with her sisters, said it was something she was working on, how she'd snap and verbally cut to the bone. But to be on the opposite end of her verbal blades. It stung.

Okay, it broke me.

Did she really think of me as a weak little boy unable to be alone? Yes, I like people, but to say I run from negative emotions? And bounce from distraction to distraction? I was livid in my pain and shock. But then what pissed me off even more is that as I sat with beer after beer, thinking about it, she wasn't wrong. I have had a relatively easy, blessed life. I don't want to deal with heavy shit, so, well, I don't.

Our first break up? I just let her go. Second break up? I haven't called or texted...I just haven't wanted to deal with it all. I'm mad again, crashing my feet into the pavement unnecessarily hard.

So it's been four weeks of unbearable silence. No call from her on Thanksgiving, no invite to her opening. That was when I really started to lose sleep.

She was so angry and hurt. Finally, after ages, she reaches out with just a location? What if I'm walking to some goodbye? What if she wants closure?

Um, hell no.

I know it as I rush to wherever she's leading me. Hurt and angry yes, but no, no, I am not letting this girl, my amazing Tiger get away again. I am not letting her slink off to some safe, boring, quiet Paul–type dipwad. Or to be alone. She'll force herself to be alone and she'll eat herself up from the inside out. *No, Tiger. N*

I should've called her, no, texted her. I should've made her talk to me, right away. But I was an idiot of epic proportions. I was wrong. I was at fault. I didn't really think much about the thing with Lauren. In my mind, I was checking off a box, a step that needed to be taken in order to set Skye and me up for success.

And I was scared.

Stupid weakling.

I was scared that if I reached out, she'd say more things she couldn't take back, tell me more of the weakness she sees in me. Now weeks have gone by, and I'm so nervous about whatever waits for me at this dropped pin, I could hurl. But I'm not avoiding this anymore.

I hope I didn't wait too long. She said I had until ten, and it's almost eight. Me and my damn meetings and calls and meals—yes, with people—all day.

My hands are shaking as I finally find the door to Beanie's. *Get it together, man.*

I walk in and take a deep breath, smelling coffee and vanilla. I look around the small quirky space, unsure of what I'm looking for. And then, it's obvious.

My breath catches.

Along the dark navy wall to my right are canvases. I stop myself from leaping closer. First is a detailed close-up of . . . eyes. Wait. *My* eyes. As she always does, she's got the canvas sparkling so much, it looks like the flecks of gold tucked in strokes of deep brown could glow in the dark. I look for the title card: "Home."

I gulp. So maybe this isn't a goodbye? *Thank you, God!*

The next canvas makes me chuckle. It's a scrawny house cat with tiger stripes, skinny and dirty, hair askew, with a sour expression, and behind it on the floor is something broken, that the cat has spilled, which is hilarious. The title is "Current Self-Portrait." *Me too, Skye, me too.*

I swallow when I see the next one. It's the floor pillows in her studio, lying as they must have been that day. Our day, our first time. The paint splatters across the pillows on the canvas look wet, as if she just splattered them there a minute ago. The title is "The First of My Best Ever." *Damn right.* I fight a smirk, unsuccessfully.

The last one on the side wall is a glowing depiction of the tiger aloe plant I got her, on the paint shelf by the window. I brace myself for the title, knowing it's part of the series of her relationships: "To Be Seen and Loved." I suck in a breath that's as shaky as hell.

There are three canvases along the back wall, and again I almost knock over the small café tables in a rush to see them. The first makes my full smile break out. It's a dimly lit first-class airplane seat, with little overhead light captured in such a way that my eyes think it's twinkling. The title card says, "Thank God for Turbulence." *A-freaking-men! Best day of my life!*

Next is a beautiful woman painted in a way I'd have to describe as soft? Like Skye took great care and painted slowly? It must be a portrait of her mother. She's frowning, but with a twinkle in her eye. I'm confused, then I see the title card: "Why I Overreacted." *What? What does that mean?*

I smile again. The last one is a larger canvas of a longhorn that looks almost identical to the one hanging in my apartment, titled: "For Your Dad." I can't believe she made another one, and then I'm struck, hard and suddenly, by how much work she's done. She just had her opening two weeks ago. *No wonder she hasn't called!*

I'm stumped for a breath, not sure what's next until I turn and realize that off to my right of the wall juts out to show another seating area. A huge canvas stretches across the whole wall.

Don't cry, you bastard. Do not start crying in this coffee shop right now.

I take many deep breaths. It not like Skye's usual work, not portrait. Instead, it's more of a modern piece, I guess, with a tex tured background color in my favorite shade of bright sky blue. And I'm not being cheesy—that's always been my favorite color, the clear Texas sky in midday. Across the whole thing are big fat block that letters read I LOVE YOU TOO.

I keep blinking back tears as I get closer. I'm grateful no one is in this little room so I can get up close, really close. And I'm not moving any time soon. Because within each letter is her handwriting, phrases, written tight together, over and over.

And there on the canvas, for any coffee-goer to see, she wrote . . . everything. It's like . . . like a love letter. It takes me forever to read it all, blinking like a fool. Then I see the card next to it that reads "Things I Should Have Said." I'm pulling out my phone already when I see the 8.5x11 series card posted next to the title card.

Series:

Send Me Your Location

Artist:

Nearby

Medium:

Words

Duration:

Forever

Forever.

I send her my location so fast I have to double-check that I sent the right spot. She says she's nearby. How nearby? How long? Should I call her? Should I text more? I decide to just follow her instructions.

I am a ball of energy, and I feel the urge to pace. But instead, reread every single word stretched across the wall. I know my face is turning purple from holding all this in—the relief, the regret, the hope. *Hurry up, Tiger, where are you?*

I hear a ding and realize she can't see me from the front door, so I turn to go out into the main section of the restaurant and there she is.

Tiger.

The love of my life.

She looks exhausted. She's run already, and her fingers are bandaged, more than just the thumbs. And she's lost weight she couldn't afford to lose.

But damn if she's not still the sexiest woman alive.

And right now, the most adorable. It's her big bright eyes. She's looking up at me with so much hope. And she's nervous. I take a step toward her at the same time she steps to me.

"I'm so sorry. I didn't mean what I said, and I didn't know how to apologize, so if we could just talk about it, I can explain everything. I was really hurting from something with my mom, if you read it." She motions toward her canvas.

Then I notice it.

And it's so perfect.

I hold back my smile.

She's still rambling.

"Skye," I say, trying to sound calm.

"So, *so* much of it wasn't about you or us at all and—"

"Skye."

"What?"

"Your backpack is leaking."

"What?"

Her face falls, and I can't help the chuckle that escapes me. I'm so relieved to see her. So in love with this girl, my girl, she doesn't have to say anything else. And, in true Skye Morgan Canton fashion, her backpack is leaking coffee all over the floor. It's not a subtle drip—it's a brown stream from her to the floor, splashing on her gorgeous runner's legs. I reach and take the straps to help her shrug out of the bag and set it on the floor.

"My coffee!" she says as I pull it off. "I'm such an idiot. I was so nervous and in such a hurry that I—"

I grab her face and kiss her harder than I mean to. I couldn't wait another second. I can feel tears on her cheeks, I can feel that she's shaking. I'm shaking too.

I kiss away everything from the past month until all that's left is us. I hold her precious face in my hands until I feel her relax. I pull my mouth away, reluctantly, and look down at her.

"I'm sorry," she whispers.

"I'm sorry too, Tiger."

"I love you so much," she says, and I wipe the tears off her cheeks.

"I love you too." I kiss her again and squeeze so tight around her that I'm afraid I'm overdoing it. I breathe her in and can't help but kiss her neck. I stop myself, stop the urge to shove her up against the wall behind us and show her just how much I missed her.

"So, you like them?" she asks.

"I love them. I can't believe it."

"Do you want to go somewhere to talk?" she asks, nervous.

"Come home with me," I blurt out.

"Okay," she says.

"For Christmas."

Her face lights up. It's the most beautiful thing I've ever seen or will ever see. I just want to do that, make her face do that, forever.

"Really?" She squeaks it more than she says it.

"Really, Tiger." She jumps up and wraps her arms and legs around me, and I'm home. And so is she.

EPILOGUE

SKYE

Eight Months Later

I adjust my big Bose headphones, happy to have made it through takeoff. *And no one is sitting next to me! Jackpot!* It's weird being on a flight without Matthew, especially in first class. Since Christmas, we've gone everywhere together. But he didn't have a reason to tag along on this trip, though I wish he had.

It was amazing, finally seeing my ideas realized at the Canton Cards warehouse. By the time we set up at the convention in a couple months, there will be a whole section of our giant display, just for PaintedSkye products.

I smile, thinking of all the subtle gloating I've been enduring, from Sam, from Susan, even Dad. *Okay, so partnering with the family brand wasn't the worst idea!* I'm not about to say out loud that they were right. I admit defeat via frequent eye rolls. As one does.

It took me awhile to get over the gap between seeing my work in the flesh and making mass prints. The magic of hyperrealism can't be captured in a photo of the work—you have to see the layers of paint and the way the colors play in the light. So, after a million brainstorming runs, and coffees, and sketch sessions— *okay, yes, I was obsessively overthinking for months*—I decided to focus on the other part of "my genius," as Maud calls it.

The titles.

Each PaintedSkye piece has a funny title somewhere on it, and, per Sally's brilliance, part of the fun of getting or gifting one is the hunt for the Easter egg. If you get one of the large coffee tumblers covered in a bright print of swirling acrylic paint, for example, and turn it upside down, you'll read: NOPE, EVEN THIS BIG-ASS TUMBLER ISN'T BIG ENOUGH. #COFFEEHOLIC.

My personal favorite is a notebook with a print of a painting I did just for my Introvert collection. Swirls of paint rage in all different colors exploding everywhere, looking angry and chaotic, except a small taped-off circle. Within the circle are soft, peaceful bubblegum clouds. Printed very small, in different locations based on the lot of prints, for example, on the ribbon bookmark attached to the spine, or on the top of the center page of the journal, you can find a print of my handwriting that says: EVERYWHERE ELSE VS. MY COUCH.

Followers love the line for Canton cards and, surprisingly, bidding wars have erupted over the originals of each piece that gets copied and made into a notebook or tote bag or coffee mug. The last few months have been amazing. Like, pinch-myself amazing.

And most of that is due to Matthew.

The man—*my man!*—is a dream on legs. He dotes on me, cherishes me, teases me, and, well, the man knows how to have sex. Like, wow. I can't believe he's mine. I can't believe the way he looks at me. I can't believe how much we laugh.

The only tiny missing piece in our perfect puzzle is our work.

We agreed to start talking about work as much as we could. We don't let ourselves argue over it, but sometimes it's tense because we can't go into details. I know we love each other enough to power through it, but I'd be lying if I didn't admit I don't want our relationship to be this way forever. And I want forever. Matthew hasn't even hinted about marriage or proposing, and I think work is what's holding him back.

We know it wasn't anyone at Postify who leaked the photo to the *Tulsa World*. We still don't know who it was, however. It's a mystery that's in the back of all our minds, but now that the secret is out, it doesn't feel so large.

That was a hard lesson for me to learn. That a wound seems much deeper and larger if you refuse to work on healing it. Secrets grow, insecurities build. I know that now.

Even with our increased communication, the past couple weeks especially have been hard for Matthew and me, which is why I wish he could've come to the warehouse to celebrate. Not only is he stressed about something he can't share (*or won't? No, don't go there!*), but Susan and Dad are keeping something from me too. I'm assuming they don't want to put me in a tough spot where I'd have to lie or evade Matthew, and I appreciate that.

Still, it's a dark cloud that seems to be chasing us.

I shake my head, looking out of the oval window, down to the tiny patchwork farms below.

My headphones, which were blaring Adele, shut off. It's odd, because I triple-checked that they were charged for the flight. I pull them off to check the Bluetooth button and *what?*

Music is playing, but in the cabin?

I look across the aisle and realize there is not one soul in the section of seats across from me. *That's not at all creepy . . .*

Then I recognize the song. "Madness" by Muse.

But it sounds super weird. *What the heck?*

I unbuckle to move to the aisle and look around. My heart flips over. There is no one behind me either, and it's oddly dark in here. *Am I dreaming? Oh, crap, have we lost oxygen and I'm about to die?*

The aisle seat diagonally from me has the light on, shining down on a gift box. There's a huge gift tag that clearly says SKYE. My pulse starts to dance in my eardrums. I glance around. I don't even see a flight attendant. *Was I drugged or something?*

I get up and go to the box and open it, because if I'm about to go down in flames, I can't die *not* knowing what's in the box, obviously. And if this is part of some trip, might as well see where it's headed. Inside the box is an article? From *Tech Insider*. This is all too bizarre. I take a shaky breath and start reading.

Gifts Giant Canton Cards Buys Postify Press for Undisclosed Amount

What!

I don't keep reading. Instead, I look up, frantically, for someone to explain the box to me. Is this real? Dad bought Matthew's business? As I launch up, four guys stand along the back of first class . . . with violins? *What the actual hell?*

They are actually playing that song, our song, in first class which is . . . empty. I turn back toward my seat and—

Matthew.

Is on his knee.

In the aisle.

In his hoodie.

With a ring box.

He is smiling his widest, happiest smile. His eyes are misty, and his hand is shaking, almost as much as my whole body. He's about to say something, but I can't contain myself.

"You sold Postify?" I blurt.

"Uh-huh."

"To my dad?"

"Uh-huh."

"When, how?"

"Last week. Sorry, I've been a little stressed."

I laugh in shock. "But how did—"

"Skye." All I can do is whimper at this point. It's crashing into me like a wave on the shore. The last thing holding us back. And 's gone. My knees are about to give out.

Matthew clears his throat, and I can tell he's emotional too. Tiger. A year ago this week, on this exact flight, I met the best ing that ever happened to me." I start crying. "You are the funest, smartest, sexiest, most wonderful woman in the world. en though you're a Sooner, you're it for me, Skye. I love you so uch. Will you marry me?"

"Yes!" He stands and puts the gorgeous ring on my finger, the tire band is diamonds, and not the tiny kind, but in the cen- r is a huge, purple, striped agate stone. A tiger stone. It's sur- unded in diamonds, giving the ring a vintage look. It's blinding d different and gorgeous, and I know he had it custom made. ok up at him as more tears escape, and he kisses me quickly.

"We have to sit down now." He points behind me. I turn and there sits Sam out of nowhere, bawling her eyes out.

"I just cannot even! Is this not the best proposal you've ever heard of in your life, Skye? In your *life*! Ahhhhh! I'm so happy for you!" She is grabbing me and hugging my neck for dear life. I look at Matthew, where he sits across the aisle, smug.

He shrugs. "It's the only way she would agree to help me pull this off."

"It's perfect," I say, hearing Samantha snotting next to me tapping up a SamStorm on her phone. "I love you," I mouth to him as Sam starts babbling something next to me. There's not a bump on the whole way home to New York.

BUT WAIT...

Who leaked the photo?
What was Matthew's hilarious nickname?
Find out in Book 2 of the Heartlanders Series!

Samantha finally meets her match in:

Things I Overshared:
An Extrovert/Introvert Romantic Comedy
kelseyhumphreys.com/thingsiovershared

WANT MORE CANTONS?

Read the parents' swoony love story for FREE!
Things I Always Wanted:
A Best Friends to Lovers Romantic Comedy
kelseyhumphreys.com/heartlanders

STORIES OF LOYA

Read the epic fantasy romance series Skye is obsessed with!
Think Hunger Games meets ACOTAR.

Written by Kelsey Humphreys under the
pen name K. A. Humphreys.
kahumphreys.com

IF YOU ENJOYED THIS BOOK

Thanks so much for reading! If you enjoyed reading *Things I Should Have Said*, please consider leaving a review on your platform of choice. For indie authors, the most important things in life are coffee and book reviews. Okay, I'm mostly kidding. But if you have a minute, leaving a rating or review will help me find more awesome readers like you.

FREE BOOKS!

If you loved *Things I Should Have Said,* would you like all of Kelsey's releases in advance and for free? Join her launch team

kelseyhumphreys.com/launch

ACKNOWLEDGMENTS

My first thank-you will always be to Jesus for my salvation, my sobriety, and my creativity.

My second thank-you will always be to Christopher, my zip-hoodie-wearing better half, for your support and patience and for inspiring all my hot, sweet fictional men.

To my family, thank you for your patience as I limped along through yet another metamorphosis while writing my first few books. To my early rom-com readers: Mom, Anita, Mattie, Morgan, Courtney, and Andi. To my team on this series: Shayla Raquel, Kayla Bruce, Shana Yasmin, and Sara Ward.

To my fans and followers who have been with me through my nonfiction writing and speaking, my YouTube talk show, my musical work, my stand up, and finally my comedy sketches, and most recently "The Sisters." Your love and support for those videos brought this series to life. I hope you enjoy reading the introvert/extrovert humor in this long format!

ABOUT THE AUTHOR

After tens of millions of video views, comedian Kelsey Humphreys has captured her hilarious, heartwarming charac ters in book form. Her steamy stories dig into deep truths abou love, identity, purpose, and family. When she's not writing ro mance or creating comedy videos, she's reading, running, mom ing and wife-ing in Oklahoma.

Follow her funny posts on Facebook, Instagram, and TikTo **@TheKelseyHumphreys.**

Made in the USA
Las Vegas, NV
16 December 2023

82948264R00215